Bridger's Run

Other Cracker Westerns:

*Riders of the Suwannee* by Lee Gramling
*Thunder on the St. Johns* by Lee Gramling
*Trail from St. Augustine* by Lee Gramling
*Ghosts of the Green Swamp* by Lee Gramling
*Guns of the Palmetto Plains* by Rick Tonyan

# Bridger's Run

*A Cracker Western*
by
Jon Wilson

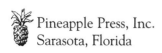
Pineapple Press, Inc.
Sarasota, Florida

Inquiries should be addressed to:
Pineapple Press, Inc.
P.O. Box 3899
Sarasota, Florida 34230

Library of Congress Cataloging in Publication Data

Wilson, Jon, 1945–
        Bridger's Run: a cracker western — 1st ed.
 by Jon Wilson.
        p.   cm.
        ISBN 1-56164-170-7 (hardbound : alk. paper). —
ISBN 1-56164-174-X (pbk. : alk. paper)
        I. Title.
PS3573.I456976B75      1999
813'.54—dc21                                98-32377
                                           CIP

First Edition
10 9 8 7 6 5 4 3 2 1

Design by Stacey Arnold
Printed and bound by The Maple Press, York, Pennsylvania

# 1

T OM BRIDGER STRUGGLED. He wanted the whiskey, as he usually did, but he had promised himself: nothing until he was off the ship. The trouble was, he felt like having a drink just to keep up with life. It had been an endless bon voyage party since he began packing for Florida two weeks ago. He was on the steam packet *Lucy Lee*, lurching into the Jacksonville harbor on a rolling sea. He had come from New York by way of Charleston—or Chahhll-ston, as pronounced by the two syrupy Southerners with whom he had engaged in small talk. He wondered if all of them were like these two—this pleasant father and daughter, who seemed so unassuming. If so, he'd have the whole country of them for breakfast.

"You must keep your wits about you, brother," Amy had teased. "One of those Southern belles will have you wrapped around her finger."

"Not very likely," Bridger had told his sister with conviction. "I'm a hard man. I grew up with our father, you know."

A thought of the hard-edged Josiah Bridger flashed

through Tom's mind, though it didn't chase away his wish for a drink. Josiah Bridger was one of the new industrialists. His unrelenting work and domineering will had built the finest foundry in Troy, New York. The Civil War had made him rich manufacturing military supplies—particularly horse-shoes. Twenty years later, he was perhaps the wealthiest man in the city, and one of the wealthiest in the state outside New York City.

Bridger thought men like his father were the reason these Southerns never could have won. But he despised his father's unsmiling, stern, and distant ways. He had thrown over his chance to follow his lead and probably amass a for-tune of his own. Money, by itself, didn't excite him. There had to be an interesting way to acquire it. So he had decided instead to follow what his father had called "this brainless, nonsensical quest in Florida."

Bridger felt for the flask in his pocket and almost drew it out. But he knew he ought to start in Jacksonville feeling fresh. He had a long way to go in a strange land—even if it did turn out to be a tropical paradise as advertised.

The ship began maneuvering into the harbor, its engines laboring. Bridger thought they sounded ragged and it made him nervous. He had never cared much for the water, anyway. "I am a land mammal," he had always told his more aquatic chums when they teased him to go for a summer swim.

Hoping he didn't look ill at ease to the other passengers, he gazed over the railing, straining to spy land. In fact, he didn't look nervous at all—at the moment. Other passengers saw a giant of a young fellow, nearly six feet four inches tall, slender enough to be called lean, but hardly skinny. Nor would anyone have called him gangly. His broad shoulders suggested strength; his carriage and every casual movement suggested an athletic grace. Most bully-boys would think twice before taking him on.

He was twenty-five, but on most days looked even younger. ("My baby-faced baby," his mother had called him until he was nearly twenty.) Today his eyes, usually an unnerving ice blue, were tired and bloodshot from days of carousing and innumerable toasts (both publicly and privately) to his self-declared freedom from home and hearth. Still, he cut a striking figure. Ginger hair flared from under a rakish, broad-brimmed hat, matched by flowing, reddish-blonde mustache. He wore a hunting jacket, twill shirt, and heavy trousers tucked into calf-high brown boots. Over his right shoulder was slung his prize possession: a Sharps carbine given him by his uncle Mike McGinnis.

It was a bright February day, cool with a crisp wind. Bridger could see other ships going in and out of the harbor: some low-slung steamers like his own, a pair of smoke-puffing river tugs, a sidewheeler, and a couple of tall-masted schooners. There seemed to be at least as much activity here as at Charleston, and Bridger relished the prospect of lively entertainment ashore.

Then things went awry. A jolt nearly knocked Bridger down, followed by a grinding, splintering sound below him. The boat lurched. A section of it where Bridger was standing cracked and tore partly away, knocking loose the railing and dumping overboard the four passengers trying to hold steady.

"She's aground!" someone shouted. "Man overboard! In the water!"

Bridger had a fleeting fancy that he would grab something to save himself, but he flailed at air. Horrified, he fell into the water, losing his hat but grabbing at the sling on the Sharps. For a moment, he shot under, then bobbed up, salt-water stinging his eyes and nose. He pawed for the bottom with his feet and sank again, still gripping the carbine's sling in one hand while he flailed with his free arm.

No bottom.

And he could feel a current sawing at him, pulling him away from the foundering steamer. He rose on a wave, then slipped into its trough, where hillocks of water seemed to isolate him from everything else in the world. Still threshing with one arm, he craned to keep his head above water and took a mouthful of it, gagging. A sudden terror smothered him. He could die. The idea washed over him like a black nightmare and he fought to think straight.

The water lifted him and again he saw the boat. A few yards away bobbed a fat man, looking about wildly but treading water. Bridger was vaguely aware of commotion on the steamer; people shouted and they seemed to be launching a lifeboat. Beyond the fat man, he could see a woman's full skirts billowing in the water. It was the young lady from Charleston.

Well, he would have to save her. He pointed himself in her direction and, hanging tight to his carbine, began a kind of one-armed crawl in the woman's direction. He was exhausted in less than ten seconds. Soaked clothes and heavy boots weighed him down. Still, he refused to let go of the Sharps. He arched up to drag in a breath and sucked in more water. A white life ring splatted close; Bridger tried to reach it but his arm felt paralyzed. He lunged but couldn't move fast enough. The life ring drifted away.

Now Bridger could barely twitch. He gasped for another breath and let himself go under again. A piece of debris from the boat smacked his head, then another. He couldn't seem to move away from it. I'll relax, he thought. Maybe this is a dream. . . . I'll let go. He thought of a spring day back home in Troy and thought of his mother and sister . . . and of Uncle Mike. And then of the words Uncle Mike had spoken to him time and again, those days when they had run miles together, when he had taught Bridger the hard facts of bare-knuckle boxing: "Never, never, never give up, Pokey. It's a sin to give up."

Bridger rolled on his back and tried to stretch out in the water as if it were a bed. The move gave him another precious breath. He glimpsed two small boats not far away, and the sight boosted his spirit. Something else floated past and he snagged it with his free arm, hugging it close. It was a box of some kind. Bridger clung to it and it buoyed him enough so that he could relax a little and take in some air.

One of the boats was struggling toward him. He could see the fat man in it, soaked and bedraggled. The other boat had picked up the young woman and the other passenger. He was the only one left in the water. But the boat and its single oarsman had to fight the breeze, waves, and current. It was having a hard go. A man in it yelled, "Try to swim to us. We don't have a line!"

Bridger kicked and tried to paddle with one arm. Inch by inch, he and the boat drew closer together. But each time they came almost within reach, a wave pried them apart.

"Use that gun for a reach!" the man in the boat yelled. "We'll pull you in that way!" Bridger managed to unsling the Sharps. When another wave lifted him toward the boat, he thrust it muzzle first toward his rescuer.

"It's not loaded, is it?"

"No," Bridger gasped back. "You think I'm . . . a fool?"

"Ye're in the water drownin', aincha?"

They fished Bridger out, dragging him over the side. He lay back in the boat, shaking from weariness and cold. Someone threw him a rag of a blanket. And the oarsman heaved and hauled toward the wharves of Jacksonville. Bridger discovered he still had his flask in a jacket pocket. He took it out, uncorked it, put it to his lips and swallowed several times. He looked around to see if anyone was watching.

What the hell, he thought. What the hell. He drank all of it down.

# 2

JACKSONVILLE IN 1885 was one of the world's crossroads, its promoters said, and on this day at the height of the winter season, any visitor might agree with the city boosters. The St. Johns River docks, a transit center for people coming and going, literally trembled under the traffic.

A huge crate, the word RAILS stamped on its side, slipped its winch halfway down and clattered onto the planks. Stevedores dodged in all directions. Carts filled with oranges, pulled and pushed by black men, rolled heavily toward a sloop tied up at another wharf. A four-piece brass band, pumped along by a thumping bass drum, stood and serenaded no one in particular with an uneven rendition of "My Grandfather's Clock."

Pomaded gents parading on plank sidewalks took care to avoid bumping mean-eyed men who seemed ready to fight anyone. A cluster of rough-and-ready boys dodged the horses drawing a car along a street railway. A few hawkers loitered and leaned against gas lamps flanking several three-, four-, and even five-story buildings near the waterfront. But most of their kind moved through the crowd trying to sell what they called "Florida treasures": alligator teeth; batches of long, exotic plumage; walking sticks made of odd, gnarled, and knobby wood.

Tom Bridger's eyes wandered over all this as he stepped down the gangplank, his Sharps still slung over a shoulder, his bag in hand, his soaked clothes clinging. He glanced through the crowd, half hoping he might spy Uncle Mike. He, after all, was part of the reason Bridger was in Florida. What if, after all these years, he just bumped into him? Maybe he wasn't really lost.

Bridger was feeling much better since taking the last of his whiskey, and now he took special care to walk straight and steady.

Immediately a man wearing a plug hat and bristling muttonchops approached him. "Florida property, sir, right here. Invest or homestead? Jack Packer'll take care of you. Here's my card. Stop by, stop by, I'm near the Park Theater." He was already looking to the next passenger. Bridger ignored him, thinking of another kind of fortune he might unearth in Florida—if he were truly lucky. He gazed around, wondering where he could go to get out of the soaked clothes beginning to chill him. He absently touched the well-filled money belt secured under his shirt. Had he been particularly alert, neither fatigued from the ordeal in the water nor dazed by the whiskey, he might have noticed several pairs of eyes appraising him. They saw a relative youngster, not exactly a tourist, but surely an adventurer—and inexperienced at that, judging from his clothes which, even soaked, retained a new, unspoiled look.

Another person appeared at Bridger's elbow, this one

claiming to be a messenger from the Grand Hotel, visible just across from the docks on a broad, dusty thoroughfare. "Accommodations, sir, compliments of the *Lucy Lee* for your trouble today. We'll clean your clothes, and your meals are free."

Oh yes, the boat crash, Bridger recalled. He hadn't known quite what to say to anyone about it, and had wandered away from the rescue boat without speaking to anyone. "How is she?" Bridger asked vacantly. "The young lady . . . the boat, I mean."

The messenger cocked his head and gave Bridger a curious look. "Well, sir, the boat will be just fine. She'll be repaired all in good time. But the line would like you to be their guest for three days. Hopin' all's well with you, sir." Through the whiskey haze, Bridger finally realized he was being offered a place to stay at no cost. "The best hotel in Jacksonville, sir, just the ticket for a gentleman such as yourself."

Bridger was about to follow along when he heard a loud pop to one side. He turned to look and saw a man fall, grabbing at his belly. Several people dodged away, bumping others. Some shoving broke out. Into the center of the fracas stepped a big man in an exotic duster-length coat. He threw a hard right-hand punch, lurching as he did, but the blow landed hard and the man who took it staggered backward, dropping something with a clatter. Bridger saw it was a pistol. The man in the coat laced the fingers of his hands together and swung his locked fists like a club, landing another solid blow. His opponent fell and tried to crawl away, but the attacker smashed him in the side of the head with his foot— no, Bridger saw it was the end of a wooden peg leg!

Two other men squared off and began to slug away. Bridger felt his blood rise. He had an urge to jump in and take up the fight. Whose side didn't matter. But the Grand Hotel runner kept pulling at him. "Come on, sir. Please, don't pay no attention. This isn't the true city."

Bridger let himself be led away, but he continued to look over his shoulder. He could see that the peg-legged man's coat seemed to have some sort of hide sewn into the shoulders. He liked the look of the slouch hat he wore, and the mustache with ends dipping past his chin. He would have been curious, though not alarmed, had he known the man's blazing eyes were boring straight in his direction.

Elijah Dicken usually didn't take care of the rougher dock business himself. Hired help did it for him. It wouldn't do, after all, for him to take part in common brawls, perhaps letting the folks on his street of fine Victorian houses learn too much about their neighbor. As far as most of them knew, Lige Dicken was a respectable businessman, a veteran of the Glorious Cause who ran the stevedore company; they would have said Dicken's enterprise helped grease the commerce of the South's next great city.

That was true, as far as it went. But men in a growing city needed money, often for such things that banks would not smile upon. Lige Dicken would, and he loaned to many—at high interest. And if men wanted gambling, whiskey, and ladies of pleasure, Dicken could supply those, too—in whatever quantity needed.

He fingered the flesh around his left knee, the place

where his peg leg fitted on. It was tender now that he had used the peg as a weapon. Sometimes it stung for no reason at all. When it did, it reminded Dicken of that damned wilderness where he had nearly grasped the dream of his life—and had almost died in the process.

He gazed across his desk at Wade Mizell, a big-fisted thug standing in front of him. Rough enough, this Mizell, but he didn't know much of life, certainly not enough to handle a problem with a competitor. That was why Dicken had decided he needed to assert his presence on the docks. Just this one rare time. The only thing was, he had not planned on a shooting—at least not then—which was why he had knocked down the gunman Barner Todd, a hothead and a trigger-happy fool.

"What about that ape he shot?" Dicken asked Mizell.

"Gut hit," Mizell smirked. "He'll squirm for a couple days, then die, likely. You know how these gutshots are, and they hurt bad. But they don't keep a man from talkin'. Want us to hurry it along?"

Mizell had a tendency toward the impulsive thought, Dicken knew. But he considered his idea for a moment. "No, let it go. He's Rotten Row scum. He'll be lesson enough as it is, and we don't have to stick our heads up again. Todd's the one I want gone. Didn't you tell him no guns? No guns this time? I wanted a beating, not a murder."

Dicken glared as his voice rose. Mizell didn't like being stared down, but he wasn't ready to scowl back. Not at this old bull. "He's stupid, a fool. Sure, I told him. He don't listen. He don't care. He does what he feels like."

"Not any more he won't. He's through, that dumb ape. I want him finished."

"What ya wanna do?"

"Whatever you want. Just make sure he knows he's not a part of this outfit anymore. Not ever again. Just make sure. You think you can do that?" Dicken continued to stare hard at Mizell.

Dicken's dark, hard eyes made Mizell think of the holes at the end of a double-barreled shotgun. "It'll get done."

"You better collect for them chippies, too. Old Sam's owin' us a bunch fer those gals. He can't pay, I know someone who can."

Mizell nodded.

"And one other thing," Dicken said. "There was a young fella got off that *Lucy Lee* lifeboat today. Real tall, had a carbine over his shoulder, big mustache. Looked half-drowned, but he was takin' everything in, real calm-like. Had a touch of the prince about him. Fella like him, he might have been headed for the Grand. Find out who he is, what he's doin'. If he isn't anybody, then maybe he has money. Least we can do is take it away from him."

Mizell left, but Dicken continued to glare at the spot where he'd been standing. He knew Mizell called him "Leg" Dicken, just like all the rest of those apes. Including the one he knew best—the one calling himself that devil-sounding name these days. He'd seen him lurking around the docks, too, right before the fight. Seeing what he could see and what he could get into.

Well, what did any of them know? Nothing about a fortune in Spanish gold, that was dead certain. So let them call him what they wanted. He had come a long way—and he planned to go further still.

# 3

TOM BRIDGER FANCIED HIMSELF a chess player. "'Knights and pawns at dawn" was how he'd challenged his college friends. Most of them at Renssalaer, his old college, couldn't beat him. Now he gazed at a placard outside a salon in the Grand Hotel:

> The Invincible Simon Puig, chessmaster
> Student of the Great Paul Morphy
> Simultaneous Exhibition!
> A Silver Dollar to challenge!
> 25 to any man or woman
> who Out-wizards the Wizard!

Bridger had been wandering the Grand Hotel's lobby and its salons, letting the atmosphere wash over him. It wasn't as opulent as many of the New York hotels he had seen, but it was more than he had expected in a war-beaten frontier state. The Grand even was awash in new electric lighting. Someone, it seemed, was doing all right in this part of the country.

The patrons here all looked affluent and not at all like broken survivors of a lost cause, as Bridger had imagined he would find. Perhaps they were from somewhere else. The ladies wore fine, flowing dresses and hats with graceful plumes; he watched one beauty peel an orange without taking off her gloves. Bridger couldn't look away from her, and didn't until her male companion raised his eyes and stared back.

Most of the men were older, portly and solid. Bridger thought they all looked like successful businessmen, and he thought of his father again. He realized he might have been the youngest among the crowd, and he was certainly the only one with a gun on his shoulder. His best clothes were now in the laundry, too. He felt a bit out of place.

Not only that, he still felt a little woozy from the whisky and ragged from the boat accident. But maybe some chess would clear his mind. Why not? His dollar got him a chair at a chessboard and he sat to wait for the Invincible Mr. Puig, who was playing eleven other opponents at once.

Puig would make a move, then quickly move to the next board. Bridger was seated in front of the white pieces, so he slapped his king's pawn two spaces to the center. Puig soon passed by and, without speaking or sitting down, countered with his king's pawn, but moved it just one space ahead.

The chess player was a small man, plump, with hair short on top and longish on the sides. Bridger thought he resembled pictures he'd seen of Steven A. Douglas, the senator who'd run against Abe Lincoln before the war. Puig, however, had a small mustache with points, which he twirled while contemplating the chess boards in front of him.

A waiter appeared at Bridger's side. "Bring you a drink,

sir?" Bridger considered a moment, then ordered a beer. "What I really need," he said, "is someone to tell me the best way to get around in this state of yours." The waiter smiled as if Bridger had told a joke, and moved away.

"Friendly, aren't you," Bridger muttered. He looked around the room for an inviting face. Two or three of the other chess players gazed back at him, but offered no greeting. One opened a magazine; another fanned out a deck of cards. They seemed barely interested in the boards in front of them.

Bridger wondered at their apparent inattention; he himself was fascinated with chess. He liked the pieces' intricate moves and their myriad combinations, and he liked the notion of commanding a miniature army to kill an enemy king. He decided to be aggressive. He pushed out his queen's pawn two spaces, side by side with the king's pawn. He wished it was as easy to plot his next move in Florida.

But then, he had no business playing chess anyway. He should be out roaming the streets, meeting people, striking up small talk, playing the jolly traveler—the kind of thing he hated to do, but would have to do here if he were going to make anything of himself. Here he was on his own, not like in Troy, New York, where he had ready-made friends and connections at Renssalaer and in the community, well-to-do and influential. But here in Florida, he wondered what he could say. And to whom? And how much should he talk about Big Mike McGinnis?

His uncle had, after all, been a first sergeant in the 48th New York Infantry, a Yankee regiment that had fought in this state and had done damage to Southern boys at the Ocean Pond battle—even though the Southern boys had won that fight, Bridger knew, and called it by another name—Olustee, or some such. But it was a subject that would be sure to arouse resentment, perhaps outright anger, if he were not careful. He had heard these Southerns held grudges and were quick to fight.

Let them, Bridger thought. He was at home in that kind of situation; fighting was easier than talking. But could he dare breathe a word of the secret Mike had told him? Probably not. Doing so would either make people too interested in him or cause them to think him a fool. How could he even begin to say why he was here? A search for an uncle he hadn't seen for five years could be as hard to explain as a quest for something that might or might not exist. Tales about hidden fortunes were everywhere.

The beer tasted good and he ordered another. It would open his thinking and make it easier to talk. Puig swung past and, barely pausing, moved his queen's pawn two spaces out. Still daring, Bridger moved his king's pawn another space forward, thrusting it into Puig's territory.

When he passed again, Puig glanced at the board and raised an eyebrow, hesitating just a moment before moving his queen's bishop pawn two spaces out. Bridger moved another pawn, knowing he soon would have to deploy some more powerful pieces. Puig jumped out his queen's knight. Now Bridger moved a fifth pawn, creating a salient in the board's center.

Puig had retired four of his opponents by now and when he passed again, he noted Bridger's move and spoke for the first time: "Fashionable, aren't we?" Bridger couldn't tell if Puig was speaking of his appearance or his line of attack on the board. Puig swept out with his queen, posting her ominously on the third rank. "What do you suppose the black rose will see?" Puig remarked, winking as if in conspiracy.

Bridger couldn't think of what to do next. He made some harmless pawn and knight moves as Puig began to position his own pieces: knights forward, a rook on an open file. He was handcuffing Bridger. And he was dispatching his other opponents rather quickly, Bridger saw. Some got up to leave. The men wore expensive, tailored clothes, some a bit snug on their figures.

One of them passed Bridger's table and glanced at his carbine. "Planning on a shootout?" he asked pleasantly.

"Only if you are," Bridger shot back. The man walked on. Bridger regretted his curt reply. Perhaps he could have started a conversation and learned something.

Puig chased Bridger's queen, hemming her in. The game was only ten or eleven moves old and Bridger could see no promising moves. He asked Puig: "You really knew Morphy, did you?"

"Oh, yes. Mad, absolutely, but a truly genius player. And he put up with my early bumblings," Puig answered. "Of course, I paid him dearly. My family hated it. They thought I should read the law. I think you're beaten, you know. You'll lose your queen, and then . . . well, why go on?" He laughed merrily and glanced around the room. The rest of his foes had lost interest.

"I'll tell you." Puig put his hands on Bridger's table and leaned forward. "You know the game, at least. The rest of these . . . these woodpushers—"he flicked a hand in contempt—"they want only to say they've sat opposite a master. They have no concept of the beauty. You, now. You have the beginnings of an understanding of the game's power planes and how they can be made to intersect. To build an invulnerable position. To mount an irresistible attack. It is a matter of spacing, and geometry . . . and music." He was going on, but Bridger found himself enjoying the chatter.

"All you lack," said Puig, "is sophistication."

Bridger's good humor vanished. "You presume to judge that?" He deliberately adopted an arrogant tone.

"Now I've injured your feelings." Puig was unruffled. "I tell you, why don't we retire to the bar. I will buy you a drink—one—and tell you all about myself. Come, if you please. I would not deliberately offend you. I meant what I said as instructive, and only in the context of the game. Come now, this salon is becoming too stuffy for my taste. One of those damnable cigars, I believe."

Bridger knew he should make his escape. But to where? Still . . . this Puig needed no encouragement to talk. "All right, then, to the bar." What the hell, Bridger thought. What the hell.

# 4

PUIG BOUGHT ONE DRINK and Bridger bought more. Many more. And whereas Puig had promised to tell all about himself, it was Bridger who did most of the talking. He decided at some point that this new companion, droll as he seemed, might show him a way to get started in Florida.

"See," Bridger expounded, "My life in New York was just too tightened up. I want more than an existence in some business already set up for me. I want to make my own way. My father said, you're not good enough, he told me. I had a reason to come south. To this place. Here I am."

Bridger no longer felt shy about talking, but he knew he wasn't speaking clearly. That was the trouble with the damn whisky.

But Puig nodded sagely. From time to time, he dug an index finger into an ear, then rubbed one of his mustache points with the residue. "I know the feeling well, of wanting to be on one's own. You say you had a reason to come here? Other than to . . . uh, seek your fortune, so to speak?"

"Uncle Mike. Uncle Mike," Bridger said. He looked

down the bar and held up two fingers. "Two more, barkeep. Uncle Mike's the reason. Mother's brother, see. Haven't heard from him. Been years."

"Just disappeared, I take it?"

"Been years. Gotta letter from him, five, six years ago. That's all. Nothing since then. Mother's worried sick. My mother. Didn't want me to come, but I hadda come. You know. Mike's more than uncle. He's like a brother, like a father. Taught me a lot about life."

He gestured toward the carbine. "Gave me that Sharps. Father sent me to college but Mike taught me how to box, made me go to Paddy Ryan's. You know Ryan? He's the champ."

The barkeep, pouring the men more whisky, looked up at the mention of the former American champion. "Was, you mean," he sneered, "Til he fought that Sullivan fella. Fact is, we got a pretty good boy right here in Jacksonville. Goes by the name of Tapper Callahan. Heard of him?"

"Fact is, haven't heard of that pretty good boy," Bridger mocked. "Don't think much at all about the roustabouts fighting down here in the sticks."

"Why, say, mister," the barman said. "You have a right high way of talkin fer such a young sprout. Who gave you yer manners?"

Bridger had an answer ready, and Puig saw him tensing. He interrupted before Bridger could take the argument any further.

"Oh, come now, gentlemen. I don't feel like hearing an argument about pugilists. Can we just have another drink or so? And Mr. Bridger, more, please, about this uncle of yours."

"Soldier," said Bridger. "Fought down here in this war of

yours, out there at Ocean Pond or some such place. Said your boys murdered all our Negro troops after the fight. Killed the wounded, shot 'em all dead right on the battlefield."

Now Puig tensed. He looked to see if anyone had heard. It didn't do for strangers, especially northern strangers, to speak in less than flattering terms about the late Confederate army. This Bridger was a bit of a handful. It was bad enough he had called the battle by its Yankee name. Floridians knew it as Olustee.

To Puig's relief, Bridger didn't pursue the subject.

"He mustered out of the Union army, finally, and glad enough to be rid of it, Mother told me he used to say. Then he goes down to South America. Joined some army or other down there, fought some kinda more wars—shoot, they made him a colonel, I think down there—anyway, he come home, come back here to Florida. I don't know. He got to some place called Punta Pinal."

Bridger knew he was starting to blither. The whiskey was working at him hard, but he was feeling good. And he was starting to feel kindly toward Puig. Why, the man must have his best interests at heart. He would confide.

But Puig spoke up first. "You see, all of Florida—especially this city right now, but all of Florida—is on the move," the chess player said. "There are wealthy people here. Northerners like you, even some Europeans, too. They've worn out their own countries, now they want to try ours. They see it as a wasteland they can turn into money. They can grow fruit and vegetables all year, citrus, cattle, they can raise timber, they can cultivate what they please. If they build railroads, they can ship whatever they raise or make anywhere in the world. And the railroads will bring more people, and those people will build more cities, and those cities will mean more money to be made. You're from the north. You should know how it works.

"Then, too, you have the health people. They're saying Florida is the place to live to add years to your life. And they're advertising it all over the world. You probably saw invalids being unloaded off boats or the train when you came in yourself. And then you have people who see Florida as some sort of exotic wilderness, and Jacksonville on the edge of a jungle frontier, just ready for the man with the good idea and the know-how to sell it.

"I myself am a mere chess player with few other talents. But this uncle of yours, whatever he was doing here, could have been seduced in a dozen ways. And if he weren't careful, he'd be used and done away with. Believe me, this is not a place to take lightly, nor are the people here to be toyed with."

Bridger tried to absorb all this. He couldn't imagine Uncle Mike being "used and done away with." Using and doing to someone else, yes. But that wasn't a point to argue now. He might as well come out with what he wanted.

"I wanna get to this place called Punta Pinal," he blurted. "Don't know where it is, or howta get there. You know?"

Puig considered. Bridger was pronouncing the name Punta Pie-nl. The chessplayer twirled his mustache. "Some relatives of mine, from New Orleans, moved to a place that sounded something like that. I don't know where it is. South of here, I guess. They said it was a wild place with no amenities."

Bridger was beginning to feel a little dizzy, but he ordered another whiskey. The bartender sullenly poured.

"And you?" Puig quizzed suddenly. "What's your secret? Are you here to get rich? I mean besides finding your uncle."

The queries startled Bridger. He had been listening to Puig, but the man talked while saying little. Fatigue suddenly rolled over Bridger. And he knew he was getting drunker. "Here to get to Punta Pinal," he said. "Maybe I will get rich. Need to get there."

Puig used more ear wax on his mustache. "If I were you, then, sir, I would first get myself to Tampa. It is across the state, farther south, a growing town but still something of a . . . well, it's not quite civilized, as we would think of that term. I suspect someone there would know of this spot of yours."

Bridger was fading. He sagged slightly on his stool and his eyes glittered glassy blue. "Tampa," he said. "Tampa. I shoul' write that down."

Some time after that moment—Bridger never knew exactly when or under what circumstances—Puig departed. Bridger might have ordered another drink, and perhaps he was served it, and perhaps he drank it, but he did not necessarily recall it.

Soon, anyone who cared to watch saw him rise from his stool, grip his carbine, and shamble out of the saloon, down a corridor and into an open mezzanine where a musical entertainment was in progress. There he stood, a baffled galoot, swaying slightly, gun hanging in his hand. His lips moved silently as the violins sang the nostalgic "When You and I Were Young, Maggie."

A man introduced a young woman named Jenny, from

Philadelphia, who began singing "Remember, Boy, You're Irish." Bridger listened and his eyes began to glisten. He thought of his Irish Catholic mother and Uncle Mike, who frequently made much of his Irish background. And it made Bridger think of another tune. He began singing it when Jenny's last note had faded. It was a soaring, romantic song, meant to be filled with daring and defiance. Bridger had learned it from Mike McGinnis and now he sang it in a loud, quavering baritone.

> The minstrel boy to the war has gone,
> In the ranks of death you will find him.
> His father's sword he has girded on,
> His wild harp slung behind him.
>
> Land of song, said the warrior bard,
> Though all the world betray thee,
> One sword at least thy rights shall guard,
> A faithful song shall praise thee.

Bridger wanted to present a serious demeanor, but he slurred and swayed as he sang. Some among those watching giggled, and others offered sarcastic response with a few slow, drawn-out claps. Some shook their heads. A man in hotel livery appeared next to Bridger and spoke a few words. He took him by the arm. He led him to a door that opened on a street. Bridger went out the door and began walking on the street, planting his feet heavily, his gun still swinging in his hand. People stared at him, but he paid no attention.

That night, as on all nights, Jacksonville toiled, laughed, bellowed, wept, brayed, gambled, whispered, caroused, and schemed. Loafers loafed, drunkards drank. Patrons left the Park Theater, chattering about Carmen and its star, Miss Minny Hawk. In a club called Sherlock's, roulette, faro, and poker went on all night. Sometime in the wee hours, several young men on horseback galloped down Bay Street, firing pistols for no apparent reason other than to make noise.

Tom Bridger was part of all the activity, and yet in his state he might as well have dreamed and forgotten it. He rambled on the city side roads, reeled up and down Ocean Street and into every dive he found. Men bought him drinks and he bought more of his own until he was so drunk he could not speak. Yet he would not fall or give up the night.

In a saloon called The Growler's Retreat—a name he would have loved but would not recall—a man promised him a woman. Bridger stumbled along for blocks, following the procurer. He tripped and started to tumble. Someone grasped him and then another took hold. They wrestled him down, punching and kicking at him.

Bridger pawed back, flailing with arms and legs, but he could find nothing solid. On his hands and knees, he retched and tried to stand, but the ground was rolling quicksand. Hands jerked at his clothing, pulled him, trying to haul him along. He felt himself falling forward, felt yanking hands pulling him up, and he could hear ugly, mirthless laughter. And finally he was somewhere else, oblivious and lost.

Those who had watched and hounded and yanked him finished their work and faded into the dark. Eventually, a kind of consciousness seeped back into Bridger's brain. Coming to, he perceived a dim, gray light—it was barely dawn. The next thing he discovered was that his head must soon explode. The pain was more than sore discomfort, it was a fuzzy, grinding, jagged thing that twisted his stomach and ruined thought.

Except for a single realization that clattered in his brain: ah God, I've done it again. Again. He remembered nothing. He had only a dark notion that something had gone terribly wrong.

Bridger sat up and looked around, wiping at the grit eating into his face. He had been sprawled on the ground. He seemed to be lodged on some kind of back pathway. A flimsy shack or two were the only structures. And he saw still flimsier quarters: tents made of blankets stretched over sticks, crates on their sides with canvas to curtain the open end.

Several men slumbered in piles of clothing and rags. The dying ashes of what had been two small campfires released sour wisps of smoke, mingling with another dank, spoiled aroma. A skinny brown dog nosed through a pile of fish heads, innards, and bones not far from Bridger. It jerked to snap at a fly buzzing its haunch.

A gaunt man wearing only trousers appeared in the doorway of one of the shacks. There were no steps up to the door, and the fellow folded himself down a leg at a time. He squatted in the dirt, staring blankly at Bridger. Who felt a sudden and helpless terror. He had lost his way. Not just taken a wrong turn. He had stumbled out of his world into a ghastly other. He had no idea where he could be or how he had gotten there.

Dread-filled, Bridger shot glances this way and that. God, no! Things were missing. No, no! His traveling gear, his precious Sharps carbine . . . Bridger slapped both hands to his middle. No! His money belt . . . gone. Nothing! And then he realized his clothes were gone, too. No coat, no shirt, trousers, or boots. How could it be? Surely it was all here somewhere. Heart pounding, breath coming in gasps, Bridger knelt in the dirt, clad only in a suit of underwear.

He turned his eyes toward the staring shack man. "Say," he pleaded, "I lost some things. Do you know where they are?" He prayed the man had taken them in for safekeeping. But the man only stared back. "Yer a joke, mister," he observed. "A real joke."

# 5

BRIDGER LIFTED HIS HEAD, then dropped face down in the dirt, nausea churning inside. His brain froze. So acute was his panic, he nearly cried. This had happened to him before. But always, friends had been near. Someone to see him home. He had had money, ways to do things. All he endured were a few gibes and a day or two of feeling jumpy and moody.

This time he had done himself in. This time he was lost, a thousand miles from safe haven. Another thought rushed through his mind: He'd have to wire his father for money. Even if he had to walk somewhere half-naked to do it. It was the quickest way out.

But amid his hangover sickness, the words of the man sitting in the shack's doorway, still watching him, came scratching back "Yer a joke." It looked like he would prove the truth of it to his father. He could already imagine the old man's smirk and his sarcastic comments. Yet what choice did he have?

Bridger pushed himself up, leaning on his knees. His

head reeled so badly that he nearly lay back down. Dirt crusted one side of his face. He wanted to heave. He tried to focus his eyes on the shack man. "All right, I'm a stranger here. I'm in a bad way. I'm willing to work. Is there something I can do? I don't really care what." Stand on your own two feet whatever happens, Uncle Mike had always told him. Well, he'd give it a try.

"Depends on what you wanna do," the shack man answered. "Or can do, more like. You a Yankee, ain'cha?"

Bridger nodded. "That's right, that's what I am. Doesn't mean I can't work."

The man kept on. "I never knew a Yankee could stand a hour a hard work. Rather stand there and tell someone else howta do his'n. 'Cept you're prolly too drunk to stand up. Was las' night, anyways."

Bridger wanted to ask how he'd come here—but couldn't muster the heart. "I'm not drunk now," he said, wondering if that was entirely true. "I need to get some work. I need to get some money, and when I do, I'll get on out of your way."

The effort of speaking—even thinking—seemed to bring on a new wave of nausea. Bridger bowed his head. Others had started gathering, rousing out of the weeds and their makeshift shelters. Seeing he had an audience, the shack man gestured toward a stained container and said to Bridger:

"Whyn't you start by takin' a drink outta that spit can yonder?"

The remark raised guffaws among the listeners. "Hey Jaw," one of them called out to the shack man, "You reckon he c'n get it all down in one string?" More chuckling.

"Maybe we oughta just toss it all on 'im," said another. "That'd sober 'im up." One or two men edged closer to Bridger.

Their mood seemed more playful than threatening, but Bridger didn't like the way things were going. He stood up as quickly as he could, still dizzy. It was a sure thing he didn't have much to offer in the way of trade. But this bunch seemed to want some entertainment. And maybe he could give them that, hung over or not.

"All right," he spoke loudly. "I was sincere when I asked you what I could do to earn money, and you didn't want any of that. So now I'll challenge you and see if any of you are men like you think you are. I'll fight any one of you to a finish. It's real easy. If I win, you give me some clothes to wear out of here. I lose, I'll be your slave, do whatever you want for a day."

Bridger couldn't resist an extra cut. "You Southerns still like the idea of slaves, don't you? Here's your chance to try it again. If you think you're good enough."

It was an outrageous offer voiced in an insulting way, Bridger knew. But it produced no shouted responses or threats. It did silence the little mob, but the men seemed more reflective than angered, as if they just wanted to consider for a while. Maybe, Bridger thought, these louts would just hand him a few dirty things and send him off.

But no such luck.

One of them called again to "Jaw"—Bridger couldn't tell if he was saying Jaw, Chaw, or maybe a bitten-off John. The man wanted to know what "Jaw" thought of a Yankee who'd come down to Florida in his underwear to try to fight folks.

"I think," said Jaw, his half-smile invincible, "That it's a job for Dognose."

Dognose was one of the uglier men Bridger had ever seen. Only the sad quality of his eyes kept him from being positively the ugliest. His nose drew quick attention. It looked as though someone had tried to jam it through his face and out the back of his head. What remained was a hunk of meat with two holes in it, smashed almost flat against the face.

Dognose had rust-colored hair—a little—that stood in bristly clumps, though most of his pate seemed shaved or naturally bald. Boil-like bumps covered his face, ginger whiskers sprouting out of some. He smelled like very old garbage, and Bridger caught a whiff fifteen feet away.

Yet the man's eyes were big and brown, wise and, Bridger thought, somehow sympathetic. Maybe this would not be such hard work, even with a horrible hangover. Maybe Dognose was some kind of buffoon these camp characters kept for amusement. Bridger could hear him humming some kind of melody as he approached.

Bridger thought the man looked like a pig standing up. He had a gargantuan belly, stubby arms, and short, oddly thin legs that seemed to bend a little too much with each step, giving Dognose a funny, bobbing gait.

He kept on humming and Bridger recognized the tune as one the sporting crowd in Troy used to sing, usually in bars and before prizefights. Maybe Dognose was one of those traveling gladiators who took on all comers.

Not good if so, Bridger thought. Such fighters often

knew a hundred tricks and styles of battle. Bridger had watched a man use nothing but his feet, kicking his opponent at will in the belly, chest, and even the head. The other man had been helpless and had nearly died. Bridger had been impressed then, but he doubted Dognose was a master of kickfighting. But he'd soon enough find out. The camp-rats had gathered, more out of interest in a possible spectacle than in Bridger's wager.

Jaw commenced the formalities. "There 'e is," he shouted to Dognose. "Have at 'im."

Bridger did not assume the classic pugilist's stance he'd learned at Paddy Ryan's. Instead, he held both fists shoulder high and faced Dognose head on, watching to see what the man's style would be. It was no surprise. Dognose lunged and tried to grab Bridger's head with his right hand. Bridger backed up, stepped to one side, and held his hands higher.

Now he looked more the boxer, even if he hardly felt like one. His head still reeled, and he thought if he were punched in the stomach he might lose everything. Still, no use in stalling. Bridger gunned a straight left, landing it on his opponent's mush of a nose. It gave way like a pouch of jelly. Bridger felt it move under his fist.

Dognose stumbled back a step, his eyes turning even sadder, as if his feelings had been hurt. He seemed surprised, and hesitated an instant too long. Bridger struck with two more lightning lefts, one after another. Dognose's head snapped back twice and blood showed around his mouth and the holes that passed for his nostrils.

The sight brought bellows from those watching, and several oafs pressed closer to the action. Bridger himself felt a rush of excitement and it cleared his head a little. He waited to see what Dognose would do next.

He charged straight on.

Bridger sidestepped, punching his opponent on an ear. Dognose whirled and lunged again, arms looping as he tried to encircle Bridger's head and neck. And again Bridger sidestepped. He's a wrestler, all right, Bridger thought, wondering if it would make his task easier or harder.

But he had no time for contemplation. Dognose rushed again—and stopped short. Feigning another head grab, he instead looped his arms around Bridger's middle, squeezing and lifting. Bridger's feet came off the ground and he felt his breath huff out.

He had made the mistake of letting a grappler take hold—and now his arms were pinned to his sides and he was being shaken like a bag of clothes. The camp hooligans laughed and shouted. Bridger was helpless—almost.

He nodded twice, quickly and forcefully, bringing his forehead down hard on Dognose's mug. Something crunched and Bridger thought he felt part of Dognose's cheekbone cave in. The lug gasped, let go, and brought both hands to his face. Bridger hooked to an ear, then snaked a blow to the ribs.

Dognose backed a step, took another hook to the face, another to the gut. Bridger double-jabbed to an eye as Dognose tried to dodge; he was afraid to move his hands away from his crushed cheekbone. Bridger, though worn from his carousing, was delivering a boxing exhibition at the expense of the camp buffoon. And the onlookers, switching their sympathies quickly, liked the action.

"Look at the Yankee work, give it to him, bo'!" shouted one. The cheering pleased Bridger. He even forgot he was performing in his underwear. He began to maneuver, trying to get in position for an ending punch. Jabbing, he side-stepped, then slid forward, backward, then to the side, almost dancing. Dognose got his legs crossed and Bridger led with a hard, straight right. It spun Dognose halfway round and dropped him to hands and knees. He lurched up, woe in his eyes, open hands trying to shield his blood-slick face.

Then it was easy. Bridger jabbed toward the injured cheek and Dognose moved both hands to protect it. Bridger jabbed again at the soft spot, at the same instant launching a short, very hard hook toward what he knew would be Dognose's uncovered jaw. It knocked the lummox flat. And the camp louts hollered and leaped, hitting the air with their fists.

Dognose lay with one arm over his face, his chest heaving. Bridger could see he was finished. He strode through the crowd, which parted nicely, and sat down on a stump, hands on knees.

"Gentlemen," he speechified, "I need some clothes."

# 6

"THEY CALL THIS PLACE ROTTEN ROW. Been here before? You don't look it." He was a small man with a side-to-side gait that reminded Bridger of a sailor's walk. He wore a bowler hat and a black vest, and tossed a pine cone hand to hand.

Bridger was wrestling into Dognose's oversized shirt and trousers and hurried to get his feet into a pair of broken brogans before one of these rascals snatched them away. Most looked shifty and hungry enough to steal a baby's biscuit.

"Not much for fashion, but guess those duds'll have to do ya, huh?"

Bridger tried to ignore the chattering man in front of him.

"Ah, ya get the scum of the world here." He gestured widely. "Grifters, killers, pickpockets, beggars, their brazen hussies, and half their drunken mothers." He looked around hopefully. "Don't see any a the ladies just now.

"But me, now, I done it all. You can't show me a trick. Been on the seas and farmed the land, fit in the war, marched all the way to Pennsylvane-aye-ay with Robert E. Lee. And they tell me they never saw such a fight that happened right here in Floradee, over by that O-lustee." He stuck out his hand. "Name of Factor. Whatta you go by?"

Bridger brushed the hand and said his name, concentrating on tying the brogans.

"You do real nice with them mitts a yers," Factor said. He said the word nice as if it were "nahss." It struck Bridger as funny.

"I been around some and I ain't seen many folks that can fight that fancy," Factor continued. "And when they is in they underwear, too. Course, then, you wasn't quite so feisty last night. Them boys brought you in, now, they mighta just left you for a dead one."

Bridger perked up. "What boys?"

"Why, Leg Dicken's boys. Thought you was with 'em. Thought they knew you, way they was laughin' and talkin'."

"They took every blessed thing I had," Bridger said grimly. "Including what I was wearing . . . and a lot more. "Who is this Leg Dicken, anyway?"

Factor tossed his pine cone.

"Oh, you are a new one, ain'cha? Who's Leg Dicken, he says." Factor turned to some loiterers nearby, spreading his arms wide, as if in disbelief. "He don't know who Leg Dicken is! Well, Bridger, Mr. Bridger, sir, let me tell you a few facts a life here. Leg Dicken runs everything worth running in these parts."

One of the loiterers moved closer. He was carrying a jar of clear liquid and he took a drink of it. Factor continued to chatter. "Ever'thing that happens on them docks in Jacksonville, that's ol' Leg's business. Anything gets loaded, unloaded, dumped, lost, or busted, he's the man behind it. He'll get ya a job, see that ya don't get one, or see that ya starve, if that's what he wants. That man is some humdinger, let me tell ya.

"Not only that. There ain't a thief in Jacksonville that don't give Leg a cut a what he steals. Same with the ladies there in the bars. They either give Leg a percentage or they best get on up to Savannah or over to Lake City. Yessir, and he'll sell you INsurance, too. Course, you pay so his bully-boys don't knock a hole in the bottom a yer boat. There's many a fisherman found out the hard way, and I'll tell ya another thing, he gets a cut of whatever they catch and sell. Why, he's the king of the waterfront."

Factor was just warming up. "I'll tell ya how he got started. Ever heard a that Texas gunfighter, Wes Hardy or Hardin or somethin'? He useta stay over by Gainesville, went by some other name, but it was ol' Wes from Texas, it was. And I hear tell ol' Leg, he and Wes partnered up, got some kind a gang together. Ol' Leg, he got hisself a pile a money."

Bridger had heard Uncle Mike talk about New York City gangs like the Dead Rabbits, bands of rough Irishmen who mostly fought each other. This Dicken seemed to have an army at his command.

"Why can't the law stop this fellow?" Bridger asked. "I might make a complaint myself, considering what you're telling me about last night."

Factor threw down his pine cone and snorted a short laugh. "Why, most people think Leg Dicken's an honest businessman, helping Jacksonville to get back on its feet. He's a Southern veteran to boot. Got 'is leg shot off in the war, over at that O-lustee fight. Rode with the cavalry, too."

One of the loiterers, the man with the jar of clear liquid, stepped up. "Looks to me," he said, "like everyone's doin' too much talkin' and not enough drinkin'." He hoisted the jar, took a pull and offered it to Bridger. "You fight pretty good, mister. Ol' Dognose there . . . " He clucked his tongue and winked. "He's the best we got. Have a swig a this. Best we got, too. It'll set you up right."

The man talked friendly enough, but Bridger saw a hard, mean set to his face. He took the jar and examined it. "Water? Willikers, I sure could use some."

The man smirked. "Low bush lightnin'," he said.

"What's that?"

"Why, drinkin' whiskey, son, homemade. Cure what ails ya."

Here was something new. I should test it, Bridger thought. Show these natives I can fight and drink with any of them. He took a mouthful, swished it briefly, and swallowed. The liquor roared down his throat and slammed into a hollow belly, empty for hours. Bridger used his will to keep from gagging and gasping. In seconds, he felt his face warm up; and a bit of the fog lifted from his brain. He felt sharper and smarter.

"I was you, I'd watch it," Factor said. "Man come in here like you did last night, he got no business drinkin' white whiskey in the mornin'." He looked away, as if offended.

"Hey, old man," said the whiskey man. "Who asked ya? You c'n shove off. Been wonderin' about ya anyway, ya yakkin' ol' goat, always hangin' around. Wonderin' what you do."

"No, he's right," Bridger spoke up. He stood and handed back the whiskey jar. His problems, he knew, were far from over. He was still tempted to send a wire to Troy. Someone there would send him money, surely. His mother or sister, for one.

The whiskey man, still smirking, moved away. He glanced behind him, looking Factor up and down.

"Maybe ya got some sense after all," Factor said. "But yer just off the boat and I'm gonna give ya some advice, friendly like. If yer gonna go around Floridee on yer own, ya better not go half drunked up all the time. You get yerself cut or shot quick as that. There's a lot more to Floridee than what you see with all them fancy people downtown and them tourists and such, and all this happy sunshine foofaraw. Wouldn't take much to get any of 'em dead, once they outta sight a them guides. It's a mean, dangerous place here."

"And these Rotten Row boys," Factor gestured, "bad as they look, they don't make up a quarter a what'll come at you in the night. Or in the daytime, either, if ya don't watch it."

Bridger listened patiently. "Well and good," he said. "You know a lot. So maybe you can tell me a few things I need to know right now. I've got to find some work, I'm flat broke, and I don't know anyone."

Factor gazed at Bridger a few seconds. "First thing, everything won't be so easy as whippin' a broke-down ol' ragamuffin. I'll tell ya that right now. But if ya want work, tell ya what. You go see Ortiz. Tell 'im I told ya to. Factor, tell 'im. He might could have somethin' for ya."

"Where?" Bridger asked.

"Ya go back to town," Factor pointed to a footpath. "Ya come in on a boat, did ya? You go back to the docks. Ask for Ortiz. He'll be down on Fisherman's Line." He bent to retrieve a pine cone. "Feller like you could learn a lot there."

Bridger nodded. "One other thing. You ever hear of a place called Punta Pinal?"

Factor stared into the distance several seconds before acknowledging the question. "Punta Pinal?" He shook his head. "Don't s'pose so. Don't know of it around here. Maybe south. Lots of wilds thataway. Plenty enough to get a man killed."

Leg Dicken, though he rarely acted on impulse, could see no clear course of action at the moment. Maybe, he reflected, while listening to Wade Mizell's report, he should go with intuition this time.

"This Factor, he knows a lot, doesn't he? Talks a lot, is his trouble. That bothers me. See what you can do about it. And this kid, Bridger's his name?"

Mizell smirked. "Yeah. A Yankee. Looks like he's bad to drink. Real bad. But he was pretty good with his fists, I heard. Had a lot of money on 'im. Nice gun, good clothes. Probly a spoilt rich kid."

Dicken mused, still curious about Bridger. He wasn't sure why. People came and went constantly. He guessed it was just coincidence. He'd been on the docks when the kid had come in off that wrecked boat; and he'd been struck by his appearance. Usually these youngsters looking for adventure didn't come in so well set up—at least not by themselves. And he had that look of confidence about him—character, Dicken guessed you'd call it—even after going through that boat wreck.

A stab of pain shot through Dicken's leg where it joined

the stump. To take his mind off it, he took out his pistol, checked the cylinder, and laid it on the desk. Mizell's eyes darted toward it, then away.

Dicken asked about the man who'd done the shooting on the dock. "Barner Todd?"

Mizell smirked again. "Died a snakebite."

Dicken raised an eyebrow.

"Remember Dub Lumpkin? You liked his style with that pimp tried to cross you," Mizell said. "He was real good with Todd, too. Took 'im on a gator hunt. Dozed off after lunch 'n ol' Dub dumped a sack a moccasins on 'im. They bit 'im and bit 'im, 'n ol' Dub said he didn't know if Todd died a fright or the snakebites." Mizell shook his head in mirth, laughing and snorting through his nose.

Dicken didn't change expression. "So Lumpkin has imagination. Ask him to see about Factor, then. I've known for a long time that he's a spy for the sheriff. Not that it matters a lot. But I'm sorry to hear he likes to talk so much. It's dangerous. We don't know who this stranger, this Bridger, might be. He's not someone ordinary, I don't believe. What if he's a Pinkerton? Or what if the next fellow is?

"Ask Lumpkin to see about this Bridger, too. But no rough stuff yet. I've got a feeling about him, and I want to know more. Make sure someone keeps an eye on him. Good as you say he is at fighting, maybe he is some kind of detective. That drunk stuff might be an act."

Mizell left and Dicken picked up his pistol, rotating the cylinder again and again, breathing deeply and closing his eyes. He imagined again that he was in a dark, hot cave bulging with Spanish gold. It was his favorite daydream.

# 7 🎇

BRIDGER LEFT ROTTEN ROW through a stand of pine trees and low bushes with pointy, fingered fronds. A breeze made them rattle as it whispered through the pine trees. Woods music, Bridger thought. It soothed him, even as his mind leaped from thought to thought. Uncle Mike . . . a lost fortune, maybe real, maybe a myth . . . who knew?

He didn't even know where or how he would eat next. Surely the docks, as busy as they were, could offer some job, however menial, enough to buy a paltry meal. College boy he was, but he wasn't afraid of work.

But what if this Dicken did control everything, down to the lowest chore? Would he have to apply to him? Could he be bold enough to demand payment for his lost gun and gear?

Then again, he reflected darkly, he wasn't even sure he had been robbed, nor of anything else that had happened that night. He remembered playing chess, talking to the chess master in the saloon—Poog, or some such name?—but little else remained clear.

Maybe he ought just get back to Troy the best way he could.

He thought he heard a vague step behind and jerked around. But there was nothing but the trail and the soft rustling of the bushes. Bridger broke into a light jog. The brogans fit loosely and would soon raise a blister, but it felt good to be moving quickly. It seemed to clear his head and he kept it up. Soon enough, the trail turned into kind of an alley with several shanties side by side. In a few more minutes, the alley turned into a street. Bridger slowed to a walk and watched the street grow busier.

A few men on horseback clumped by, the animals kicking up puffs of dust. Their riders didn't so much as glance at Bridger. A cart driver swore at the two mules pulling it, trying to bully them around a knot of cattle lumbering up the street, a dog patrolling their flanks and a man with a whip walking behind.

Bridger followed the cattle until they turned onto a major avenue. It was Bay Street, Bridger saw, where he'd begun sometime . . . yesterday. Yes. Now he would start over.

A squadron of pelicans, glaring down their bills, stood guard over several small boats roped to pilings. A man sat in one of them, working his fingers over a net. Bridger hailed him. "Looking for a fellow named Ortiz. Know him?"

"I am Ortiz." He was a small man with knotty, strong-looking arms.

Bridger felt encouraged that he had been lucky enough to find Ortiz so quickly. He came right out with his plight. "Fellow named Factor said you might have some work."

"Oh, shoor, that Factor, always sending me ees problems. Hah." Bridger heard no rancor in the remark. "I tell you," Ortiz went on. "You ever feesh?"

"With a pole, some," Bridger said.

"Hah!" Ortiz exploded. "I mean feesh with the net, haul em een all day, mullets, trouts, them croakers, everything you haul in. Get you strong, lak me." He flexed an arm, showing a bicep like a big potato. "I tell you. You work one day for Factor, cause he walk off when I need eem. I feed you, no pay. Next day, you work me again, I pay you, maybe feed, too. Plenty a feesh. You sleep in a boat, under canvas.

"You see 'at crapper there?" Ortiz pointed at a beaten-down structure at the edge of the dock. "You go een there, slosh out, buckets a water. Use mop, ay? You come out, you not throw up you stomach, I feed you. Then you start clean-ing my boats. You learn how to be feesherman."

Bridger did Ortiz's bidding for three days. He cleaned several boats, learning the hard way about the sharp-edged creatures that stuck to the hulls. Barnacles, Ortiz called them. Bridger used other names. He scraped his skin bloody before learning to take care chipping them off. Ortiz showed him how to caulk weak spots on the hulls and began teach-ing him how to inspect nets for tears and frayed sections. The fisherman said he owned four boats and that he was getting them ready for new crews, two men to a boat. He seemed willing to help Bridger learn the trade.

"You work good," he said. "I can make you feesherman."

"Let me think about it," Bridger replied.

The notion was tempting. He could at least spend a few weeks earning money and acquiring skills and knowledge he could probably use in his travels around Florida. Still, he was wary of delaying his search for Mike McGinnis. Already, the trail was old and probably cold. And another thing: Bridger had spied a man lurking around a nearby skiff, fiddling with its lines, trying to appear as if it were his own boat.

But Bridger thought the man looked more like a Rotten Row denizen than a fisherman or a boatman. And he didn't like the secretive glances the man threw at him. He wondered if he had imagined someone behind him when he had come to town the other day—or if he had in fact been followed. Eventually, the loiterer left, but the episode left Bridger uneasy. He could think of no reason someone would shadow him. But he wondered if he shouldn't push on, money or no money.

At least he was getting two meals a day—raw oysters and fish smoked, a cooking method Bridger had never known before. It gave the fish an aromatic, tangy flavor and Bridger loved it. He asked Ortiz where he'd learned the trick.

"Always knew," said the fisherman. "My father, ees father, we all know. Catch feesh in keys, Cuba, New Smyrna, all over. Always smoke em."

Bridger liked the fisherman enough to tell him a bit of his own background, and after a while he posed some questions. Had he heard of a place called Punta Pinal? Did he know Leg Dicken?

But Ortiz's mood darkened when Bridger mentioned the one-legged man.

"That fella cost me," he said. "'Hees man sank one a my boats one time I pay heem not enough to tie up here. Now I save a leetle ev'ry catch, geeve Leg Dicken ees money. I don't, he sink all my boats, maybe he sink me."

Ortiz looked away, scowling. Later, he merely grumbled a reply when Bridger asked again about Punta Pinal. So Bridger said no more. At night, curled among canvas sails, he contemplated how best to get south. If he traveled in that direction, working along the way, surely he would meet someone who could point him right.

Ortiz said he had no plans to fish south along Florida's Atlantic coast. Bridger decided his best hope would be to travel inland down the peninsula. His chance came suddenly.

On the morning of the fourth day, Bridger was unrolling a net, checking for tears, when his gaze skimmed over a steamboat moored a few boats away. Learning against the bow railing was a tall man wearing a frock coat and a slouch hat pulled low. Bridger stared, squinting.

Dicken!

Without a thought, he threw down the net, sprinted down the dock and barged up the steamer's gangplank. He charged toward the bow. "Hey, there! You, mister!" Heart pounding, Bridger realized what he was doing. It was too late to back out. He'd just have to take on Dicken man to man.

The tall man turned, very deliberately. "You're speaking to me, young man?"

It stopped Bridger dead. This man's mustache didn't seem quite as long as the one the man fighting on the dock had worn. Bridger glanced down. There was no wooden leg. The best Bridger could do was clear his throat.

"I . . . I'll have to apologize, sir. I thought you were someone else. I shouldn't have come up to you like that. I just . . . well, I'm sorry. I made a mistake."

"I daresay you did, son. Who did you think I was?"

Bridger wasn't sure he wanted to say. But he spit it out anyway. "I thought you were someone called Leg Dicken. Would you know him?"

The man looked down his nose at Bridger. "I would. And I take it as no compliment to be mistaken for him." He sighed and handed Bridger a card.

Sam Satin, it read. Entrepreneur.

"You may call me Mr. Satin," he said. "Some people pronounce the name with a long A, you know. They make it sound like the word for the devil." He watched Bridger for a reaction.

"You, however, may come to see me as your savior."

Bridger couldn't believe his ears. Mr. Satin repeated the offer.

"Yes, two dollars a day wages, plus meals. And yes, what you do is . . . be my man Friday, more or less. That could, you know, cover a lot of territory. Some days you may be little more than my companion in conversation.

"Other times . . . well, you are well set up as a pugilist, I know, and I'll wager you were a good shot with that rifle you say was stolen from you. I like having someone around who can take care of himself . . . and of me, if necessary."

Bridger frowned. Mr. Satin's apparent insight troubled him. "How is it you know so much about me?" He felt yet another twinge of regret about what might have happened the night of his binge through Jacksonville. "How do you know that I can box? Or that I had a rifle?"

Mr. Satin chuckled. "Oh, Tom—may I call you that?—this is a town built on intrigue and speculation. There is money to be made in Florida, and Jacksonville is its gateway. There are some of us who find it of good fortune, shall we say, to pay attention to who is coming and going, and to what they do once they're here. Information—gossip, some might call it—is not hard to come by.

"The fact is, I've been on the lookout for someone like you for some time. I learned of you, then learned of, shall we say, your most recent whereabouts. My problem was how to approach you. Then you solved that yourself, approaching me as if you had assault on your mind."

Bridger heard what he took to be traces of the south in Mr. Satin's speech. And he spoke like someone who had had an education, a bit like the chess player. He didn't like being the subject of speculation—but perhaps he could open up a bit to this man.

"Then you probably know I'm in Florida for a reason, not just a lark. I'm not sure why anyone would be interested in me or what I'm doing, but if they are, I wish they could tell me how to get to a particular place."

Mr. Satin raised an eyebrow. "I might be able to do that. I do know Florida rather well—I'm in real estate, you might say—and I'm well familiar with the ways we have to get around. Some, I must say, are rather primitive.

"But you haven't told me if you'll accept my offer, and you're not likely to get one any more handsome. And speaking so, if you'll pardon me, that is a reason you were interesting to many people. A new young man, travelling alone, obviously well-dressed, obviously well-armed, obviously quite handsome. There were many eyes that took note of your arrival, Tom."

Such talk made Bridger uncomfortable. He looked closely at the man who called himself Satin. He wondered if he had met the man during his first night in Jacksonville, and simply didn't remember it. But he felt a small rush of pride at the flattery. Maybe he'd sign on with this fellow. He knew a lot about Florida. Maybe he could learn from him.

"Mr. Satin, I'll accept your offer, on the condition that you understand it is a temporary arrangement. I have a responsibility and a mission here in Florida, south of here, I believe, but I'd like to work long enough to raise some money. I lost what I had, and in a way, I'm starting over. I'm working for a fisherman named Ortiz, but . . . that's temporary. I should tell him I'm moving on."

Mr. Satin smiled. "Well, it's a happy circumstance that I'm heading south myself. To Tampa, actually. Maybe we can learn something of your destination on the way. But I don't know that it would be a good idea to speak with this Mr. Ortiz just now. You probably haven't seen him this morning, and the reason is that he is speaking with a detective. The same detective who happened to speak with me earlier, in fact. You have been acquainted with a Mr. Factor, I gather? It seems that he has been murdered. And it seems that you are wanted for the crime."

Leg Dicken took pride in his telephone. The new contraption was one of the few in Jacksonville, although he thought the thing made callers sound as though they were crumpling paper near the mouthpiece as they spoke.

But only the rich or influential owned one and Dicken fancied himself both, at least in his own world and maybe—one day—in the world all Jacksonville's high-and-mighties walked in.

What Dicken didn't fancy at the moment was the chess

player. "You are paid to pass along information as you get it, not wait until it's convenient for you," Dicken shouted into the phone. His heart pounded. What the chess player had told him was shocking. Someone else was on the trail of a hidden fortune—perhaps the one he'd considered his own secret.

"And you are paid to tell me what these slick strangers talk about. I'll do the deciding what's interesting."

Still shouting, Dicken began to tremble. The chess player said this Bridger had talked about Punta Pinal—Spanish words that meant the Point of Pines—and had asked how he could get there. That he had been mysterious about his reasons for going there.

Dicken could feel the ragged end of his leg throbbing with every heartbeat. Never—never!—had he heard of anyone coming to Jacksonville with that destination in mind, unless they were running and wanted a new life lost in the wilderness, or were some of those hornswoggled English people lured to what they thought was going to be a paradise. Bridger didn't seem to fit either of those categories.

No, there had to be a powerful temptation. Who would go to that ornery wilderness on the Gulf if not? Surely, someone who simply wanted to get lost wouldn't lay a deliberate trail along the way. Unless, Dicken mused, he was actually bound for someplace else and was trying to mislead anyone who might follow. Unless he was a plume-hunter . . . a naturalist . . . a surveyor of some kind?

Dicken heard the chess player's voice rattling in the telephone, but now he hardly listened. Ah gad, the leg! It was screaming again, as though a knife were in it. He forced himself to speak. "Never," he said. "Never hide something from me again, ever. Or I'll finish you!"

Dicken hung up the telephone and gasped. God forbid that Mizell had taken it that this Bridger should be killed. He had to live. Maybe Bridger could even lead him back to the treasure. But how could this pup really know anything?

How didn't matter. Dicken had been curious about him since spying him on the dock. Maybe that curiosity was telling him something. He would have to get a message to Mizell. Do . . . not . . . kill Bridger. But catch him, and keep him caught.

Oh, but that leg. It hurt so bad he nearly passed out. He started to stand, but dropped back into his chair, dizzy from the pain. He would fight it down, as always, and then think clearly. Perhaps a fullness of time demanded he try again for the fortune. He had come so close before. Hadn't he? The ancient lore he'd at last taken as more than myth, his lone quest to the eerie wilds on Tampa Bay. . . .

It was an accident that he had found it at all. He had literally stumbled into a grotto, dug into the side of a mound, concealed by low jungle growth and reinforced with wooden beams and uprights. Someone had taken pains to build a hiding place, for inside lay box upon box filled with gold coins and what appeared to be jewels. The sight had made Dicken's heart pound.

He had scooped a few coins into a little leather bag—just as the chatter of people somewhere outside the cave stopped him cold. He slipped back out of the grotto, somehow unseen, lurching down a bank through thick curtains of vines. He could hide—or perhaps ambush anyone who heard and pursued.

But there in a creek bed, startled like a fawn not five feet from where Dicken stumbled down the bank, crouched a little girl no more than seven or eight years old, molding sand dams to hold back a tiny stream. She started to smile, then realized she did not know this breathless intruder with the funny leg. Dicken saw she was on the verge of screaming. She would give him away in a moment.

He cursed and picked up a rock, so big he could barely wrap his fingers around it, and moved toward the girl. He raised the stone to strike just as her face lifted to his. It was round and soft and her lip quivered as Dicken glowered. He saw her eyes widen as they stared into his. He tensed his arm to bring down the rock—and at the last moment cursed and threw it aside.

Instead, he put a finger to his lips, turned and moved as fast as he could down the creek bed, which bent, narrowed, and vanished into a wall of tangled brush. It looked like a hiding place—except he knew the little girl would betray him.

Even now, he heard voices back around the bend in the stream, a child's excited caw among them. A man burst around the curve and snapped off a pistol shot. Dicken felt suspended in time; a fraction of a second seemed to stretch for a dozen heartbeats. He felt his shoulder sting just as he perceived a wisp of smoke from the gun barrel. It seemed to spiral straight at him.

Dicken managed to pull his own pistol and fire. His pursuer lurched backward, his gun flying. Dicken gasped in pain and shoved into the bushes, crawling at first, then sliding down on his belly where the growth reached across the stream, branches and leaves crowding down until they dabbled in the water.

He inched through the mud, shouts ringing behind

him, the muscle between his shoulder and neck on fire where the bullet had nicked it. Damn the girl! He could have—should have—brained her. He could hear men lashing the bushes just a few yards behind. Another gunshot thundered and he heard a wild bullet rattle branches off to one side.

They wouldn't see him for a while in this hidden, half-dry bed—but another lucky shot might finish him. Dicken checked his pistol. He felt for the little bag of coins. Then he pressed as close as he could into the rivulet, part slime, part mud, part water. He plastered some of the mud to the rip in his coat and shirt, letting it soak through to the wound.

His leg throbbed where the peg joined it and he was scratched and cut from slapping through bushes. But he bellied through the creek bed, sliding like a snake inches and feet at time, hidden from his pursuers. Through a night and part of a day he crept, never letting go his bag of coins.

Dicken remembered it, almost as if he were remembering a dream: how he had at last reached the bay at the creek's end, how he had gotten into an abandoned boat and drifted in it for sun-baked hours until the tide brought him ashore near Tampa, still clutching his bag . . . .

It had been years, Dicken thought, massaging his upper leg. But maybe the time to return was now. And this time, he swore, he would show no mercy to anyone in his way. No mercy at all.

# 8 🎇

"WHAT DO YOU MEAN, MURDERED?" Mr. Satin's casual remark jolted Bridger. He'd just met the fellow and now he was saying there had been a killing he was wanted for. "Man, you must be joking! I talked with a Mr. Factor, that's all. I couldn't have killed him. I left him back at that camp . . . that Rotten Row."

Mr. Satin raised an eyebrow. "Maybe so, but it's you that detective wants to see. You may well have an alibi. But you're a stranger with no apparent connections, no money and no means of support. I don't know whether you would be wise to linger here.

"Now this steamer leaves for Palatka within the hour. From there we're bound up the Ocklawaha for Silver Springs and Ocala. You can be on your way and lost in the wilderness. I thought I might be able to persuade you to come with me. And in my infinite preparedness, I have in my cabin clothing that looks smarter and will fit you far better than those rags you are wearing. You may retire to my stateroom, if you like. I'll buy you a ticket and we'll be done with this city. I've grown weary of it, at any rate."

Bridger, thoroughly frightened, glanced toward Ortiz's row of boats. He didn't see the fisherman. But what if he came looking with a detective? This Mr. Factor had been Ortiz's friend, after all. He half expected to see a squad of lawmen heading toward the steamer.

But it was business as usual on the docks. Maybe, Bridger thought, he should just turn himself in. He'd done nothing. He could clear himself, have some money wired, and be on the way home. Be done with this Florida adventure.

"I can't help but think a young fellow like you might make a fortune in Florida," Mr. Satin smiled. "In fact, I can offer you a little advance toward it, if you'll accompany me."

Bridger made his decision. Within the hour, he was dressed in new clothes and bound for Palatka. Coins jingled in a pocket of his new trousers and he began to feel like a new man. Standing next to the steamer's small pilot house, gazing quietly over the St. Johns River, he could almost feel as though he were a mere traveler again, and not someone fleeing from questions about a murder.

The river was smooth and slow moving, relaxing, and so wide in spots it seemed almost like a bay. Where it was sufficiently narrow, Bridger saw bluffs on both sides, forested by widespreading trees draped in flowing gray moss and taller trees he judged to be some kind of pines.

Other steamers plied the river, as did a profusion of sailboats, barges, rowboats, pole boats, and other smaller craft. Occasionally, Bridger's boat passed a village. Stately, two-story homes seemed to drift past at intervals. Once, Bridger spied on the eastern shore a cluster of deliberately spaced trees with thick green foliage. He could see dots of orange and thought he must be looking at one of the famous Florida groves.

The steamer pushed upriver all day. Bridger had read the St. Johns was one of the nation's few northern-flowing streams, but the current seemed too gentle to greatly impede the craft's passage. A bit after dark, the boat docked at what looked to be a growing town. Pine knots burned on posts, and Bridger could see a small business district and, not far from the docking area, what might have been a small shipyard. "All out for Palatka," Bridger heard the pilot bawl. It was a place to spend the night and nothing more, Mr. Satin declared.

Mr. Satin's fare included a cramped stateroom. But as it had but one berth—which Mr. Satin quickly claimed— Bridger was left to rest upright in a chair or find a spot on the deck. There it was cooler, but at least as uncomfortable. Bridger wished for a drink. The pine-knot torches silhouetted the waterfront and Bridger could hear laughter from a hotel ashore. He wondered if it had a bar.

In the morning, gritty and stiff from his night on deck, Bridger followed Mr. Satin aboard another steamboat. A nameboard nailed to the pilot house declared it to be the Okeehumkee.

"Named after an Indian who once roamed these parts," Mr. Satin informed.

The steamboat was an odd craft, not at all like the grand Mississippi boats Bridger had seen in romantic paintings. This one was built low and narrow with three decks, no longer than a distance Bridger thought he might cover in fifteen or twenty regular strides. The first deck housed the engines and what freight the boat carried; the second a tiny saloon and a series of cramped compartments where the passengers could retire; the third more cabins and a pilot house squatting in front of the passenger area.

"Not a prepossessing craft, and by no means majestic," observed Satin, who seemed to see himself in the role of tutor. "And she's small because this river we'll travel is narrow and twisty as a cottonmouth. She needs to be small to get by all the bends and bumps."

A paddlewheel in the stern would propel the Okeehumkee, Bridger saw. He peered into the engine room and spied a boiler-and-furnace combination that would build the steam to power a pair of wheel-turning engines.

"Of course, the railroads will soon render these boats obsolete," Satin said. "I myself hope to hurry that development along." He seemed to expect no response to the comment and Bridger offered none.

Under way before dawn, the steamer huffed upriver, "makin' three, maybe four miles an hour," the black pilot bragged. Several passengers, tourists judging from their craning and constant pointing and commenting, stopped their chatter long enough to nod sagely.

Bridger himself felt like gawking. The St. Johns was narrowing and the scenery changing. There were fewer houses and no more villages, and what dwellings did come into view were smaller, unpainted wooden huts, far removed from the bigger houses nearer Jacksonville. Bridger realized he was closing in on the Florida frontier.

A half-dozen dark-headed birds with broad wingspans wheeled over a small lagoon washing into a section of the riverbank. They made Bridger think of buzzards—perhaps they were a Florida variety—and he wondered what might be dead or dying.

The chain of thought carried him into a seizure of melancholy and he began sorting through dark notions. He shouldn't be here. He might have company, but what did he know about Mr. Satin? In truth, he was lost and in trouble, probably wanted for murder. His Uncle Mike was gone, he'd never find him. This lost Spanish treasure Mike had written about in his last letter—it was probably a silly fairy tale. What if he was killed? He would be swallowed forever by Florida.

"Look at this," came a voice at his side. It was Mr. Satin. The Okeehumkee was turning toward a broad, gentle slope to make a landing. Ashore stood a tall, straight, dark-skinned man wearing a bright shirt. At his side was strapped a long knife in a sheath and he held a rifle.

"Seminole," said Mr. Satin. "Probably selling alligator hides downriver. Going home now, maybe up around Silver Springs, with a belt full of money. You don't trifle with those fellows. They fought three wars with the U.S. Army, and the soldiers never could lick them. There aren't enough of them to do much harm now, and they mostly stay to themselves, off in the jungle."

The short lecture brought Bridger back. He eyed the Seminole's rifle, which he saw was an Enfield, of military issue from the war. Uncle Mike had taught him how to recognize most military weaponry. He wondered how the Seminole had gotten his.

"Are they still wild?" Bridger asked.

"No more than any other man of the swamps. I'd trust them more than a lot of white men."

Many of the passengers stared at the Indian in his colorful regalia. One man got up and offered his hand. "George Barker," he said. "Stereo photographer. I'd be obliged if I could make your picture." The Seminole said nothing and walked away, leaving the photographer baffled. The other passengers looked amused, except for two who seemed to take no notice at all. Bridger thought they were staring at him. They were two hard-eyed men who looked as if they couldn't smile. Both wore coats and derby hats.

Imagination, thought Bridger, moving away. Imagining people are after me. But he kept an eye on the pair.

Not long after a noon meal of venison cutlets served in the second-deck saloon, the steamboat loosed a rolling blast on its whistle and swept into a slow right turn, moving into another river.

"The mouth of the Ocklawaha," said Mr. Satin. "It'll take us through a jungle all the way to Silver Springs. We'll see civilization again at Ocala, I trust. Then we'll take the train from there to Brooksville. And after that, we go to Tampa."

Immediately, the river scene changed. The Ocklawaha, also a northern-flowing stream, narrowed dramatically. Huge, spreading trees, branches laden with flowing moss, grew right to the edge of tea-colored water. In particularly narrow spots, the forest canopy blocked out the sky, turning the river into a flowing tunnel through the jungle, which looked otherwise impenetrable.

Several times the pilot had to slow the boat and, once or twice, even back it up to avoid snagging the craft on stumps poking out of the water. In places, it was difficult to discern a bank, and the river melded into swamp colored in shades of green and brown, thick with reeds, rotting logs, twisted branches. A rich, penetrating aroma of damp earth and rotting vegetation mingled with the oily stink of the boat's engines, whose chuffing blended with the shrill yelps and squawks of birds. Never had Bridger experienced such a scene.

Tall, skinny birds on stilt legs waded near nubby stumps, plunging their beaks into the water like spears. A sheet of sunlight dropped through the canopy, lending a green-gold sheen to the forest and illuminating a young deer, not much larger than a fawn, browsing in a patch of swamp.

Bridger watched, entranced, the eerie beauty of the jungle creeping around him. It was like nothing he had imagined, living in New York and thinking about what he might find in Florida.

And then the water exploded. Bridger flinched at a violent thrashing near the deer. Amid the roiling water he saw a long creature lash like lightning toward the deer. The hapless animal buckled, gave an odd little cry and jerked two or three times before it vanished underwater. Bridger thought he saw a pair of gray jaws drag it down.

"Alligator!" someone shouted. Passengers crowded to the rail for a glimpse. The Seminole paid no attention. Mr. Satin was at Bridger's elbow again. "A desperately beautiful place, wouldn't you say?" he mused. "And quite, quite deadly. As you can see."

The alligator sighting sent a tremor of excitement through the boat. There were perhaps a dozen passengers aboard, and many of them retrieved guns from their sleeping compartments or pulled them out of their gear.

They returned to the rail with an astonishing array of

weaponry: old military rifles, including a vintage .54 caliber Mississippi, target rifles, shotguns, a new Winchester '76 repeater, two or three Colt pistols—even an ancient flintlock piece Bridger thought he recognized as an Adirondack rifle, once popular in his home state. Several people had more than one weapon.

He wished for his stolen Sharps, but almost laughed aloud at the arsenal this supposedly peaceful tourist group displayed. Impressive enough, he thought, to stun a squadron of dragoons.

Again, the Seminole ignored the activity, as did the two men Bridger had noticed earlier. He thought the pair moved uneasily at the dash for the weaponry, but now they had settled down, watching alertly. At least they didn't seem to be watching him, Bridger thought.

Then a shout: "There's some!" On the bank—in fact, on both banks—lay alligators big and small, foot-long youngsters among fat, mossy leviathans that looked like they must weigh a ton, and every size between. All were sunning themselves.

A shot cracked, then a second and a third. Then came a fusillade, and after that, ragged volley after volley. Every passenger with a gun, which included most of the men and one or two women, blazed away. The forest vibrated, shook, and echoed. So close was the range that Bridger could hear bullets thumping into the gray-green creatures ashore, some of whom twitched, or slid into the water, or simply lay immobile as shots peppered them.

A regular shooting gallery, Bridger thought. This target practice in no way resembled sport. There wouldn't even be a chance to use meat or hide. The steamer chugged on, the animals left to expire where they lay.

Bridger saw a man with a shotgun gun down a shiny, white bird flapping into the air to escape the commotion. The Seminole rose and ambled to the stern, not looking at the slaughter. Bridger decided he, too, had seen enough. It was time to retire to the saloon. Perhaps he would enjoy a beer.

He wondered about Mr. Satin, who, while not wielding a firearm, remained outside on the deck, apparently enjoying the shooting spectacle. Who was he, really?

He had suggested he was in the real estate business, and perhaps that he had an interest in railroads, but Bridger had seen no evidence of either. The man was more professorial in his demeanor. He spoke as if he had been educated, and Bridger confessed to himself he was somewhat surprised at that. He was learning that not all people in the south were ignoramuses. But what could he want with a young fellow inexperienced in the ways of Florida? Someone who would simply listen to his pronouncements?

Bridger decided he may well have been retained for the exact purpose Mr. Satin had suggested—as something of an errand boy and perhaps as a bodyguard. But what kind of errands? And what could Mr. Satin be doing that might require protection?

Out on the decks, the shooting had abated. Now only an occasional shot cracked, as most of the gunners grew weary of the easy practice or decided it might be prudent to avoid blazing through their entire ammunition supply.

Bridger grew restless and testy, once trying to nap in the tiny sleeping compartment, but failing due to constant chatter and movement outside. He wished he was the sort who could easily strike up conversation with strangers; but he had always shied from small talk.

Of course, he thought, things were different when he had access to beer or spirits. They loosened his mind and tongue, and he became gregarious and jolly—to a point. Maybe he should have a drink or two now and see if he could get to know that Seminole fellow. No doubt he knew every cranny of Florida; maybe he could map a route to Punta Pinal.

He had nearly decided to pursue that plan when a gunshot echoed, followed closely by another. Several cries of alarm came from the deck. "Say," Bridger heard. "Is someone shooting at us?"

Not particularly thoughtful of his own safety, Bridger strolled outside. "What is it?"

"Crackers, probably," said a man who had pulled a revolver from his waist and was checking its cylinder. "They'll take potshots at the boats now and then, I understand. Just their way of saying hello. And goodbye, they hope. A lot of 'em don't take much to all the newcomers moving into their country."

Satisfied with his load, the man pointed his pistol and fired twice into the forest, wildly. "Pow-pow," he said, laughing. "That'll keep 'em ducking."

As if in answer, another shot crashed out of the woods. Bridger heard something slam into the boat's side, drawing more startled yips from the less stolid tourists. The captain bellowed for them to get inside. Someone laughed wildly. Indeed, there seemed to be no undue concern, as if the episode was merely part of the excursion.

The boat moved on and the shooting stopped. Bridger

peered into the forest, darkening as late afternoon crept in. There was nothing human to see. In the diminishing light, tangled creepers snaked through thick canopies, roping them to gaunt trees, the omnipresent gray moss swaying like ragged curtains.

The steamboat's whistle bawled. "Henry's Landing, five minutes," the captain sang out. The boat shuddered as its engines began to slow. Bridger looked around for Mr. Satin. He wanted to go ashore for a few minutes, but felt he should let his employer know. If he was indeed to be a bodyguard, it didn't seem proper to simply walk off the boat.

But Mr. Satin wasn't visible. A few minutes, Bridger decided. Just a few minutes. He probably won't know I'm gone.

The steamboat came ashore by turning toward a wide, gentle slope on one bank and simply running aground. Bridger felt more of a grinding than a jolt. When a gangplank went down, he went ashore with some deckhands unloading boxes. No one seemed to notice.

He scrambled up a high section of the bank and took a few steps into the forest. It was getting dark and it occurred to Bridger he could easily become disoriented; even a few yards away, he could no longer see the river through the tangle of trees and bushes.

But he walked farther in, knocking away vines, stopping to stare at a whiskery, gray plant that looked to be growing out of a tree trunk. Then he heard the shouting.

Some kind of commotion was going on back at the boat: Bridger heard two gunshots, angry yelling, then three or four more shots. He froze for a moment, poised to run back, but uncertain. He heard another shot and something rattled through the bushes, cutting past Bridger knee-high.

The boat's whistle boomed, one steady blast reverberating in the forest. Bridger saw movement in the dim light. He dodged behind a tree and a chunk of it seemed to fly apart in his face, knocking him backward just as the report of a gun hammered his ears numb.

He was hit!

# 9

BRIDGER FELT BLOOD SLICKING ONE SIDE of his face, which began to throb and burn. Dizzy, he dropped to his hands and knees. More gunshots crashed; the boat's whistle continued to bellow. He could hear shouts to board; the boat was going to leave him!

Head ringing, Bridger rose and stumbled toward the commotion. Limbs whipped his face, lashing viciously into the wound on his cheek. He cried out and flailed at the slashing branches.

Now the sound from the steamer seemed to be coming from another direction. Bridger charged that way and crashed into a net of tough, thorny vines. Stickers bit through his clothes.

Panic ripped at him. The boat was leaving and he wasn't even sure what direction to run to reach it. He forced himself to think. If he could move parallel to the river, surely he could find an opening to hail the boat. That was it, he decided, listening carefully for noise from the river.

Instead he heard a crashing through the forest and men

talking. For a moment, he thought he was rescued. But then he heard a voice clearly: "I'm tellin' you, one of em's out here. I mighta shot 'im."

"All right, all right," came the response. "We'll look around. If you shot someone, maybe he's got money on 'im. I still think you shot a tree stump."

Bridger dropped down again, creeping close to one of the low green bushes with the spreading fronds. It rattled as he squeezed next to it and he tried to be still. His head was beginning to throb; he could hear at least two men moving through the woods. He could hear nothing from the river.

But now he thought only of the two men hunting him.

He remembered old tricks: stay still, still as wood, and even if you see your hunters, they may not see you. He smeared his face with dirt, over his skin, over his blood. Mike had taught him that to blend in, you don't want the sun shining off your face like a signal mirror.

It was getting darker, though. Bridger could hear his pursuers thrashing awkwardly and cursing. Then one of them fired, sending a bullet crackling through bush and bramble.

"Maybe I'll flush 'im." The words floated far above ground, disconnected. Bridger, head hammering, tried to think of who these men might be.

Surely deputies would not shoot without questions. Would Factor's friends, thinking the worst, chase him for revenge? It didn't seem likely anyone from that bunch would. But who could tell about people in this crazy place. Maybe they were just people from the boat, believing they were shooting at one of those crackers, or a hold-up man.

Bridger heard a crow: awk-awk-awk-awk. Its squawk gone silent, Bridger's ears reached into the forest. He was a cat listening for the tiniest tick of a twig, the silken slide of a boot upon earth.

No thing, no sound did he hear. Yet no move would he make. Perhaps his enemies hid, too, waiting for the tell-tale tremble of a leaf or snapping of a branch. He would not fumble into their trap. Here he would lie, curled in the forest's belly, still as a log and silent into the night.

He would rest, if his torn face would let him. The bleeding had stopped, but the wound felt as though someone were grinding glass into it. As night came, then deepened, he skimmed the surface of slumber. Too much tore at him: fear, pain, hard ground, chill, damp, noises in the ground. In and out of sleep he dodged, never wholly unconscious, never fully awake.

He came to long before dawn, jittery, alert, afraid. Dry blood, dirt-caked, pulled at the skin on his face. His jaw throbbed. His lips stuck together. Thirst raked his gullet. The river. He must find the river. It would sustain him, and it would guide him.

He got to his knees, hands on thighs, straining all his senses. Something smelled, a combination of old vegetables and something dead, Bridger thought. He heard the whine of a bug in his ear, a night bird's three-note whistle. But not the sound of a stalker. A waxing moon, skittering through thin clouds, threw pale light on a patch of swamp where nubby stumps reflected.

In water.

Bridger surged forward, fighting an avalanche of dizzy nausea. He groveled before the stinking liquid (something vegetable, something dead), thrust his face into it, swallowed in gulps. Belched air. Soaked his head and hair. Tried washing his crusted face, wincing as he touched it.

What would Mike McGinnis have told him?

"Time will come, boyo, when you've run to the end of your rope. You'll be wantin' to lay down and die. When it happens, ya take an inch at a time. One thing at a time. Ya do what ya have to do to live right then."

So he would wait for the sun. He would see it in the east and move to meet it, and he would find the river. (For hadn't he come ashore on the west bank?) He would find the river and follow it south, and he would walk out of the jungle. Walk wounded out of the jungle.

A fire raged on his hurt face, his head spinning and splitting. He retched a mouthful of water, catching it in a hand. But there, certain light, surely from the east. He grabbed a tree with both hands, dragging himself up. He stood, in balance, belly calming after a spasm.

Toward the light he would go, one step at a time. But there was no straight path. Twisting tree trunks, a bramble wall, a bog with jagged stumps; all forced Bridger to sidle and dodge, slapping, pushing, forcing a track through the jungle.

Everywhere now the gray dawn light came, but nowhere could its source be seen; in it, enveloped, Bridger moved. He was no longer sure of direction. He stopped, listened, straining to hear a current's ripple, even to smell the river. He thought of its tea color, thought of a mild tea, sweet tea, thought of a home in Troy. He had been deep in the woods before, close to his home. He was an outdoorsman, unafraid of any trek. Competent and strong. He would get out of this.

Yet deep down Bridger knew this was different. Home in Troy he knew all the paths. His sense of direction was unerring. He could always find his way home, no matter how dense the forest or how dark the day. Back home in Troy. But this was the jungle. And for the first time, he realized that he was lost.

He felt a sudden quaking in the knees, saw gray and black and floating shapes before him, felt a pounding, a pushing behind the eyes. He stumbled, reached, grasped thorns, tore his hand.

Weak, Bridger thought. Weaker than I thought. But . . . think. Think.

He could not hunt. With what could he hunt? The plants. Mike had told him forest plants could be eaten. He would think of which ones, soon, when his head did not spin.

Bridger counted steps. Left foot strikes: one, two, three, on to a hundred, and again, knowing at least he was moving, and through the morning he plodded, stopping, starting, weaving through the brush and bog, counting his steps.

And at last giving way to a dark and swelling doubt: He had gone away from the river. Too far away. One thing at a time to live, thought Bridger. One inch at a time. A rustling in a bush, and Bridger flinched as if ambushed. Scuttling away, something gray and small and quick. He could not have hit it with a rock, even if he'd had one in his hand. He could not hunt in this jungle, Bridger knew.

But the low bush with the rattling, palmy fronds on the green and jagged stalk, were they the ones a man could eat? Deep inside, Mike had said, get at the pulp, at the heart of it. Perhaps this was the forest food. Bridger knelt to explore. He pushed fronds aside, seeking the plant's core.

The snake barely had time to sound its terrible warning. And Bridger never heard it. Something thrashed, lashed, retreated, coiled. Bridger perceived only an explosion of movement, as if he had triggered some awful jungle reflex. His gut clutched. For the tiniest instant, his vision blurred. Then he focused, and he saw, and what he saw froze his heart.

Three feet away, coiled and winding in the dirt, a giant rattlesnake flicked its tongue, tasting the air. The snake's spade of a head swayed on a body thick as a firehose, feinting toward Bridger, dodging back. Gold and black triangles and diamonds rippled on its skin, its scaling so rich it looked like sleek fur. Even in his terror, Bridger nearly moved toward the creature, so gorgeous was its body, so hypnotic its movement.

Then the head drove straight at him.

Bridger threw up a hand in reflex. Spikes drilled through it and white-hot pain burned up his arm as the snake struck and withdrew, its rattle singing.

Bridger had a flashing, insane thought: That's it, over, no worries now. The snake writhed an arm's length away, its hideous hissing so resonant it seemed to Bridger he rattler issued a growl.

In reflex, he twisted and kicked away and scrambled, thrashing dirt, scuttling on knees and elbows and belly.

He glanced back, saw the snake now two bodies' length away. Again he hurtled through the dirt, giving up a gasp of fear. Another look back, and a glimpse of the snake retreating, slipping backward, rattle relaxing. Bridger stood and stumbled headlong, careless of direction, heedless of creepers tripping him, blind with horror and hopeless of salvation.

In his flight, Bridger wept. He would soon die, he knew, alone in a Florida wilderness. His family would bear another loss, never knowing what had happened. Maybe this is the way Mike had died, alone and unknown. He imagined his mother staring into the night, unmoving in her chair.

Yet on he charged, as if he could outrun death. He collapsed, finally, gasping. His lungs pumping, he waited for the inevitable. Would it be paralysis? Would he die in a blaze of pain? His hand and arm still throbbed, but the burning sensation had abated.

Bridger looked at his bitten right hand. The skin between his thumb and forefinger was ripped and bleeding, and his hand was swollen. But he could still move his fingers. He tried, and found he could move all his limbs, shake his head, shrug his shoulders. He didn't know how a deadly snakebite should feel; his hand felt more like it had been torn by blades.

But the thirst. Ah God, he had to have water. Again, he pulled himself up, grasping a small tree with his good hand. He lurched a few steps. And a few more. Inch by inch, one thing at a time to live. He thought: If I can do nothing else, I can refuse to surrender. Let the jungle beat me. But I will refuse to give up. He thought: I see the direction the sun came up. I can reckon a course 90 degrees to the right of it. I can try for south.

He moved on, slower now, hoping. Still dizzy, a fever smoldering in his head, he knew enough to stop and look, to sniff . . . perhaps there would be a trail, a hint of a path, the odor of a campfire.

He felt his wounded face ooze, itch, burn as the ache spread into his scalp and neck. A throbbing pulse drummed in his bitten hand and it hurt as if punched through with thorns. Once he found water. He drank, gagged, drank more. He stomach coiled and rejected it. Still he drank, almost lying in the puddle.

Again he moved. Through the day he fought toward what he thought must the south, dodging, stumbling, altering his dead-reckoned course only if forced. In the woods, birds called and unseen creatures rustled. But he saw no human, and no thing save the everlasting jungle.

An inch at a time.

It took Bridger into the night, his energy at an ebb, his will slipping into the dark. It made no sense to go on now, and so he rested . . . and then he moved again, or so he thought. He began to dream, and it was day, and in the distance a tree burned, and he moved toward the fire in the south, and then it was night, and still he moved, swimming in dirt, and he saw himself sprawled in a tree, and Mr. Satin handed him a cutlet of pork . . . but it slipped out of his grasp as the steamboat's whistle belched, and he was swimming in the river, floating, and a smiling snake curled around his legs . . . .

And in the night he was floating, he was off the ground, yet he was warm, and a horrific stench boiled about him, yet he was safe.

And he slept.

Leg Dicken looked at the telegram, read it again, threw it down and swore.

Lost him! Two men lost him, let him loose in the forest while their fat bottoms stayed glued to a boat seat! Mizell's two best detectives, fah! City boys, scared of anything that didn't have a stinking street with a bar on it!

Two supposedly good men couldn't cage one scared

pup! Bull! Or maybe this youngster wasn't so scared, after all. Maybe he was more than his rich-boy appearance suggested.

But now things would be difficult. Maybe he could pick up this young Bridger's trail; maybe not. If he came out of the woods—and that might be a large if—he would probably wind up in Ocala. Chances are, if he were bound for Punta Pinal, he would go through Tampa.

Well, then, Mr. Mizell would have a little stay in Tampa. As for Ocala . . . he knew who he could use there. They'd been wanting a little work—all they'd have to do was keep a lookout for a few days. And if it came to kidnapping— well, that was right in their line, too. Or, just maybe, the jungle would swallow the boy forever. Yet unless he knew for sure . . . .

Dicken felt a twinge in his leg, and it made him think of the time he was himself lost in the wilderness. He had gotten away through sheer perseverance. He wondered if young Bridger were as determined.

# 10 ✺

THERE WAS LIGHT AND WARMTH, and gradually Bridge. s half-dreams turned to deep sleep. And finally he awoke but did not understand for several seconds. He was on a bed, in a room in a rough house. He became aware of a comfortable aroma, baking perhaps, or mulled cider with spices. It mingled with a meaty smell, and Bridger noted that he felt as though he might enjoy food, and after that, he thought of how half-sleepy snug he felt, and after that, he realized that no pain tore at him.

And he began to remember where he had been. He flashed through recollections: No, he had not been on a drunk. Nonetheless alarmed, he glanced around and spied his clothes cleaned and neatly folded on a trunk at the foot of the bed. Almost fearfully, he reached for the trousers. Relief! He felt coins in the pocket and his money folder was intact. But he had been lost. Vague twinges reminded him he had been hurt.

His hand went to his face. A dressing covered the torn side and Bridger felt a tingle when he pushed on it. He looked at his hand, and remembered a snake had bitten him. It was swollen, as if he had dropped a bag of bricks on it, and it was numb. A kind of salve covered the ripped area between his thumb and finger.

Bridger began to haul himself out of the bed. Who had taken him in? He had to find out. But the movement made him dizzy and he fell back.

He saw his boots and socks had been stripped off and that he was naked to the waist. He ran his hands over his torso, touching, looking. He flexed his muscles and wiggled his feet.

He had come through something, that was for sure. He lay back on the bed and stretched. Perhaps there was no hurry to find out where he was now. At least it wasn't Rotten Row this time. He would rest a few minutes more.

And then the door opened and a woman holding a rifle came in. She glanced at the bed, then at Bridger. His eyes locked on hers.

"Hello," Bridger spoke first.

"Welcome," the woman answered. "It's good to see you're awake."

"Do you know where I've been?"

"Before you slept?" She smiled slightly. "Lost in the forest, it seems. Maybe we can get to the why of it in a little while. You'll be hungry?"

"Yes. I . . . I'm not even sure when I last ate."

The woman leaned the gun against a wall, and Bridger saw it was a .44-caliber Winchester, a powerful rifle suitable for hunting. He watched her go to a cupboard and take down two or three knives. "Maybe the shot woke you," she said. "Bobcat. Been after my animals. I waited for it all last night, got him just before dawn. Dang thing. Skin it down and we'll throw it in that stewpot." She nodded at a kettle suspended over the hearth, where a pile of embers glowed red.

Bridger saw that she was tall, likely not much shorter than he, and strong-looking, built just a shade more solidly than what he would call slender. She had black hair, falling below her shoulders but held in place by two combs. She wore a skirt that looked made of some animal hide and it reached just below the tops of her boots, also crafted from hide. She had on an ochre-colored long-sleeved shirt made of some lighter material, and Bridger noticed a pendant lying over her bosom.

He decided to use his best manners.

"Ma'am," he said, "Thomas Bridger's my name. I'd like to thank you for helping me out. I was in trouble out there."

She took a few steps toward him, and Bridger could see her eyes were a startling light blue. He looked directly into them, entranced by the contrast with her hair and dark complexion.

"You are welcome," she said. "My name is Regal Lily Frazer. Younger gentlemen such as yourself usually call me Miss Lily."

She had dragged him inside from her front step a morning earlier, she told him. Pulled him onto the bed, yanked off his boots, removed his shirt and treated his wounds.

"You were twice lucky," Miss Lily said. "That bullet broke up on something, close enough to put chunks of it in your face. It was a big piece of lead that cut you, though, and there were some pieces of tree bark in the wound, looked like. Might leave a scar.

"Then there's that snakebite. Only saw one happen that

way one other time. That snake—was it a rattler or cotton-mouth, do you know?—he hit you between your thumb and finger and his fangs went right through the skin. He dripped his poison right down your palm. I saw the stain of it. But all he did was tear up your hand. Must of been a big one, the way that hand is so torn up."

Bridger asked what she had put on his face and hand.

"A poultice on your face," she said, rather primly, Bridger thought. "Made of oak bark, lemon and some other things. A little cayenne and some ivy and bay leaves mostly. It's chickweed ointment on your hand. I make them myself with things I grow on my own land. And it's just as good as all your modern medicine. I suppose you know all about that, where you come from. Not from the South at all, by the sound of you."

Bridger stayed quiet and thought. He had surely fallen into the hands of a backwoods Southerner. He wondered if she were married. He had to admit this Miss Lily had a raw beauty, and she seemed well-spoken. But her garb, her dwelling, her manner of living—they all bothered him. He had never met—never seen—a woman such as this one. And she made him feel uneasy.

She pulled out a pipe and stuck it in her mouth, look-ing at him straight in the eye as she lit it. Bridger looked away, shocked. He fought down an urge to leap up and flee the house. Of course, he couldn't, he realized. And the thing was, this woman had taken him in, given him her bed, dressed his wounds as best she knew how. He had to admit he was feeling pretty well, under the circumstances.

"Now that you're up, I'll make you an oak bark tea," she said, "in case any snake poison got into you. It probably wouldn't be much, but the tea will take care of it for you."

She fed him vegetables and pieces of meat from the stewpot, making sure he ate slowly. Bridger felt nauseous at the first bites, but then hunger engulfed him. He ate slowly, but steadily. And steadily. And steadily.

"I swear," said Miss Lily. "We'll have to get to butchering that bobcat if we're to keep us in meat."

Bridger shot her a glance. "Ma'am, I forgot myself. It's delicious, and I . . . well, I'm forgetting my manners. I've never skinned a bobcat, but if you'll show me where it is, I'll do my best."

Now Miss Lily laughed, a girlish giggle that surprised Bridger. He would have expected a lusty guffaw. "Oh my," she said. "I didn't mean for you to skin the bobcat. It was just a way of me tellin' myself I'll have to get busy. But if you're strong enough, you can come and look on. D'you think you can pull on your boots?"

Bridger thought he could, and did. A bit unsteady, but declining Miss Lily's offer of an arm, he walked outside. As she walked beside him, he again noticed her pendant. It suspended a cross with a circle behind the crosspieces.

"Captain Frazer gave it to me before he died," she said, gently fingering the cross. "It was some kind of swamp fever that took him. A big, strapping man like that."

"Captain Frazer was . . . a relative?" Bridger didn't want to come right out and ask.

Miss Lily turned to look at him. "He was my husband," she said.

Bridger studied her. She had referred to him as a "younger gentlemen," but she didn't look so much older than he. He looked at the way her hair swung below her shoulders when she moved her head, and decided it was the prettiest hair he had seen in a long time.

A pleasant mid-morning sun filtered through pine and oak trees, warming a brown and green carpet of moist leaves and needles. Bridger saw a small, squarish rail-fenced pen corralling some pigs. A few black-and-white chickens fussed in the yard, which contained a variety of plants, several of them flowering—in February, Bridger marveled.

Woodsmoke from the fireplace drifted around the homestead, tickling his nose. On the far side of the clearing from the house stood a plank barn. Bridger looked back at the house. It was solidly built with the trunks of trees like those he had seen on the Ocklawaha.

"Palm tree logs," said Miss Lily. "Good and strong. Roof's made of their fronds," she said, pointing. "Got everything I need here. Garden grows squash, yams, beans, all kinds of vegetables, herbs. Got pigs and chickens and eggs, down the trail not a half mile there's a pond with fresh fish, and a clear spring a few steps beyond that."

Bridger spied the bobcat. It hung tied by its rear legs to a tree branch, dangling at Miss Lily's eye level. She went to work on it with her knives, starting by making small slits around the cat's paws and claws, then peeling the hide off each leg. She continued the slit-and-peel process, pausing to cut away the tissues binding skin to muscle, then pulling the hide off a little at a time.

Bridger eyed the pinkish blend of flesh and muscle and smelled the sharp, coppery aroma drifting off the carcass. "Where'd you learn to do that?" he asked.

"Growing up in Florida. Didn't the women learn how in your part of the country?"

"Why no, they didn't, actually. Of course, that's fine. I mean, that's fine you know how to do that. We just didn't have much chance to do it. Where I come from."

"And where is it that you do come from, Thomas?"

"Why, New York. Troy, New York. It's north, up north of the city. A small town. Small city, actually."

"And what did you do there?"

"Oh, I went to school. Some. Uh, worked a little in my father's factory. I really like contests. Games, you know. Running matches. I boxed a little."

Miss Lily did not respond or react, but went on working at the bobcat.

Bridger read her unspoken question. "I didn't like working for my father. That's why I'm in Florida. To make my own way, in a new place."

He found himself hoping she would be impressed with his ambition.

"I could see you've never worked with your hands. There when I was soothing you. They're soft, like a schoolgirl's."

Bridger contemplated a moment the idea of Miss Lily soothing him. The thought pushed out any annoyance about his hands being compared to a girl's.

"But then," she continued, "There's many a man in Florida these times who's never bent to real work."

Bridger thought of the hours he had spent poring over textbooks, or his father's ledgers. Or, more to the point, loitering with his sporting friends.

"It's true," he said, "I've never had to work hard. I've been fortunate. But I also think I've missed out on something. Everything has always just been . . . there for me."

He took a deep breath. He wanted to be honest with this woman. He found himself wanting to win her respect. "But so far, I guess I haven't done too well on my own, either." He tried to smile, but the right side of his face was too stiff to allow it.

Miss Lily used a stubby knife to make an incision in the bobcat's middle, then reached in and began pulling out innards. They spilled on the ground. "Well, Thomas," she said, "We all have different stories. It doesn't mean that because they start out one way, they always stay that way."

They talked for two hours.

Bridger told of his privileged background; she of her upbringing in the Florida wilderness.

"I did well in school," he said. "Fourth in my class at Rensselaer. But classrooms and offices and factories—ah, they were like prisons to me." He talked of his family, of the love of his mother and sister, the stern, distant ways of his father.

She told of her marriage at seventeen to a United States Army officer, Captain Henry Frazer. "A lovely man. No one was ever kinder to me," she said. Bridger watched her as they talked. Occasionally she moved a hand to touch the pendant on her breast.

"My people have been here as long as history has been written of Florida, and before," she said. "Since before the Spanish came, the Seminole, the English, the Americans. Now, all their blood is my blood. And so is that of people you've never heard of—Timucuan and Calusa is how they are called now. People here before the Europeans came. My mother told me the stories, and her mother's mother told her. We have our own spoken history."

She talked proudly and Bridger liked the way her blue eyes flashed as she did.

He began to see her in a different way. Rustic ways or not, Miss Lily had a captivating way about her. Bridger caught himself staring at her. He couldn't help but wonder how she would look in a fine dress.

She told him her Captain Frazer was a Scotsman by birth whose mother had been Irish. His family had come to America seeking a better life. Young Henry had joined the Union army in time for the war, had won an officer's commission and found a career. After the war, he had been posted to Fort Brooke in Tampa.

Bridger told her of Mike McGinnis, his wild Irish uncle. "My mother's brother," he said. "Just the opposite of everything my father was, just the opposite of everything my father wanted me to be. My father taught me figures; Mike taught me how to shoot a gun. Father wanted me to learn the way to run a factory, Uncle Mike taught me to box, showed me how to run for miles without getting tired. He gave me an idea that I wanted to see a little of the world. Father wanted me to stay home in Troy. 'Try to amount to something,' he'd tell me."

And he told the rest: his own quest to find Mike McGinnis, lost in Florida. Miss Lily listened to the speech. "How will you ever find him?" she asked.

"The only thing I know to do," said Bridger, "is go to the spot he mentioned in his last letter. Punta Pinal, somewhere in Florida."

Miss Lily glanced at him sharply. He wondered if he should tell her about the lost Spanish treasure.

"I know Punta Pinal. It's a Spanish name, meaning the

Point of Pines," she said. "I grew up there."

It was a peninsula, she explained, between the Gulf of Mexico and Espiritu Santu—the old Spanish name for Tampa Bay. People nowadays mostly called the peninsula Point Pinellas, she said.

"My family, my mother's people mostly, lived around there for years. Generations of us. We have stories about when the first Spanish came. In their ships of white wings, the old people said. We lived close to the water, in a bayou, in a kind of a village. There weren't many of us, and we didn't stay there all the time. Fishermen, hunters, white men and black, Seminole sometimes. People of the land and the sea. People who live and die, and their stories are never told.

"Years ago, in my mother's mother's mother's time, it was a pirate camp. You probably never heard of John Ross. He was a seaman, called a pirate by the government. It was his camp. He may have been my great-grandfather. As the story goes."

She looked at Bridger, as if waiting for a reaction of distaste. Bridger, instead, was entranced. Her story intrigued him, all the more because she had lived—grown up!—exactly where he hoped to find answers to his mysteries. Before he could frame a question, Miss Lily continued.

"I learned to read and write from a poor, old man who'd once been servant to a man who called himself a European count. He lived on a hill next to the bay. There was a quarrel, a misunderstanding, and he had to leave the family. There was no place for him to go, so he lived with us. And he became my teacher. He taught me better English, and French, some Spanish. And how to figure, and some notions about the earth and the sun and what he called our solar system. He talked to me about the countries of Europe, and all the huge lands to the east of it."

Bridger decided to ask a question.

"Did you ever hear stories about lost treasure? It just . . . it seems as though the Point of Pines must be a place for a lot of stories, a lot of legends. . . ."

Miss Lily shot him a hard look. She did not reply for several seconds. "There are stories about all of Florida. And people do not hear what is said and they hear what is not said. Men have always come to Florida looking for riches. Most of them have gone away, if they lived. They took their scars with them, and questions without answers."

Then she fell silent and went back to the bobcat, nearly butchered now. She severed the haunches and rear legs and cut chunks of meat from its chest. "Something more to put in the stew, anyway. And no more bother to my chickens."

Bridger puzzled at Miss Lily's refusal to answer directly. He tried again. "What would you advise me . . . or who should I talk to who might be able to tell me something about Uncle Mike?"

"I'll have to think about that one." She shook the bobcat's hide—nicely removed—to its full length and handed it to Bridger. "I'll dry it," she said. "Nail it up on the side of the cabin. Maybe it'll help scare the lily-livers out of the country."

Mercy, thought Bridger. One minute she's a handsome woman talking about her life like it was a poem, and the next she's a hard, old crow. He looked at the cat's skin and wondered if she thought he was a lily-liver. He looked at the hide very closely, and for a long time, feigning great interest, though he didn't like the odor.

Something else was on his mind. He thought he might

as well ask. "Miss Lily," he said. "You told me you thought someone carried me to your cabin. Who was it, d'ya think?"

Again, she didn't answer immediately. And when she did reply, there wasn't much to it. "Thomas," she said, "I couldn't tell you that. I don't know."

Bridger gave up on answers. He was feeling weak again, anyway.

Young Thomas Bridger troubled Regal Lily Frazer. As she lay down to sleep on a pallet near the hearth—insisting her guest take the bed again—she reviewed the day and her impressions.

Thomas is a good young man, she reckoned. But naive, almost boyish in some ways. She promised herself not to be short with him again. He seemed to want to talk. Perhaps she could help him in ways other than simply healing his hurt body.

But had she done right in taking him in? She really knew almost nothing about him, although he seemed honest when he had talked about leaving the boat, being shot at, gotten lost. But she was fully aware that an innocent front could conceal a scoundrel's heart. She had learned that much growing up in a rowdy camp of free spirits.

Still, she was confident she could take care of herself. And Thomas aroused in her a protective instinct. Because he was still lost, she told herself. No, be honest.

She wanted to know more about him. She had been abrupt with him today. The truth was, she wanted to draw him out. He talked lovingly of his family, yet he was determined to be separate from them all. He talked of himself in a way that hinted he didn't believe he quite measured up—maybe in his eyes, maybe in someone else's.

It touched her—and it troubled her because it did. She had not wanted to know much about any man for . . . what had it been now, seven years? When the captain died, Regal Lily had buried any desire she might have felt to be close to another man. And now a stray one had showed up on her step. She knew she wasn't falling in love. She could tell herself that with certainty. That business didn't happen overnight. But it had been a long time since she had been interested in—or willing to let—a man know something about her.

She smiled as she thought of old Abner Banks. Captain Frazer's protective first sergeant had quit the army and lived nearby. But theirs was a longstanding, nearly formal friendship. She had no desire to know him on a deeper level. Somehow, she felt that desire when she thought about Thomas. That troubled her, too. And she had to admit something else.

Thomas had awakened another nearly forgotten feeling. She had noticed it when she had partly undressed him and touched his body, applying the healing herbs. He was young, true—but not that young, and he had a man's strong physique, and he was fine looking. When he had awakened, and begun talking to her—and, she admitted, listening to her with interest—she had felt the yearning again. Perhaps that troubled her most of all.

She smiled to herself. He was so full of questions, so intrigued by the country, so . . . like a wild, young animal, and in a way as innocent. He needed someone. To guide him, and yes, to protect him if possible.

Regal Lily was snug near the hearth, and she was soothed by the idea that another person lay in the cabin, her cabin, comforted by its warmth. She slept well. In the morning, she woke first. Thomas lay quietly, breathing easily. She lightly touched his forehead. It was cool. Her medicine was working.

But he would need time to mend. He could stay on here for a while; no need to rush him off. Perhaps she would answer some of his questions. But not all, surely. What she knew of hidden fortunes was best kept to herself.

Nor did she know who—or what—had carried him to her door. Old Abner Banks lived close enough to walk to her cabin, but surely he wasn't strong enough to carry a big, dead weight of a man for any distance. And he would have let her know, somehow.

There were other men, she knew, virtual hermits who lived deep in the woods, living off the land. Perhaps one of them? She smiled to herself, thinking of some of the old-timers' stories she had heard: stories about hairy giants that lived in the woods and were supposed to be shy of men and smelled of rotting meat. She had never seen one, but . . . who knew? Florida had more mysteries than she had answers.

Yes, she thought, Thomas Bridger could stay awhile. She had a plan, but she needed time to think it through.

# 11 ⚡

By the third day, Bridger's strength began to return and stay with him longer at a time. He did some light work in Miss Lily's gardens, and he met her two mules, Sarge and Marge.

They rolled their eyes and shuffled their feet when he cleaned their stalls. It was clear they didn't care for him and he worked quickly, ready to dodge kicks or bites. But the chores were new and he liked the outdoor work. It relaxed him.

"I'll have to try to find my employer one of these days," he told Miss Lily. He had spoken of his arrangement with Mr. Satin, and she had listened without comment. Nor did she encourage his departure. He continued to sleep in the cabin's only bed; she on her pallet by the fire.

They talked during the day and into the night. Bridger began to lose his shyness and talked about the athletic contests he loved. Miss Lily listened and smiled. Bridger did not bring up the subject of the treasure again.

One morning, a man stopped by. Miss Lily was outside

chopping wood shavings for the breakfast fire, and Bridger heard someone call out. "Mornin, Miz Captain Frazer."

"Why, good morning to you, Abner. How is it that you're by so early?"

Bridger, hidden by a curtain, peered out a window. He could see an older man dressed in rough clothes, certainly another backwoods character. He held his hat as he spoke. "Miz Captain Frazer, the marshal came by from town last evenin'. Talked about a man jumped off a steamboat the other day, wanted for something up to Jacksonville. I was a little worried. No one been botherin' yeh, have they?"

"No, no one's been bothering me, Abner. What did the marshal say he was wanted for?"

"Didn't. Just said he was wanted and jumped off the boat and ran into the woods. Down the river a ways. I just wanted to see yeh was all right."

Bridger waited. Neither Miss Lily or her visitor said a word for a while. Then: "Abner, can I ask you in? There's someone I'd like you to meet."

Bridger panicked. He considered squeezing under the bed. He wasn't ready. He couldn't meet anyone who thought he was wanted. Never mind. Too late. In they came. He fiddled with the buttons on his shirt.

"Thomas, I'd like you to meet an old friend of mine. Abner Banks, Thomas Bridger. Abner was a sergeant in Captain Frazer's command."

Bridger noticed Banks wore a holstered pistol belted around his waist. "Sergeant," he said, "A pleasure to meet you." He bowed slightly but did not extend his hand.

"Abner'll do, young'n. Yeh a military man?"

"Why, no. Ah, I had a, have an uncle who was. He was

in the war. On the same side as you, I imagine." Banks grunted. Miss Lily spoke up.

"Abner, I have something to tell, and Thomas, you may be interested, too. I'll pour some coffee. Hungry, Abner? I can stoke up the fire a little more. There's stew."

"Coffee'll be fine, thank yeh, Miz Captain Frazer." He looked down his nose at Bridger and glanced around the room, sniffing for a sign of trouble.

"Oh, sit, Abner. You too, Thomas. I need some coffee, then I'll tell you both something."

Miss Lily got busy and soon had rich coffee poured into three cups. "If I had a cow, Abner, you'd have cream, but you'll have to make do with syrup and like it." She settled into a chair and came right to her point.

"Now, I'm planning a trip, Abner, and I'll need your help. I want to go to Tampa, to Fort Brooke, or what's left it, and see some old friends, maybe even some relatives. It's been a long time since I've visited. And Thomas, maybe we can find out something about your problem."

Surprised, Bridger noticed Miss Lily's use of the word "we." And he wondered which problem she meant, considering she might now believe lawmen were after him.

Banks evidently thought much the same. "I'll go along with yeh, Miz Captain Frazer," he said, scowling at Bridger. "I'm thinkin' yeh might need protection."

Miss Lily shook her head. "Now Abner, you know I need you to look out for my little farm here. I won't be gone long, and I don't want to trouble you much. You can take Sarge and Marge, of course, and then just look in once in a while. Maybe just see that the gardens aren't too overgrown. And I'll bring you tobacco from Tampa, or anything else you might want."

Banks brightened at that, but still he grumbled.

"Yeh mean yeh're gonna travel with this fella?" He pointed at Bridger, but didn't look at him.

"Abner, Thomas is going there anyway. We can travel together. At least we can if he explains to me again how he came to be lost in the middle of Florida." She looked at Bridger expectantly.

He cleared his throat, glanced at Banks and then at Miss Lily. He didn't especially like the idea of taking on a travel companion, when it came down to it. On the other hand, Miss Lily might be able to help him if she still knew people around that Punta Pinal area, that Point Pinellas. Anyway, everything he had seen made him think she was pretty independent.

But now he was on the spot. Miss Lily waited for him to speak. Banks glared. He decided to be as honest as he could. "Everything I told you about the steamboat and getting lost is absolutely true," he said. "Miss Lily, you saw the wounds I had to prove it. Only thing is, I did leave out something that happened in Jacksonville. Oh, it wasn't anything I did," he added hastily, realizing his listeners might take him wrong immediately.

"I met a man named Factor and talked with him. I heard later he was killed—murdered is what I heard, exactly—and that maybe the law wanted to ask me some things. But I never heard that from any policeman. It was only what someone told me. I mean, where I'm from, if the police detectives want to ask you questions, they just come get you."

Banks grunted. "PO-leese," he said. "Where yeh from, boy? We don't have no PO-leese here."

Bridger ignored him. "And I had a job. The man I was

going to work for was leaving on the boat. I needed to go with him."

Banks humphed again. "Lost, and still out of work, huh? Say, where are yeh from, anyway?"

"Troy," Bridger answered, a bit defensively. "Troy, New York."

Banks spat. "New Yorkers."

"Well, where the devil are you from?" Bridger flared.

"Born in New Jersey," Banks answered.

Miss Lily jumped in. "I doesn't matter where either of you are from, and I don't know who cares. You're both in Florida now, and you're both friends of mine. And I'm telling you both I have plans, and Abner, you can help me by watching the homestead, and Thomas, if you're still interested, maybe I can help you with your mysteries. But I am going to Tampa regardless. If I have to, I'll just close up the house. You can take the mules in any case, Abner, whether you want to help or not."

"And Thomas, you can choose to travel with me or not." She paused, then added: "I don't think I'll lead you into any trouble. But I do wonder how you happened to be acquainted with a fellow who was soon murdered. It makes me wonder what kind of company you keep."

Banks smirked. Bridger sighed and plunged in. Why not? He had come this far. "Miss Lily, I lost everything I had in Jacksonville. The boat wrecked coming in, and when I got to shore, I decided I wanted to celebrate still being alive. I guess did a lot of it, and I got robbed, and I got left in a, in a bummer's camp, I guess you'd call it."

He wondered if either of them had heard of Leg Dicken. "They were some pretty rough characters, so maybe it doesn't surprise me that one of them got killed."

Said Banks: "A drunk, huh?"

The word hit Bridger like a slap. "I told you I felt like celebrating. A lot. You ever do that, Mr. Banks?"

The old man chuckled. "Didn't say I was talkin' about yeh, boy. Maybe you got somethin' worryin yeh." Bridger was quiet, but Miss Lily spoke up again.

"Well, what about it, Thomas? Is there something worrying you? You should talk about it. You'll be the better for it."

Bridger rolled the notion over in his mind. It seemed to have the ring of wisdom . . . but he wasn't ready to talk about all his shortcomings, real or imagined, and certainly not with Banks sitting there. "Something's worrying me," he said. "Part of it has to do with what happened in Jacksonville, and whether anyone thinks I might have done murder. But the truth will come out about that, I'm sure. And it'll show that I didn't do anything wrong.

"Truth is, I'm more worried about finding a way to stand on my own in Florida, so that I can find out what happened to my uncle. That's why I'm really here, and that's why I've got to get on down the road. Maybe I still have a job with Mr. Satin, if I can find him again."

"You should leave tomorrow," said Miss Lily. "You're strong enough now. And I'll take you to the train in Ocala. I'll take it tomorrow myself."

Banks studied his hat.

Bridger thought he did indeed feel well. His face was scabbed over—he would have a scar—and his hand was a little tender. But there was no fiery throbbing. His head was clear. He felt fine. There was no sense in waiting.

The conversation had sapped some of his energy, though. He felt subdued. If Banks hadn't made the remark about drunks, he might have asked the old man if he had a drink.

Regal Lily had known drunken men before. She had seen them in the army, of course. Some of the officers billeted with Captain Frazer were notorious imbibers. Growing up in a village of transient people of many backgrounds, she had known men, and some women, who remained intoxicated as a way of life.

She carried mixed feelings about them. Some of the old fishermen and the vagabond sailors acted no differently whether swilling water, coffee, or rum. She had seen others who turned wild and mean after a few drinks, especially those who drank the raw, clear, woods whisky straight out of the jar.

She remembered from her childhood a bellowing man who had broken into her mother's hut, overturning furniture and clawing cups and dishes off a shelf, threatening to kill them all. Her mother had thrust a bowie knife into the man's belly. It took him three days to die.

Young Thomas worried her. Listening to him confide fragments of his experience, it was clear he had arrived in Jacksonville well set up, had been careless, had drunk too much, had been robbed, and had gotten into circumstances that apparently had led to murder. Furthermore, he seemed to have no good recollection of all that had happened.

Perhaps he had used bad judgment on that particular day. After all, he had been through a lot. Or maybe it was a weakness of character that lay at the center of his uncertainty and wandering, and maybe he was to be avoided like an evil spirit.

She decided she would reserve judgment. For now. She would try to help Thomas. He intrigued her. He was someone unusual, perhaps a refined man who still had some rough ways. He reminded her of her late husband. Both had been educated, not brought up in hard circumstances. Both could have had comfortable lives. Yet each had chosen to prove himself by taking unfamiliar, difficult roads.

She, on the other hand, could be somewhat refined when she chose, though she had been brought up around, and by, rough people. She had found a degree of sophistication first through the old servant, then her husband. She toyed with the cross around her neck, and thought of what she must to do get ready, and the people she would see in Tampa. Mother was gone, but surely some of her kin remained, if not on the Point, then maybe on the keys offshore, or down on the Manatee River. And there surely would be old friends around Fort Brooke.

She hummed as she went about her chores, a lilting melody she knew from somewhere. She didn't know all the words. It was a song about a minstrel boy, a tune she had learned somewhere years ago.

In the morning, Bridger rose, dressed, and found himself shooed out of the house. "I won't be long," Miss Lily said. "You can keep Abner company." The old man was waiting. He had the two mules, Sarge and Marge, hitched to a wagon.

"Guess yeh're one of these light-travelin' fellas, ain'tcha? No need to make room fer any a yer belongings, cuz yeh don't have anything," Banks cackled.

Bridger just shook his head. There wasn't much he could do about Banks. "Nice mules Miss Lily has," he said. "Any relation to you?"

"What're yeh sayin'? I'm a mule?"

"Why, I didn't say I was talking about you. I mean are you any relation to Miss Lily? Maybe you've got something worrying you?"

"I don't think much of young'ns without manners," Banks grumbled.

Both settled down to wait, and Banks lit a pipe. Bridger liked the smell of it; he had even gotten used to Miss Lily's puffing, although she had only lit up a few times in his presence.

She came to the front door and called.

"I'm going to shut up the house now, if you two can load my things."

Stunned, Bridger stood and gaped. In place of her hide skirt and homespun shirt, Miss Lily wore a cream-colored, high-necked dress. Bridger recognized it as a style several years old, but it accentuated Miss Lily's dark skin and hair. She wore a small hat, high-heeled slippers, and, around her shoulders, a light blue shawl. And she had on white half-gloves, with no fingertips.

Banks never missed a beat and started heaving items into the wagon. Bridger recovered in time to lift the last bag.

"Yeh know," said Banks, "Yeh'd look better without the mustache."

# 12 🌾

THE STATION DID NOT MUCH IMPRESS Bridger. The depot was made of wood nailed up in a hurry. The name of the town—Ocala—was nicely painted in green block letters. The sign was easily the station's most attractive aspect.

Bridger thought the locomotive looked better. It had a long cowcatcher and a smokestack that flared at the top. Two sets of small wheels led two sets of bigger ones, and the engine's name was printed on its side: Sherman Conant. It pulled two cars filled with crates and three faded passenger cars. One bore the letters F. S. Ry. "Florida Southern Railway," Banks said. "Them crates are for oranges." Bridger saw cracks in the passenger cars' sides, and one had three windows out.

But a dozen or more passengers waited to board. It was supposed to take four hours or more to travel about 50 miles to the town of Brooksville, and Bridger wondered if this strung-together contraption could make even that speed. Nothing like they had up North, he reflected. But he supposed this scene was probably typical of the South.

Several of the male passengers tipped their hats to Miss Lily and smiled. Bridger, for some reason feeling a pang of jealousy, stood by and looked stern. Banks, who insisted on seeing them off—all the way off, Bridger thought grumpily—nodded to some of the men. He gazed a little longer, but didn't nod, at a lounger near the station door. Then he nudged Bridger.

"Yeh know that fella by the door? He's lookin a hole right through yeh."

Bridger glanced, shook his head. "Never saw him before now."

But he saw a chance to be bold. Maybe Banks—and Miss Lily—would notice. He strode over to the man. "Do I know you? Or maybe you think you know me." He hadn't meant to sound so blunt, but there it was.

The other man let a wet, brown gob of tobacco drop out of his mouth. It plopped on the station platform. "Don't know any Yankees. Don't want to know none."

The remark further annoyed Bridger, already feeling feisty. "You ought to," he snapped. "It'd do you good to know some. Might better your outlook. Tell me your name. Maybe I can introduce you to some people who could lift you up. Help you make something of yourself."

Bridger was hoping the man would take enough offense to fight. He didn't like being stared at, first of all, and he didn't like the fellow's attitude.

The man said nothing, but kept staring back, his face expressionless. Others on the platform watched. Bridger knew his own next move or comment might determine what would happen next. He decided to push, and stepped closer to the man.

"Why don't you pull your gun?" he said softly. "Pull it. You Southerns like to use guns, don't you? Are you a coward?"

The man's face hardened and he moved slightly, a little to one side and away. Bridger could see he was a moment from yanking the gun. He braced to go for the man's gun hand if he tried to pull a weapon.

"Thomas!"

Miss Lily called out. She was fumbling with one of her bags. "Come help me, please! I've lost something." Bridger hesitated; he glanced at Miss Lily, then back at the man.

"Please! I need your help."

Bridger took one more look at the man, then sidled toward Miss Lily. Though brief, the interruption had taken the edge off the situation. The man glared at Bridger, then moved away.

"What is it?" Bridger whispered, bending to look in Miss Lily's bag.

"My ticket," she said. "I've misplaced my ticket. Did I give it to you?"

Bridger felt in his coat pocket and found only his own. "Did you put it in your other bag, that little one there?"

She looked; yes, it was there. "Thank you, Thomas. Sometimes traveling makes me absent-minded."

"I see."

Banks spoke up. "Well, now, aren't yeh a humdinger. Fight a man if he looks at yeh crossways, will yeh?"

Bridger didn't answer. In truth, he was a little surprised at himself. No, he didn't mind a fight in the least. But he realized this stranger had done or said nothing really offensive to warrant his sudden pugnacity. Now he felt deflated. He contemplated Miss Lily's sudden absent-mindedness. He'd never noticed it before. He suspected he was being looked after, and didn't like that, either. He thought a fight might have done him some good, and wondered if this Ocala might have a saloon.

Miss Lily was watching him; he put away the thought. There was no need to start the trip by having a few drinks that might lead to something more. Anyway, he wondered if he had already behaved badly.

The cars swayed and rattled, and the train was slow but it huffed steadily on. The countryside surprised Bridger. Instead of the unbroken swamp he expected, he saw rolling meadow-land, open fields with scattered stands of trees, and here and there, grazing cattle. Funny. He had thought of Florida, at least away from the beaches, as one vast jungle. This part didn't look very different from parts of his own New York.

Banks had stayed behind, much to Bridger's relief. It appeared he had wanted to get on the train with them, but Miss Lily had insisted he would help her more by looking after her homestead. And Miss Lily was acting differently. Usually, she conversed in a deliberate kind of way, never say-ing much at a time and pausing to let him respond. It was in tune with the steady, capable way she worked her little farm.

But now she talked animatedly, and the topic was bor-ing Bridger. It was, oh, Captain Frazer this, oh, my husband that. She met him when he and such-and-such companions wandered into her camp. Oh, what fine-looking men. He was on a hunting expedition, away from the fort. Oh, so polite. Oh, so handsome.

Maybe the journey was making her a bit nervous, Bridger thought. He managed to smile and nod at her conversation while his mind wandered. In a while he saw a horseman galloping across one of the open vistas, coming toward the train at an angle up ahead. He vanished for a moment as the terrain dipped. Then he reappeared on the rise. He was definitely heading for the train. A messenger? Bridger looked closer. The rider seemed to be wearing a headgear of some kind that covered his face.

Bridger leaned forward in his seat, squinting to get a better look, just as the train began to slow. Too rapidly. Wheels squealed and passengers lurched in their seats, several crying out in alarm.

The train stopped with a jolt. Bridger peered out a window and saw the rider near the engine, waving a pistol at the cab. He heard a shot.

"He's blocking the tracks!" someone yelled. "It's a holdup!" The conductor entered from the car just ahead, panic filling his face. "Get down," he pleaded, gesturing toward the floor. "Get down!"

Some of the passengers dropped. Others, including Bridger, craned to get a better view. Miss Lily fumbled in one of her bags. Bridger finally got a clear view of the rider. Over his head was a white hood of some kind, a pillowcase or maybe a bag. It had slits cut for the eyes. Besides his pistol, the rider had a rifle slung over his shoulder. He rode down the length of the train, sidling his horse close to look into the cars. Then Bridger heard him shout, and the words stunned him.

"I want one man. Tom Bridger's his name, and he's traveling with a woman. He's the one I want. He comes with me, the rest of you go. Let's go! I want him now!"

Bridger fought back an impulse to drop to the floor and hide. But no, he decided he had to meet this head on. But even as he thought so, he couldn't help but think it was some kind of joke. Who would come after him in this way? Surely not the law. And this fellow looked ridiculous wearing that white bag.

Then the rider fired a shot into the roof of Bridger's car. Most of the passengers screamed and a man began praying. "I'm not funnin'!" the rider bawled. "I want Bridger and I want him now!"

Bridger leaned partway out the window. "Hold on!" he called. "I'm your man. What do you want me to do?"

The rider jerked his horse back roughly and pointed his pistol. "Hold your hands in front of you!" he ordered. "Stand up and step down out of that car." Bridger did as he was told and began walking toward the door.

"Hurry it!" the rider bellowed.

The "it" had barely gotten out of his mouth when a blast shook the railroad car. Miss Lily had pulled a gun from her bag and shot the rider. The bullet struck him in the left knee, tearing his leg backward out of the stirrup. It caused him to lurch forward just as the horse shimmied and bucked. There was no chance to stay in the saddle and the man slipped off, landing on his hurt leg and collapsing. But he held on to his pistol.

Miss Lily had fired and moved, and now she aimed through another window and fired again. This time the shot struck the gunman's arm and his gun went sailing. He sprawled in the dirt, shaking and moaning.

Bridger jumped off the train, hurried to the gunman and ripped off his hood. It was the man he had wanted to fight at the depot! Now he looked pale and beaten. Bridger pulled off the rifle slung on the man's back.

The conductor huffed up, his earlier case of the nerves apparently gone. "Here now," he directed. "Tie this man up. Somebody get some rope. Let's see what made us stop. Get to the front of the train."

There was no one just then to follow the orders but Bridger, and he had no rope or any idea of where to get some. So he headed toward the engine and met the engineer coming back.

"Wood junk," the engineer said. "Tree limbs. Some rocks. Could have been dangerous, but there wasn't enough of it. Just one man, I guess. We can move it quick."

Bridger saw a few more men venturing off the train. "Go help the engineer," he told them. He was more interested in learning why someone was intent on snatching him off the train.

Was this odd rider simply angry about the exchange of words at the station? Did he just want to get even, maybe with a pistol-whipping? Why was he wearing that ludicrous bag? And come to think of it, how did he know his name?

Bridger meant to ask some of those questions, but his would-be kidnapper had passed out. "Why, I think I know that fellow," said one of the passengers, pointing at the unconscious man. "I was gambling with him a few days ago. Up in Jacksonville. I swear it's the same man."

"Gambler, is it?" said another man with a bristling mustache. He looked at Bridger accusingly. "You a gambler too? Wasn't he the one you was arguin' with at the station? You do somethin' to him? Steal his money?" Several others looked as though they were ready to blame Bridger for the incident.

"I never saw him before today," Bridger said. "I have no idea what he wanted with me. But if some of you know him, maybe that's why he was wearing the bag. Some of you saw him at the station, too. He was about to kidnap me. He probably didn't want anyone to recognize him."

Obviously, his pursuer wasn't a lawman, Bridger thought, unless lawmen wore hoods in Florida. But he had a feeling the man was connected to what had happened in Jacksonville. But who would have known his name? Had he even mentioned it in the bummers' camp? Still . . . Mr. Satin had known it. And there was Leg Dicken and his gang. Of course, there was no telling what he had said while running drunk through Jacksonville. And if the gossip mill was what Mr. Satin claimed it to be . . .

He had meant to ask Banks or Miss Lily if they had ever heard of Leg Dicken.

Miss Lily. In the flurry he had forgotten her. She was still in the train, sitting alone quietly. Bridger rushed back aboard. Two other women who had remained in the car were ignoring Miss Lily, and they looked away from Bridger when he entered.

"Miss Lily! Are you . . . all right?" He realized it was a stupid thing to say. She was uninjured and seemed perfectly composed. She still gripped the pistol, a big Army Colt, in her lap. "Of course I am, Thomas. That man . . . is he bad off?"

"Passed out. He should be all right if they don't let him bleed to death."

"I wasn't going to let him hold us up. Or you. Or whatever he was going to do."

Bridger heard the hint of a tremor in her voice and looked at her closely. Her blue eyes were flashing. But he thought she looked a bit pale. He wanted to take her hand or hug her or touch her in some way. But he held back.

"Thank you for doing that," he said. "If you hadn't, I guess I'd be gone by now." He thought: Gone for good, maybe. "Where'd you get the gun? It's a good one."

"I'm a woman and I don't like to travel without a weapon," she answered. "Captain Frazer had two of these. He taught me and we practiced together. He told me I was a natural shot."

"May I see it?" He took the pistol and examined it respectfully. He saw the chamber was full. She had fired twice—and reloaded. He handed it back. Respectfully. "I think it's going to be all right now." He pointed to the engineer hurrying to the front of the train as a hastily formed squad of track clearers trooped back to reboard.

Three men carried the rider, still unconscious, toward the baggage car. Crude tourniquets circled his leg and arm. The conductor, still huffing, swung aboard the car where Bridger and Miss Lily sat.

"Ladies and gentlemen, we apologize for this. This sort of thing doesn't happen on the Florida Southern Railway." He glared at Bridger. "We're going to move along now, to Brooksville. You, sir," he nodded at Bridger, "And you, ma'am," he tipped his hat to Miss Lily, "will have to report to the authorities there."

The train heaved forward, rattling the cars and unsettling the conductor, who grabbed the back of a seat for balance. "And all of you can rest assured," he said, "that the

Florida Southern Railway will get to the bottom of this."

Bridger looked away. What a gabber the conductor was. The train slowly picked up speed. Miss Lily leaned against him. After a while she closed her eyes. A bit later, she seemed to be asleep, still leaning against him, Bridger noted with pleasure.

# 13 🌿

After a jolting, rattling, grinding eternity, which tense passengers spent darting glances out the windows, the train finally reached Brooksville. The engineer and conductor, who both wore pistols now, saw to their prisoner. This was a railroad to nowhere, Bridger thought. But it must be making someone money.

Brooksville seemed drabber and smaller than Ocala. The village was built on a hill, which at least offered a view of rolling pine woods. But a cluster of wooden buildings, haphazard and dry and dusty as the street they fronted, added no cheer. Bridger spied a hog lumbering through the dust, stopping now and then to snuffle in the dirt.

Bridger looked closely around the shack that served as the livery, half-worried that some other character might be waiting for him. He could see no one but a man who looked like he ran the stable. One of the passengers sprinted down the street, eager to shout the news about the holdup attempt.

His racket brought a few more people outside, some of whom began to hurry toward the stable. Several others were content merely to amble over, and in that latter group Bridger saw someone familiar. He wore a long coat like a duster and a slouch hat. It was Mr. Satin, no doubt about it.

Bridger felt a surge of elation. It was like seeing an old friend. "Huzzah!" he hollered. "Mr. Satin! Over here!" He thrust up his hand in flailing wave, then turned to Miss Lily. "That's the man I'm working for! What a piece of luck. Excuse me, would you?" Miss Lily said nothing as Bridger almost ran to Mr. Satin, who smiled a half-smile and said:

"Dear boy, where have you been? I have work for you. I was wondering if you had quit me. Without notice, I might add. I wondered if I might have made a mistake with you."

The comments, spoken as though he had been absent but a few hours instead of more than a week, confused Bridger. "I don't know. I thought you might know."

"Know where you've been? And you don't know yourself? It sounds as though you've been off carousing."

"No. I meant I didn't know you had work. Or if I could still even work for you. I mean . . . I haven't seen you for days. I'm not even sure how long it's been. The boat left me back there in the jungle."

"Apparently," Mr. Satin said with faint sarcasm, "we were under some kind of attack. A robbery, evidently. Some even thought you were in cahoots. I had to do some talking myself since I was the one who brought you aboard. Bought your ticket, you may recall."

"No!" Bridger said. "That's not true at all. Yes, I know you bought my ticket. But I was the one being attacked. Look!" He pointed to the wound on his face, which had lost most of its scab and was beginning to scar. "I got shot. They chased me through the jungle. I got lost. A snake bit me. I almost died out there. If it hadn't been for Miss Lily . . ."

Miss Lily.

He looked around to find her and saw her walking, back straight, carrying two bags, down what passed for the village's main street. He started to move away from Mr. Satin. "Can you excuse me for a minute? I've got to go get her. I can't let her just walk away. We can talk a little later."

Mr. Satin glowered and caught Bridger's arm, looking up at him as he spoke in a hard voice. "We'll talk now, young fellow. I've paid you for a job you've yet to perform. You're late. But that's better than never. Now you can start earning your money. Or maybe I should tell the judge here you've defrauded me. And once he's heard the whole story, he might just be interested in shipping you back to Jacksonville. Under guard."

Bridger felt his throat tighten and his heart started pounding. It had not occurred to him that Mr. Satin could make such an ominous threat. He dared not even think about going back to Jacksonville. He did not dare cross Mr. Satin. His throat throbbing, Bridger asked: "What is it you want me to do?"

Mr. Satin smiled and let go Bridger's arm. He was once again the friendly mentor. "Something I think you can do very well. Race a stagecoach. From here to Tampa."

"You mean riding on a horse?"

"Oh, no. I mean running on your feet. I made some inquiries about you in Jacksonville, and a few more during my stay in Ocala," Mr. Satin told Bridger. "I am not without connections among the New York sporting fancy, you might say. I count Mr. Richard Kyle Fox of the National Police Gazette among my correspondents. And I'm told you are quite the accomplished athlete, particularly in pugilism and pedestrianism," Mr. Satin chuckled. "That's fisticuffs and running to the unwashed, of course. But in fact, I was told you are skilled enough in either to have pursued a professional career if your interests, and your background, I might add, had directed you so. But the point: I've taken the liberty of making a wager based on your talent, assuming you did indeed come back into view. I was not altogether certain you would, you know. But I knew you were headed south. So I've been meeting the trains, and hoping, while trying to raise some interesting prospects hereabouts."

Bridger started to interrupt but Mr. Satin waved him off.

"You are to race the stagecoach from here to the Tampa station. It's, oh, I don't know, maybe twenty-five or thirty miles. The point is, the stage is slow. It's old-fashioned transportation. It will soon give way to the railroad, as it has in other parts of this state and in Europe and our own American West. It will give way, that is, if forward-thinking men like myself can persuade others of this inevitability. That's where you come in. If a man can outrun the stagecoach—and I have no doubt that you can, given the nature of the roads and the stage itself—then people will begin to see the foolishness of clinging to the outmoded. The publicity will embarrass the stage lines and give hope to potential railroad investors. Men with money—maybe some of these cattle barons hereabouts —will be inclined to invest in the future, the coming thing. Get in at the beginning and get richer, they'll think.

"And I," Mr. Satin concluded proudly, "will be the guide and agent to promote their interests. I'll get rich. And," he said, leaning confidentially toward Bridger, "perhaps you will, too."

Bridger tried to digest the scheme. He had questions, but he had to admit he liked the idea. It was the kind of physical challenge he enjoyed. He had indeed built something of a reputation in New York for his athletic prowess. He had, in fact, won a professional prize fight, not that his opponent was anything special. But then there was running. If anything, he loved that sport more. He recalled fondly the ten-mile race he'd won not long before leaving new York. He and eight other of the state's best amateur runners had contested the distance along the canal between Troy and Albany. He had won it in fifty-five minutes, eighteen seconds, a time that had astonished the New York sporting crowd. Writers were comparing him to Deerfoot, the legendary Seneca runner of the previous generation. Even he had not always managed the ten miles in so fast a time. And more than one promoter had approached Bridger about a professional tour of England and the continent. He'd make a fortune, they'd said.

Just now, though, Bridger wondered what kind of shape he was in. He had not trained and he had just gone through some hard, draining experiences. Twenty-five (or thirty) miles was longer than he had raced, although he thought he had sometimes covered that long a distance when running for hours in the woods and pastures outside Troy.

"I don't know if I can beat it," he said to Mr. Satin. "Win the race, that is."

"You don't necessarily have to. A tie or even a near loss would likely prove my point. But if you won—especially by a large margin—it would drive the point home. Think of it. A man afoot traveling faster than a commonly used public conveyance. It would make these short-sighted yahoos—wealthy yahoos, if you'll pardon me—sit up and take notice.

And very likely be the last little push they need to invest their money in the future—and in me. You'll have an incentive, Tom. Fifty dollars if you win. That's on top of the fifty just for the race. You can't say I haven't been generous with you, and it's because I believe in your talent."

Bridger decided he had very little to consider. This was an astounding sum of money to do something he enjoyed anyway. At this rate, he might soon be able to afford a guide to help him look for Mike. Mr. Satin must be well set up to be able to offer such payment. "I don't know what I'll run in. I don't exactly carry a kit with me."

Mr. Satin chuckled. "Never fear. An acquaintance of mine fancies himself a bit of a harrier. English fellow, several of them settled here and there around Florida. In fact, at first I'd thought he might be interested in this proposition himself, but he claims poor conditioning these days. At any rate, his togs ought to fit you. A bit small, maybe, but his feet are big enough. Gunboats, really. His shoes shouldn't give you bunions."

"When do we do this?"

"Why, now that you're here, I think tomorrow," Mr. Satin said. "My gentlemen friends were beginning to tire of my yammering. I believe they want action."

With Mr. Satin dogging him, Bridger began to ask around for Miss Lily, noting that his benefactor was hardly encouraging. "You can meet her in Tampa and say everything you have to say," he fussed. "She'll just distract you. Remember, there's a lot at stake in this race."

Besides hoping to make a dramatic point, Mr. Satin apparently had made several side bets. Knowing so made Bridger nervous. But he couldn't bear the thought of simply walking away from Miss Lily. He owed her much. She was offering to help him more. And, he had to admit, he was beginning to enjoy her company.

He finally found her in a boarding house, one of the nicer buildings he had seen in Brooksville. It was a two-story structure, with ornate woodwork gracing its porch railings on both the first and second floors, and it was freshly painted white. Miss Lily received him in the drawing room. Mr. Satin had retired grumbling to a saloon.

She was attired in a crisp gingham dress and looked elegant, Bridger thought, as though she hadn't just dealt with a harrowing train ride. The cross glistened on the swell of her bosom. She hardly seemed the same woman who smoked a pipe and had gutted and skinned a bobcat.

Bridger felt uncomfortable and didn't quite know how to start. He also thought of himself as educated and articulate. And he always found it easy to talk with the gay ladies who seemed always to be near his crowd of jovial companions, while he, drink in hand, drew giggles and smirks with the simplest, even crudest, of jokes.

This woman was different.

"I didn't mean to seem rude this afternoon," he finally got out. "I was . . . excited about seeing Mr. Satin. My employer."

"I saw him. He looked like a businessman. I hope he is an honest businessman. A lot of them aren't."

"Oh, I think he is. He must be."

"Why must he be? Because you think he must? What is

it about him that makes you think he is?" Miss Lily's tone was more critical than curious.

"Oh, why, he . . . he has a lot of wealthy friends. He knows a judge. He's even in the railroad business. He's a visionary."

Miss Lily was not impressed. "And are you going to be his secretary? Or valet?"

"Not at all." The remark annoyed Bridger. But he tried not to show it. "I'm going to . . . help him make money."

Miss Lily said nothing.

"Actually, I came here, I wanted to apologize for jumping up and leaving you. I still haven't thanked you enough for, well, for looking after me, frankly. And protecting me there, on the train. Maybe you saved my life, I don't know. But it seems like I've had nothing but trouble since I've come to Florida."

Bridger was disgusted with himself. He couldn't seem to help stammering in front of Miss Lily, and couldn't get out a reasonable string of thoughts.

She sighed. "That reminds me, too. The sheriff wants to speak with you. I told him what happened on the train, and the conductor and some of the passengers vouched for me. But they wonder about you, and the sheriff would like to hear what you have to say. I'm surprised he hasn't looked you up already."

"Well, I'm not hiding," Bridger said, a bit defensively.

"You still haven't told me what kind of work you're going to do."

"I'm going to race the stagecoach tomorrow," said Bridger, thinking how odd it sounded. "To Tampa."

Miss Lily seemed not at all surprised. "Are you well

enough for that? I wouldn't say you've been practicing for hard exercise."

"I'm a little worried about that, actually," said Bridger, pleased that Miss Lily was not incredulous. "I'm hoping I've never gotten too far out of condition. At least I'm reasonably rested. The main thing I'm worried about is getting enough water along the way. I'm told it's twenty-five or thirty miles."

Miss Lily looked skeptical. "More like thirty-five, I'd say. And you actually plan to run it. Have you gone that far before?"

"Oh, twenty or twenty-five," said Bridger, not wanting to be too precise. "I entered a three-day race once. Those three-days and six-days, people like to do them in New York right now. I walked most of mine."

Miss Lily contemplated. "I saw a race at Fort Brooke once. Between some soldiers and a Seminole, and I knew the Seminole. Charlie Turtle, the soldiers called him, for a kind of joke. But he could run fast, and for a long ways, too. There were some boys from the North—Pennsylvania, I think— who liked to run, and some of the officers bet money they could beat Charlie. Did this businessman bet money on you?"

Bridger nodded.

"Charlie Turtle raced ten miles, it was twenty times around a path through the fort, and he beat the soldiers, but the officers got mad and wouldn't pay. They said Charlie cheated by not going around the path enough times. But Captain Frazer had counted and knew Charlie had run the ten miles. He made the others pay up, but there were bad feelings about it. Charlie had to stay away from the fort after that. I just wonder if there won't be trouble for you. This businessman sounds more like a gambler, like the one who came after you on the train."

Bridger realized he hadn't actually considered that. True, he really didn't know all that much about Mr. Satin— except that he was willing to pay generously. He had yet another fifty dollars to prove it, and prospects of more. He didn't know quite how to respond to Miss Lily's concerns. Instead, he repeated: "The thing I'm most worried about is getting enough water. Assuming I'm able to run reasonably well."

"This race is tomorrow morning, then." Miss Lily pondered. "I should be on that stage anyway. And I shall arrange to have water along. How much will you need? A bottle?"

"More like two quarts, minimum. Better three or four," Bridger said. It was early March now, and Florida's weather was relatively mild, he had seen, but he wanted to take no chances on running short of water if the day turned hot.

"I have something for you," said Miss Lily. "I'll be back in a moment."

When she returned, she handed Bridger a heavy package tied with string.

"Just take it," she said. "Open it when you're alone. I'll see you in the morning."

Bridger, wanting rest, slipped away and rented a bed in a stable room near the stage stop. Not fancy, but no one would be able to find him, he figured, not even Mr. Satin. He heard laughter from the saloon, not far away. Maybe just one beer would taste good, maybe help him sleep. But no, it would be smoky in the saloon. Better that he rest. Anyway, he had the package. A gift from Miss Lily, and it intrigued him.

When he opened it, he found a cleaned and oiled Army Colt, and a leather pouch filled with ammunition. And a handsome pocket watch with a sweeping second hand.

# 14 🌿

BRIDGER, UP EARLY, DRESSED FOR THE RACE and wrapped his clothes and the weapon. Several men, including Mr. Satin, were milling around the stage stop when he arrived. Miss Lily was there, too—and angry.

"These men," she said in a deliberately loud voice, "bought all the tickets and say there's no room for me." Bridger saw the stage. It wasn't as nice looking as the ones with the high seats and graceful round frames Bridger had seen in pictures from the West. This one looked more like a closed carriage, with the rear wheels bigger than the front, but there was an extensive set of springs underneath.

"Looks pretty uncomfortable," he remarked. He noticed that Miss Lily had several bottles of water in a basket. "Better to load it up with those fat-bottomed galoots anyway," he said. "They'll slow the thing down and it doesn't look fast as it is." Still, he noted the four broad-chested horses hitched to it. They looked strong.

Mr. Satin saw him and ambled over, barely touching the brim of his hat to Miss Lily. "You look ready," he said to

Bridger. "Are you?"

Miss Lily jumped in. "I was to be on this stage to Tampa today. And I have water for Thomas." Mr. Satin looked at her with contempt. "If you didn't book ahead, you wait—like everyone else. And as for Thomas"—he said the name mockingly—"I'll look after his needs." He turned and abruptly shouted. "Come on. Let's get going. I thought this stage had a schedule, such as it is."

Word of the race had spread. Quite a few townspeople had gathered, and several men on horses awaited the start, apparently intending to follow. Four men were riding in the stage, Mr. Satin among them. The others Bridger took to be the local gentry with whom Mr. Satin had wagered. The judge, said Mr. Satin, had fixed it with the sheriff not to trouble Bridger with questions about the train episode, at least for the time being.

Bridger, meanwhile, noticed there was almost no baggage aboard. If there were any genuine passengers this morning, they traveled lightly. The driver, a short, stocky fellow carrying a coiled whip, glanced at him once or twice, showing curiosity but no hostility. Well and good, thought Bridger.

It was a pleasant morning, comfortable for the light running garb Bridger had on. But the air felt damp and Bridger suspected the day would heat up. He'd better drink water now. Miss Lily, a bit to Bridger's surprise, had given up the argument about getting on the stage. But she was standing nearby with the basket of water bottles. Bridger walked over.

"I'll look for you in Tampa," he said. "And thanks for the loan of the gun. And the watch. I can use the timepiece, but I hope I won't need the gun."

"You may not, and then you may," she said. "But know that it's reliable protection, if it's kept clean. It's one of a matched pair Captain Frazer left me. The other is the one I used on the train yesterday." Bridger drank deeply from one of the bottles. "I still want to thank you."

But Miss Lily cut him off. "How long are you going to keep thanking me? I wasn't going to see you taken away, and none of the others wanted it either. Even though they were unfriendly about it later. I was only the one who had the means to stop it."

*And the gumption to use it*, Bridger thought. "I'll see if Mr. Satin will guard this," he said gently, taking the basket.

"I'm sure he will. After all, he has money on you."

Someone blew a few high, quavering notes on a horn and Bridger turned to see a man straining at a cornet. He gave it up and bawled: "All ready. Morning stage to Tampa. And a race between man and beast. To see who's the better man. Or beast, that is."

Guffaws smothered any further remarks and the man retired, stepping back among several other musicians. It looked to be a ten- or twelve-piece band, Bridger noted with surprise, and he smiled when it struck up a spirited "Bonnie Blue Flag." This was becoming an event, and he liked it. He tossed Miss Lily a light salute and strode over to Mr. Satin, still holding court with his coterie of dignitaries.

"If you would, please sir, take custody of these?" Bridger handed Mr. Satin the basket of water bottles, holding onto one to carry as he ran. "I'm as ready as I can be." Indeed, he had not felt so excited since leaving Troy. This was the kind of atmosphere he loved: a lively crowd and a contest about to begin.

He realized he would have to be careful and not try to run too fast at the beginning. It was going to be a long haul over unfamiliar territory. Mr. Satin cocked an eyebrow "Good luck to you," he said, almost warmly. "Luck to us."

The driver bustled around. "Men—you too, Judge—get on in there, now. We are ready." He directed Bridger to stand beside the lead horses. "Not too close. They may shy when the gun goes off." Bridger looked for Miss Lily but could not see her. He thought of the Army Colt now among his possessions stashed on the coach. One of a matched pair, he thought. He noted the time on his watch, then stuck it in a pocket. The starter fired his revolver in the air. The lead horses lurched sideways, then strained forward. And Bridger lunged into the race.

# 15

HE CHOPPED AHEAD OF THE HORSES, which took longer to get going. Then the team got rolling, quickly passed and moved ahead of him, the stage swinging from side to side. Bridger watched it go past and heard the shouts and laughter inside as the wagon built a steady lead. The band, its noise fading, had struck up "Dixie."

These Southerns, still fighting the war, he thought. Funny, Miss Lily never said anything about it, one way or another. But then, her Captain Frazer was in the federal army. So was that old geezer of a sergeant that hounded her. She probably thought it prudent to say as little as possible about her military connections, at least in most company.

He took a swig of water and settled into a comfortable stride. He knew he would have to find a steady pace, keep it up and hope the stage couldn't maintain a consistently fast speed. It was a fact he could never beat it at the rate it was going now. He had to hope the terrain would slow it down.

On either side, mostly ahead of him, rode men on horseback. They looked to be following the race. But Bridger thought of the horseman of the previous day. He was vulnerable, running in the open like this.

His breath came hard at first, but after a few minutes he fell into a pleasant rhythm. It felt good. He eased into a pace he thought was about eight minutes per mile, hardly as fast as he could go but a decent ground-eating lope for an uncertain long distance such as this one.

In a while, the trail sloped down, at first gradually, then sharper. Ahead, the stage braked, taking the descent cautiously. Bridger closed the gap, then began catching up rapidly as the horses began hauling uphill. He caught the stage halfway up, his lungs huffing and thigh muscles burning. But he waved gaily as he slogged past.

"That's my boy," yelled Mr. Satin, laughing wildly. Bridger glimpsed him talking and gesturing.

The hill was a bit steep, but short. Surprising, Bridger thought, even to see one in Florida. He had pictured the whole state as marshy and flat. At the hill's crest, the trail funneled into a forest, leaving the open vistas behind. Bridger relaxed through the modestly rolling contours and thought about what Uncle Mike had said about running long distances.

"Go easy," he'd said. "Think of yourself as a lone wolf, loping all day, you can go on forever, you got long muscles, strong ones, like fresh saplings. You can go forever." Bridger smiled at the memory. But he hadn't thought that much lately about Mike, he realized, not since he'd come out of the jungle and stayed at Miss Lily's. He wondered if he were getting any closer to finding his uncle, or at least some clue as to what had happened to him. And perhaps a hint of whether that treasure was real or merely a legend.

A clattering jerked Bridger's wandering mind.

The trail had leveled and gotten narrower, and the stage was coming up behind, hard and fast. Bridger saw there wasn't room for him and the stage side by side. He looked for a place to move over, but the trail was banked on both sides and there were spiky plants that would make a quick jump into the woods treacherous.

The stage thundered closer. Bridger looked back and saw the driver swinging a long whip and shouting. He picked up his pace, looking for a way off the trail. It was going to be close. Now Bridger was almost sprinting. He could hear the horses' heaving breath and the squeak of their harnesses. A knot of fear began growing in his belly. This was serious business; money had been wagered. He doubted if the driver bore him any personal ill will, but what was it to the rich landsmen aboard the stage whether he was trampled into the dirt?

Bridger looked once more over his shoulder. Foam boiled around the lead horses' mouths. Wild-eyed, they tossed their heads and groaned. At the last second, Bridger scrambled up an embankment, but there was no place to go. He leaped and wrapped his arms around a young, skinny tree, clinging to it as it swayed and the coach thundered past. He dropped his water bottle, which shattered on a rock.

"Damn it!" Bridger roared. He wanted to pitch something at the stage. He could hear its passengers hooting. All —save one, no doubt—sounded breathless with hilarity. He groped for the watch and pulled it from his pants pocket. He breathed relief. It wasn't damaged. Bridger noticed he'd been running for a little more than half an hour, or maybe about four miles if he was keeping to his planned pace.

He jumped back on the path and, adrenaline pumping,

chased the stage. It was anger at being nearly trampled, not an effort to catch up, that spurred him through a hard quarter mile or so. Then he got himself under control and slowed down. He would burn out if he weren't careful, and now he was without water. And because he was, he immediately wanted a drink.

Where were the horsemen? Bridger realized he hadn't seen them since the road had penetrated the forest. Maybe one or two of them had extra water; but what if they'd taken another route? He'd worry about it later. He settled back into a steady jog, concentrating on the trail and looking ahead to each curve as soon as one came into view. Once around, he looked to see if he could spy the stage, or some sign of an outrider.

But he saw nothing. Once in a while, he thought he could still hear the team of horses, but the racket had faded. He heard only his own breathing, his own footfall. Yet once again, he seemed to have fallen into a pleasant rhythm, as though he could go on forever.

Abruptly, Bridger found a dip in the road, then an immediate rise, and when he had negotiated it, he noted a series of ups and downs lay ahead. They weren't severe enough to tax him—but he knew they would slow the coach. Ever so slightly, he picked up his pace. If only he had water.

In a few minutes, the trees began to thin out. And in a while longer, Bridger glided into a rolling, open space. He saw wild grass beginning to green up in the mild late winter, and a few solitary trees spread shadows on the hillsides. But the hills kept him from seeing far down the road. The coach was not in sight, nor could he hear anything but the occasional two-note call of some unseen bird. Then, glancing backward, he saw a horseman, riding off to the left and a ways behind. He was still too far away to be seen clearly, but it looked to Bridger as though the horse was angling toward him.

It made him a bit nervous, but maybe he could get some water. He wasn't terribly thirsty, but Bridger knew from experience it was best to drink before he was. The horseman seemed in no great hurry, and Bridger slowed a bit, still looking back. The rider was definitely coming his way. Bridger decided to keep running easily and let whoever it was catch up.

It took just a few minutes. The horseman slowed and trotted alongside Bridger.

"Mornin'," he said, half smiling. "You doing all right?"

"So far. But I could use a little water if you can spare any." He noted a large canteen hanging over the saddle—and also that the man wore a gun. Seemed like half the people down here carried guns with them, like he'd heard they did on the Western frontier. Then again, Florida was a frontier itself, he guessed.

"I'll get ya some, but I need to get down." The man reined in, dismounted and offered the canteen. Bridger took the heavy jug with both hands and drank. And the man pulled his gun, pointing it at Bridger's chest. "This is all the further yer goin," he said.

Bridger cursed silently. Not again! This was getting ridiculous. But this time, he felt not a hint of fear. Instead, he let a scene unfold in his head. He visualized it: himself knocking aside the gun, himself hitting the man in the face. In a heartbeat, like a reflex, he made it happen.

He flung the canteen into the gun, at the same time

snapping a straight right-hand punch square on his assailant's jaw. He didn't have all his weight behind the blow, but it was hard and fast as a spear, and it knocked the gunman flat. He dropped the pistol and lay still on his back, his horse whinnying and shying.

It occurred to Bridger he could mount up and chase the stage, close the gap, then get off and run again—but he put the thought away. He might be among thugs and maybe cheats, but he didn't have to become one himself. Instead, he snatched up the dropped pistol and set off down the trail at a hard trot, heart pounding, completely forgetting the canteen of water. That entire episode, he thought, couldn't have taken a minute or two.

But now what? Was he still being pursued? Maybe the man he knocked down had another weapon and would come chasing after him. Maybe it would be better to dodge into the forest and hide. But no, not after his adventure in the wilderness after the steamboat episode. Better to stay on the trail unless he absolutely had to conceal himself.

Anyway, he had a gun. He checked the cylinder; loads in five, and the hammer rested on an empty chamber. So here he was, running down a trail, chasing a stagecoach, carrying a pistol. Well, he had come to Florida for adventure. But why did it seem that everyone in the state was chasing him?

Maybe some of the men wagering with Mr. Satin had arranged to delay him. That didn't explain the masked rider who stopped the train, though, or the ones who'd shot at him when he'd gotten off the steamboat. Well, whoever it was, he'd managed to defeat them. With help from Miss Lily. Thinking of her made Bridger pull out the watch she'd given him. He was a little more than ninety minutes into the race. Even with the bumpy terrain, and accounting for all that had happened, he thought he must have gone about ten miles.

And still he felt strong, though his legs were protesting a bit, as they always did at about this distance. Bridger knew it was just a phase of any distance run. The fatigue would go away—for a while.

Then he saw another horseman. Maybe a half-mile ahead, waiting alongside the trail. Surely the man he'd left knocked cold couldn't have gotten ahead of him so quickly! Bridger slowed and contemplated getting off the road. His stomach jumped. He wasn't sure if it was fear or growing anger. This was getting on his nerves. But he remembered: This time he had a gun. He'd get rid of this fellow, too. Speeding up again, he focused on the horseman and stared at him as ran closer. The concentration eased his misgivings.

And he made sure he swung the gun in front of him with each stride. When he was twenty or thirty yards away, the horseman hailed him. "Hullo there. Shootin' snakes?"

Bridger slowed again. "Not unless I need to," he said, adopting a hard voice. "Who might you be?"

"Hey now," said the rider, grinning. "I'm just watchin' the race. No one said there'd be shootin'." He pointed to the gun. "What's that for, anyway?"

Bridger saw the man carried no gun and relaxed a little. "Back down the road. Somebody tried to yank me out of the race. I knocked him out and took his gun. I'm still on the nervous side, though, so I hope you don't want to try anything."

"Hey now. I just started ridin' along. I'm a watcher, that's all." He raised both hands, palms out. Bridger saw he was a youth, maybe sixteen years old. He had floppy, reddish hair and a wide grin plastered on his face. His legs were too long for his stirrups, and his knees rode high like a jockey's. "That stage isn't very far ahead of ya, y'know. Maybe a mile, or a little more, but it's hard goin'. I don't see how you can run this far."

Bridger relaxed some more. "Would you have any extra water? I broke my bottle a ways back."

"Hey, now. Give ya a swig, I guess. You think ya can really beat that thing?" The youth unstrapped a bottle and handed it down. He rested his hands on the saddle horn. Bridger took a swallow, then another. He watched the boy carefully.

"The only thing I can do is try to stay close to it, then hope for some luck." He handed the bottle back up. "I need to keep moving right now, though."

"Well, my name's John Joseph, but people call me Cheese on account of I ate so much of it when I was young. Whattaya think of that? I'll ride along with ya a ways, too. I'm just goin' to the Becker Station up here, where they change horses. It's about halfway. Road gets real bad after that."

Bad for horses or men, Bridger wondered. And change horses? He'd be running against a fresh team. Of course, they'd have to take time to change. He picked up a faster pace again.

Cheese said no more and the two moved in silence as Bridger ate up another two miles or so. Then, topping a modest rise, he saw the stage. It had slowed and now, maybe a half-mile away, appeared to be laboring.

"There she be," remarked Cheese. "That road got too soft for her to go very fast. Hey now, you can move over there off the road, where it's harder ground and keep on goin'. You can go around the stumps and such. That stage, she can't."

This was good, Bridger thought. He'd keep up a hard surge and see if he could overtake the stage. The thought excited him. "Watch this!" he yelled, running even faster. The trail indeed turned sandy, and Bridger cut over onto the harder ground alongside. Striding hard, swinging his arms, he was eating up ground. The stage looked like it was coming back toward him, as though he were reeling it in.

Cheese's horse was cantering. Bridger was within a quarter mile of the stage and gaining rapidly. "It's all bogged down," puffed Cheese, his voice throbbing with the gait of the horse.

The stage driver, flogging his team and cursing, hadn't time to look back for Bridger, and none of the passengers knew he was catching up. He went past the stage without a sideways look, as if it weren't worth noticing. There was no immediate reaction. Then Bridger heard a shout, followed by a loud hail he knew was Mr. Satin.

"That's the way, there he goes! I knew he could do it! Keep it up, son!"

Bridger thrust up an arm in greeting and called to Cheese: "Ask him if he has my water. See if you can get the bottles." Cheese dutifully rode alongside the stage, bending for a moment to the window, then jouncing back alongside Bridger.

"Hey now, just one left," he said, showing Bridger a bottle. "He says the rest broke because of the bumps." Bridger swore.

"How much further to the station?"

"'Nother four miles, maybe. Can ya make it?"

Bridger swore again. This addled bumpkin had no idea. "Yes, I can make it. Will any water be there?"

"For horses, anyway. Don't know about folks."

"Well, give me the bottle," Bridger snapped. "Here, carry the gun, will you?"

The youth flinched and accidentally reined his horse, which shied. "No! I don't touch guns. Too scared of 'em. Daddy says I'm a weak sister because of it, but I don't never hold one!"

"Well, for the love of . . . just hand me the bottle!" Bridger snatched it, pulled the cork with his teeth and spat the stopper on the ground. He gurgled down several swallows and took off running. Besides being annoyed, Bridger was starting to feel foolish. Out in the middle of nowhere, racing a stage on foot. His companion a benighted rustic called Cheese. And here he was, the grand Northern adventurer, rushing along with a sloshing bottle in one hand and a loaded pistol in the other. At least he had the pistol. And Cheese, bless his heart, must be the only soul in Florida who wouldn't carry a gun.

Bridger decided to see if he could bury the stage behind him, and in so doing, bury the absurdity of it all. He charged ahead, running as fast as he had all day. After a few hundred yards, he was breathing hard, but he kept up the pace. In a while longer, he felt better again, though he was running as fast. He realized his body had adapted to the faster pace, and it pleased him to know he still was in fairly good shape. Maybe he could afford a few beers when he got to Tampa.

After a while, Cheese spoke up in his crazy, horse-bounced voice. "Ca-a-n't see-ee the sta-age no more, Mis-ter . . . Hey now, what is your na-ame any-how?"

"Water," Bridger answered. "On account of I want to drink so much of it." He took a swig and kept on running.

Bridger concentrated on getting to the halfway station as fast as he could. He shifted the pistol to hold it by its cylinder, took another drink, and lengthened his stride. He ran hard, deliberately hard, testing himself. He would pay for it later, he knew. In half an hour, maybe less, Bridger saw the station. It consisted of a shack, a pen with several horses, and a watering tank.

He slowed, huffed up to the tank and leaned against it, draining the rest of his water. Cheese came thumping right behind. Bridger looked back down the trail. He could barely see the stage as it vanished behind a hillock. It might have been a mile behind, even more. He sloshed some water over his head and neck, then cupped some in his hand to drink.

"So you're the runner." The voice came from behind and Bridger turned. He saw a fat man who needed a shave. A red, long-sleeved undershirt slopped over his trousers, and unhitched suspenders hung dangled at his thighs.

"Yeah, he's that runner, he's beatin' that stage by a long shot, he's gonna go all the way to Tampa, too, I've been with him," Cheese babbled. The station man ignored him. "Hope you like the water," he said to Bridger. "No one else does. Not even the horses, much." His laugh was a hacking, liquid sound that came from deep in his chest.

Bridger drank a little more and refilled his bottle. However dubious, the water would have to do. He took a few deep breaths, but he wouldn't be resting long. "They'll change horses here," said the station man. "See those with the big chests?" He pointed to the pen. "They're the strong ones to pull through the sand. 'Course, it's rained a little.

Road ain't as bad as it can be. It'll harden up again after ten, eleven miles, and them big boys'll fly then, you'll see. Don't guess it matter much to you, though, hey? No man can run that far anyhow. You must be pretty near spent now." He laughed his wheezing laugh.

Bridger gestured up the road. "When that thing finally gets here," he said, "Tell the gentleman named Mr. Satin that someone tried to stop me. Had a gun." He held up the weapon. "But I've got it now, and everything's fine. Tell him his bet's safe." And he took off running, sticking to the hard ground.

Cheese clomped after him, trying to run, too. "You can do it, Mr. Water," he hollered. "Just keep on running, hey now!" Bridger couldn't help but smile. But it would be a tough haul now, he knew. He hadn't stopped long enough to stiffen up, but he'd be approaching twenty miles soon. He knew from experience: for some reason, it always got very difficult to run hard after twenty. And he'd spent a hunk of energy on his charge into the halfway station.

At least he knew what to expect. And it wasn't long before he felt the first signs. He legs weren't moving with quite the same ease and he couldn't seem to get back into a comfortable breathing rhythm. It wasn't enough to make him hurt. But on top of it, he could feel hot spots on both feet. Blisters rising. Well, he thought, it was going to be work from here on in.

Bridger thought about tossing away the pistol, but reconsidered. The way the things seemed to be, he'd no sooner get rid of it than someone would ride up and stick another in his face, demanding this or that. He managed to pry the watch out of his pocket with two fingers. He'd time a half-hour and that would surely bring him to twenty miles or a little more. Then he'd focus on running a half-hour at a time. With luck, and if he didn't flag too badly, he ought to reach the finish line in less than two hours more—if the distance was indeed around thirty miles.

He let his mind wander, a trick he'd learned from Uncle Mike that sometimes worked when relentless focusing on the run only seemed to wear him down. The thirty minutes went by nicely. Then the cramp struck, a stabbing pain through his lower belly. It abated, then returned in a minute or two. The water, Bridger thought. It had to be the water out of the horse tank.

The cramp ripped at him again and doubled him over. He looked around wildly for a bush or a tree to hide behind, then almost laughed when he remembered there wasn't anyone around to see him anyway. In a few minutes he got back on the road, but less than a mile later, he made another forced stop.

Now he faced a dilemma: Drink the water he'd brought from the way station and likely continue to fight cramps. Or go without water, which would probably weaken him as badly. He'd worked up a good sweat, even on a relatively cool March day, even if it weren't particularly sultry. He knew he might sweat out the rest of his liquids until his muscles, squeezed dry, would quit on him. End of race, good-bye money.

But maybe he could get away with it. He figured thirteen or fourteen miles to go. It shouldn't get any warmer, at least. And that water he'd been drinking. It might make him sicker. He flicked the bottle away. And immediately felt thirsty. He thought: Put it out of your mind. Now's the time to put that stage behind you. But his legs were losing their lift. He glanced at the watch again. This time, he'd figure a half-hour would get him a little more than three miles at his slowing pace. Then he'd have ten to go, maybe fewer.

He looked over his shoulder. There, far back, he could see the stage! Maybe it was still two miles away. But it was plain as day, inching across the land, which was now broad and flat as prairie. Sand like fine sugar still marked the main road, and Bridger still ran to the side on harder ground. But he could see solid patches showing up on the road. He was probably not far from where the stage stop man promised the road would get better. And that meant the stage would pick up speed.

Bridger looked again. It seemed closer. He wanted water. The sun glowed and the heat seemed to tumble down in waves. He was oily with sweat and a new cramp knifed at his chest and up through his neck, constricting his breath. The blisters, full-blown now, brought stinging pain with each step. But he launched back into the run, trying to find a comfortable stride. It wasn't fast.

But somehow he got through a half-hour. Maybe he had ten miles to go. He dared not think of the distance. He'd concentrate on the minute hand of the watch. He'd make it his goal to run nine minutes, and consider another mile done, and then go another nine minutes more after that. His stomach alternately pained and turned queasy, but Bridger kept on slogging. He kept the watch in his hand, keeping track of every minute gone. He got through nine, and nine more.

The road had dipped and curved and Bridger couldn't see the stage. But now the trail was solid. Here's where the stage would make good time. He'd try to run the next mile hard; he'd need every spare yard to win this race. And he realized for the first time that he believed he might win. The notion had seemed outlandish at first, and just finishing, maybe not far behind, might have been enough for his pride —if not for Mr. Satin and his wager.

But now he'd come almost thirty miles, and he was actually in front. With luck, who knew? He thought about the stage driver nearly running him down, and the image made him angry, and the anger gave him energy. It drove him through the next mile. What now, maybe seven more?

He ran another, stopped, bent, hands on knees. Sharp pains burned in his back, just inside his shoulder blades. His knees wobbled and his lower back throbbed. The bile in his stomach rose every minute, and each time he forced it back down. Can't stay still for long, Bridger thought, I'll never get going again. Dizzy now, he broke into a labored jog. At least he was moving forward. But for how long? . . .

. . . As long as he could . . . another tortured mile. And another. Limping now, he forced himself forward. He wanted desperately to stop. Nothing, he thought, can be worth this. As quickly, he forced the thought away. He thought of Mike. "Never give up," he'd said. "It's a sin." He stumbled, going down on his knees. He willed himself upright and slogged on. He tried to imagine himself a hero, a soldier in the Scots Greys, charging at Waterloo, he'd seen them in a painting. . . .

. . . And at last, ahead, he spied the station. Couldn't be a mile. Bridger stumbled again, almost falling. Behind came the stage. He could hear it pounding. Why did it go by him? Then he could pass out and die. A mile. Infinity. Ah, help me, he prayed. He felt his vision fading, a dark curtain creeping from the corners of his eyes. Little by little, it was closing out his sight. Perhaps he was dying. He did not know, could not think. Hot pain ripped at his heart and shafted his lungs. Dried spittle stiffened his lips and sweat-salt crusted his mustache. He had stopped breathing long ago; now he merely gasped.

Step by step he came, forcing himself on, while the stage hammered behind, an everlasting nightmare. A hundred yards from him; now seventy-five; and now fifty. Men came trotting from the station, a half-mile now, straining to see, shouting as they came. And they saw a wild-eyed specter of a man, a lurching, flailing wraith. They drew closer and heard his awful breathing, somewhere between a moan and a cry. And as he staggered by, they saw his pistol still in one hand, a watch in the other. Some men, alarmed, shrank back.

A few hundred yards to the finish, the stage driver reined in his team. "Out!" he bellowed. "All you lard-bottoms out! Now!" Doors flew open and passengers tumbled out. "Now!" the driver screeched, ripping his whip cruelly, urging the horses for one last charge with the much lighter coach. "Yah! Yah!"

Bridger heard it coming. With the last of his will, he raised his head, bared his teeth and tried to shout. Those near him heard it come out as a snarl. And they saw him wrench his body forward, grimacing as he went, growling and gagging. And on came the stage, its nightmare horses heaving yards behind. Numb, his legs dead, Bridger heard nothing. He spied the forms of two men just ahead. They looked like phantoms holding some kind of string between them.

Those who saw it talked about the finish for years.

They said later they would never know what kept the man standing; that he ran like someone mortally shot, that he ran insanely, wildly, as if in the twitching reflexes of death.

At the end, his knees buckled. Nearly falling, he jerked upright. His mind told him he was floating. He knew he wouldn't fall because he could fly. He flapped his arms. He lunged, intending to glide above the ground, as in a dream. He sprawled into dirt. With thunder and grinding, the stage crashed past, spewing dirt on Bridger's kicking legs.

Somewhere, men shouted and cheered. Dimly, fading in and out of his vision, men were shoving each other. He could hear cursing. Somebody fell. It didn't matter. It had nothing to do with him. Bridger blessed the soft bed of the ground. Around and above him, voices bleated and blared in argument.

The stage, someone declared, had won.

# 16

P EOPLE LIFTED HIM, and there was water at last, a lot of it, and sweet as wine. Someone offered him candy, someone else two oranges. There was backpatting and kind, proud words, as if strangers were made better by touching him or speaking to him. Respectfully, someone offered to hold the pistol he still clutched. How could he run so far, they wanted to know.

Bridger smiled drowsily. "Just keep going and be patient," he panted. "You'll get there by and by."

His gasps sounded like the rasp of a saw, but in a few minutes he was able to salvage a deep, heaving breath. He was able to stand by himself, and he lifted his hands overhead, hoping to open his lungs and draw in a much air as he could. Gradually, his heart eased its locomotive pace. He gulped cup after cup of good water and poured more over his head. He let a boy throw an entire bucketful on him, causing the crowd to explode into laughter. He walked stiff-legged to a barrel filled to the brim and plunged his head in, bobbing up whooshing and shaking. He turned his back to the barrel and slowly slid down its side, exhaling loudly and sitting down hard. He toed off the shoes he had run in and stretched his legs.

"Pretty good shape for the shape I'm in," Bridger allowed, a broad grin beginning to spread under his mustache. "Say, do I have to race it back?" The remark drew more laughter. All watched his every move, and Bridger was starting to relish what he had done. His temples throbbed, his muscles ached from dehydration, and vague spots and shadows crept in and out of his vision. He thought he still could faint if he didn't move with care. At least his cramps were gone; he thought he must have sweated out the bad water he'd taken in earlier.

Mr. Satin was ecstatic. "No matter they said you lost. You proved our point." And he pressed a hundred dollars into Bridger's palm. "Well done," he said. "And well-earned." He pleaded then. "Come back with me to Brooksville. Now we'll finish persuading these backwoods barons that the railroad's time has come."

Bridger begged off. "Dead tired," he said. "I can hardly move, let alone talk some kind of business." He'd rest here at the relay station, he said, and rejoin Mr. Satin in Tampa. Maybe he'd even do some fishing on the river nearby. Without saying so, he hoped Miss Lily would be on tomorrow's stage. He'd rather see her without his employer hovering.

In the end, Mr. Satin agreed and boarded the return coach to Brooksville. In tow were his potential railroad magnates, by now drunk and arguing loudly. Bridger reflected that he could use a beer himself, but decided against searching for one. One would certainly lead to two, and then more.

He wanted to be fresh for Miss Lily. He knew a good night's rest would leave him stiff and sore but otherwise pretty much recovered from the run.

But Miss Lily was not on the next day's stage. Puzzled, Bridger pondered his next move. Perhaps she had decided to go back to her homestead, after all. Or maybe she still couldn't get a ticket. This coach had been crowded, too. At last, rather than take the relay coach to Tampa, Bridger decided to pay for the use of a boat and float down the river the rest of the way. He could be there by dark, the boatman told him. It was downstream, and he could row if he wanted to go faster. And Miss Lily had, after all, said she would meet him in Tampa—not at some dirty stage stop.

For the time being, the boat proved to be a happy choice, though considering all that had happened, Bridger kept a lookout for any approach of a stranger.

It didn't keep him from enjoying the river—the Hillsborough, the boatman had called it. The day was warm, the sun shining golden off green trees. Turtles slid off rocks. Fish leaped. Graceful white birds with long, wiry necks stalked along the banks. Several times Bridger saw alligators there, too, and each time they made his heart tighten. But the big lizards hardly seemed alive and showed no interest in his boat.

Bridger took off his shirt and lay back, letting the current move him, occasionally dabbling an oar to guide the boat. His mind wandered, kicking over the questions he wanted to answer. First, Uncle Mike. He would have to renew his search in Tampa, with or without Miss Lily. But from what she had said, Tampa was close to Punta Pinal—the Point of Pines, Point Pinellas, Mike's last known location.

Somehow Bridger felt as if he were close to finding some answers. And if he found out what had happened to Mike, maybe he was getting close to solving the mystery of the treasure. Bridger had never been absolutely sure what he believed about it. Uncle Mike liked to pass along tall tales, but he never had been one to fabricate a story out and out. On the other hand, Bridger didn't know for sure if he had actually seen any treasure. Maybe he was just passing along rumors.

What if he found Uncle Mike? Then maybe he'd find a lost fortune and be rich—or maybe he wouldn't. In either case, what would he do next? Go back to New York? Stay in Florida and make a new life? And what about Miss Lily? He realized he wanted to see her again, to talk to her for hours. The feeling surprised him. He had never felt any such desire for serious female friendship. But this woman was different. Bridger pictured her in her dress: tall, graceful, her elegant face wearing an expression sometimes amused, always wise, conversing on every subject. She was a backwoods princess, that's what she was. Bridger realized he wanted very much to see her again.

But so much else lay unresolved. Would he continue to work for Mr. Satin? Who were these men who continued to chase him? For that matter, he still didn't know how he'd gotten to Miss Lily's doorstep days ago. And was he still wanted in Jacksonville?

Bridger cut short his daydream. He noticed his boat's bow had begun to swing in a gentle, but very definite arc. He saw that he had drifted into a whirlpool. He pulled several times on the oars, hauling out of the spin. Looking back, he gazed at the languid whirl, and saw leaves revolving in the eddy, going around like riders on a carousel. Odd how such a small thing could seem so peaceful, Bridger thought. He looked up and saw what looked like a hawk or an eagle gliding, catching air currents and rising with scarcely a wing movement. He took an easy, deep breath and lay back. For the moment, life was good. He half-drifted, half rowed into Tampa. He began paying attention when he saw a row of wharves and warehouses on the riverbank.

It took a day or two for Leg Dicken to get the latest "full report" from Wade Mizell, who, it was obvious, wanted to minimize the difficulties his agents had in coralling Tom Bridger. The first telegram read: "Missed Bridger on Ocala train. Missed again during stage run to Tampa." Mizell knew his boss would hardly accept such an accounting. He merely wanted to stall until he could think of an acceptable story.

Dicken didn't give him the chance. His own wire demanded "all details now." When he received them, Dicken smacked his desk and swore. This Bridger, this pup, had somehow bested an experienced gunman who knew something about holding up trains after a crime career in the West. Or so Mizell said, the ape. This "experienced gunman" didn't sound like much now. Whatever had happened, the gunman had been shot, either by Bridger or someone else on the train, and later been arrested.

Dicken fumed as he read. After that, as if the first episode hadn't been folly enough, another of Mizell's fools had tried to kidnap Bridger during some kind of a footrace involving a stagecoach. And the kid had flattened him!

Gotten away again! Damnation!

In spite of his fury at Mizell and his band of misfits, Dicken shook his head and almost smiled. Who was this pup? Someone determined, someone with gumption. Someone who could survive in hostile territory, Dicken reflected. Someone a bit like himself. And therefore someone capable of turning ambition into reality. Treasure. Treasure into a personal fortune.

"This kid is dangerous," Dicken muttered aloud. Dangerous enough because he'd helped get one of Mizell's apes put in jail, where he might start pointing accusing fingers. Dangerous because he could be sniffing after the fortune Dicken himself continued to dream of.

Fifteen years ago, he'd gotten a fraction of it out of that cave in the wilderness. It had proven to be his stake for a career. With a little money to start, it was easy enough to make more from human weakness in post-war Jacksonville. Some might look down on him if they knew all. But, Dicken reflected, at least he had made his own way.

He had used some of his windfall to buy an interest in a saloon. Then he'd fed and clothed several women and girls, drifting paupers, really. He put them to work in the saloon, taking a nice hunk of their earnings. Soon he was able to buy out his partner. He bought another saloon, established them as gambling houses, and set up high-interest loans for big losers.

He began selling "insurance" to small-time fishermen whose boats were their livelihoods, and later, to larger marine interests. It wasn't unheard of for a boat to sink or burn at its moorings if an owner refused to do business with Leg Dicken. He made allies along the way—men like himself who wanted money and didn't care how they made it. Dicken considered it a point of pride that for a time, he had had dealings with Wes Hardin. The notorious Texas gunman, calling himself J. R. Swain, set up temporary camp in Florida's unsettled interior, southwest of Jacksonville. It was never proven that the pair actually collaborated in a major crime, but it was said within the underworld that Hardin's gun had enforced Dicken's word more than once.

Eventually, his network of criminals, toughs, informants, and would-be thugs stretched as far west as Lake City, and nearly as far south as Tampa. Some said he had influence in Tallahassee, the state capital. But he wanted much more. He never let go the idea of the fortune, the jungle-hidden treasure on the remote Gulf of Mexico peninsula. He thought of it daily. He brooded for hours. With it, he would distance himself forever not only from the rotten outcasts he dealt with daily, but also from those half-rich Jacksonville snobs who would never quite accept him, even though they were polite enough to his face.

And riches and fame would be the best revenge he could think of on Mr. Sam Satin. Oh, how far back they did go. Dicken nursed in his heart a sweet hatred. He fed it every day, just as he nurtured his dream of lost treasure. Soon the day would come when he would be ready to try for it again. But now there was this Bridger fellow, this brazen pup, untested and therefore unafraid. He would have to be made afraid, then.

# 17

BRIDGER TOOK A ROOM AT A HOTEL called the H.B. Plant, named, he was told, for the man who had brought the railroad to Tampa a year ago. Railroad building did indeed seem to be the vogue in Florida, Bridger observed. "Good reason for it," said the hotel clerk. "They're opening up this state. Good for business, good for towns."

Mostly because of this Plant fellow, the clerk said, Tampa was starting to hum. Bridger could see it was far from being a Jacksonville, but it was trying. Small boats, some carrying fresh catches of fish, nosed into the docks. A shallow-draft schooner dropping passengers was just in from some place called Cedar Key up the Gulf of Mexico coast. On the dirt streets, wagons drawn by mules and oxen kicked up dust. They carried lumber, barrels and boxes of oranges, a piano, a huge safe, glass for windows, and even a cornet band—they were everywhere in Florida, apparently.

Some horsemen, their long whips uncoiling and snapping like rifle shots, harried skinny cattle toward the docks. It was the second drive Bridger had seen. He'd had no idea of it before, but Florida seemed quite the place for cattle, though this bunch looked anything but well fed. He saw an elegantly dressed lady being driven in a carriage pulled by two black horses, and a four-mule-team ice wagon. On posters, entertainment beckoned: A reading of Sidney Lanier's works at the Ladies Improvement Society. Bongo Jones, The Key West Slasher, a pugilist to take on all comers. Now open, a roller skating rink, "the newest diversion," said the poster.

Roller skating. Bridger shook his head. He'd tried it once during a spree in New York City. He had flailed wildly around the rink, causing general panic while bowling over several sailors ashore from a U.S. Navy vessel. And he had vowed never again to put wheels on his feet.

But then, what to do? Other placards advertised a diversion at Branch's Opera House, and the Tampa Rifles militia would "hold a public spectacle" at a place called Ballast Point. The name made Bridger think again of the Point of Pines. But he doubted it could be the same spot. Nothing sounded just right to do. But it was a crisp, clear evening and, bathed and trimmed, Bridger was feeling rather good about life. After all, he had run a heroic race against beast and machine, nearly winning. Maybe he'd help change the course of Florida history! And even if not, he'd run further and faster than ever before. He had money. And he had two guns stuck in his belt, underneath his coat.

He stopped to buy some spicy, breaded crab meat from a street vendor, then he had some smoked fish like he'd tried in Jacksonville. It made him want a beer, and why not? Bridger swaggered a bit as he stepped into the first saloon he saw. A leathery, one-eyed man drank at the bar, and, after two beers, Bridger struck up a conversation. Corkeye Slim was what the man called himself, and he said he was a fisherman, sailor and general waterfront roustabout. "It's a hard life," said Corkeye, straight-faced. "I'm only twenty-three."

Bridger guffawed. Corkeye was white-haired, and a scattering of white whiskers glazed his wrinkled face. He said he got his name because he had a trick of holding a whisky bottle cork in his empty eye socket. "Have a drink on me," Bridger said. "And I'll have one myself." He ordered whiskies backed by beers and the two men drank up.

"Another round here," called Bridger. At a table across the room, he saw two men arm-wrestling. One of them in particular stood out. He was an older man, maybe about Mr. Satin's age, but he looked wiry and hard. A long black beard hung down his chest. "That's Nathan DeBell," said Corkeye. "Lives over acrost the bay, old pioneer, a real woodsman. Fit in the war, too, and a right fearsome soldier, as I hear it."

Bridger watched DeBell slam down his opponent's arm, then pocket a coin the other man gave him. Well, a little sport, a little betting! "I think I'll try this fellow out," said Bridger. He ambled over to DeBell's table. He had a fierce, scowling look about him, Bridger saw, and there wasn't a hint of humor in his black eyes. He was bigger than Bridger had thought at first, and long and lean. "Evening, sir, care to try your luck again?"

"There won't be no luck. Let's see your wager." The man's voice rumbled deep inside his chest. Bridger took out a coin, pulled off his coat and sat down. The butts of his pistols showed out of his trouser tops, and Bridger saw DeBell's eyes flick to the weapons. One was Miss Lily's, the other the gun he'd taken from his assailant during the race. A few of the saloon's other patrons, including Corkeye, sauntered over to watch.

The two locked hands. There was no signal, but both contenders, as if reading one another's minds, seemed to know the instant to begin. Bridger meant simply to hold steady for a moment, gauging his opponent's strength—and was stunned at the older man's sudden, devastating power. DeBell hammered Bridger's arm to the table and almost threw him out of his chair. The onlookers whistled and shouted. And DeBell stared right through Bridger, never changing expression.

"I guess I'll try again," said Bridger, masking his embarrassment. DeBell merely nodded. Again, the two locked hands. This time Bridger anticipated DeBell's lightning attack and he held the first surge. But the man had the strength of an animal. It was overpowering, almost unreal, Bridger thought, and he knew he had no chance. He just kept pushing as best he could until DeBell forced down his arm.

"Well, that beats all," said Bridger, handing over another coin. "Buy you a drink, too?" He wanted to know more about this strange, silent fellow. "Don't need it," said DeBell, abruptly pushing back his chair and rising. He stalked out the door without another word.

"Ah, don't mind him," spoke up Corkeye. "He's just put out because that big cow chaser Booter Powell didn't come around. He's the only one hereabouts ever has a chance with Nathan. And lemme tell you, it's no disgrace to lose to Nathan, either. 'Cept for Booter, and him not often, don't know as I've ever seen Nathan beat."

"Who is he again?" asked Bridger.

"An old-timer, like I said. Lives over on the point, acrost the bay there, out in the jungle. Been there years, him and his family. Don't much like the newcomers movin' in, I hear. And he's not a man to cross." Bridger mulled Corkeye's remarks. Hostile or not, dangerous or not, DeBell seemed like someone who might know about Big Mike. Who might even know about a lost treasure. And what about this point Corkeye mentioned? Could it be the Point of Pines?

Bridger decided he'd make it his business to pay a visit to Mr. Nathan DeBell. But first, he thought he'd have a few more drinks. Just to be sociable. After all, there was no telling what he might find out right here. Bridger bought a round of drinks for everyone and someone struck up "Shoo Fly" on a fiddle. The musician followed that with "Maggie"—"Wrote right here in Tampa," he bragged—and moved on into "Bonnie Blue Flag," which brought a chorus of whoops and shrill hollers. Bridger wondered if he was hearing the notorious Rebel yell Northern war veterans still recalled. In a while, he sang "Minstrel Boy," and the fiddler picked up the tune with ease. More cheering, and this time, applause.

This was the ticket, Bridger thought. They recognize me as an adventurer, a man of the world. He could see it clearly. They respected him. He smiled broadly and ordered another round of drinks. He bought himself a bottle of whisky. Corkeye held the cork in his eye socket while Bridger poured a shot into a small glass and lit a match to it. The alcohol flared up and Bridger drank the blazing liquid at a gulp. "Smoo-o-th," Bridger said with exaggerated pleasure, rubbing his stomach. The gesture brought more applause and general hilarity. Bridger was feeling grand now, on top of the world. Say, he might just swim across the bay and beard old

DeBell in his den. Beard him, he sure had a beard for it. Hee.

He noticed a fellow sitting alone at a table, unsmiling. Unfriendly, like. Well, what was the matter here? Bridger stuck his bottle under an arm, grabbed another glass, and walked over. "Have a drink, sir, on me. It's a lovely night inside tonight and may you live to see many more."

The loner made as if to spit, then ran his eyes over Bridger. "Person like you ever do any real work?" Bridger's smile faded just a twitch. Some of these folks down here . . . well, he'd try again. "Now and then, sir. But I do take my pleasure when and where I can."

"I'm a cardplayer myself. What is it you do exactly? Besides drink."

This time, Bridger couldn't ignore the jab. This fellow was rude, looking for trouble, or didn't care if it came his way. Bridger set the bottle and glasses on the table, making sure he cracked each one down hard. "Some men would vouch that I do any number of things," he answered. The cardplayer smirked.

The others watched. Bridger knew they were waiting to see what he would do next. The man at the table answered back. "Rich kid on a lark, huh?" It was the kind of remark calculated to annoy, and it did because Bridger feared it was close to the truth, no matter what other reasons he had for his trip. He knew he was in Florida for good cause. But still the words ate at him. He calculated his own reply.

"There isn't much about this part of the world that resembles a lark, as far as I can see." Bridger let a beat or two of silence go by. "Unless it's cleaning out petty card dealers." Most in the little audience grew quiet after Bridger's response. He was on display now, Bridger knew, and maybe he hadn't won any friends with his last remark. But he had meant to be friendly. He could see no reason why this person seemed bent on picking a fight.

He glanced about, checking to see any of his drinking friends had turned hostile. He failed to notice one man at a corner table, another loner not joining in, quietly sipping a beer. The gambler seemed to take no particular offense at Bridger's comments.

"High-low's the game, if you got the stomach for it," the gambler challenged. He pulled out a thin leather case, pale with the outline of a skull burned on it. He yanked the cards and fanned them on the table. "Your pick, rich boy."

A silly game, Bridger thought happily. He'd always heard real gamblers wouldn't bet on something of such apparent pure chance. Then again, maybe this deck was marked. But . . . so what if it was. He was here for some adventure. And he could always quit if he started losing badly. Bridger drew an eight of hearts; the gambler pulled a jack of spades. Bridger drew again, this time the ace of diamonds. The gambler chose a three. Then Bridger went on a run. The card sharp was picking medium high cards, and Bridger suddenly had a run of royals. He won five straight times.

If they were playing with a marked deck, the gambler must be stringing him along for something. Bridger poured two shots of whisky, drank one and lit the other on fire. He was giddy, almost as if he could feel the winning cards before he picked them. He knew he was on a streak. He gulped the flaming whisky, and could see the gambler's temper rise.

Bridger thought he'd offer a game of his own, especially since this so-called gambler didn't mind wild games. "Tell you what, card man. Let's play an old college game. Ever been to college? Let me show you something. It's called go-between. Kind of a version of monte."

Bridger described a game that called for dealing two cards. Then each player in turn bet on whether the next card dealt would be something between the first two. "Say there's a king and a nine on the table, you need to draw a ten, jack, or a queen to win. Bet what you want or match the pot. You win, take your bet back and that amount again. Lose and the pot keeps your bet. You follow all that, card man?"

The gambler looked at Bridger with poison in his eyes. "You deal 'em, pretty boy." Deal them Bridger did. He won the ante money three times in a row, then lost twice, feeding the pot. The gambler, still stinging, bet the pot on a four-and-Jack frame. But up came an ace and he had to match the kitty. Then it was his turn to deal. The gambler turned stingy with his bets. Bridger was not quite as careful, and put in more than he took out. He got the deal back and the gambler watched him through angry eyes. Bridger won a couple of small bets. Then he tossed a king and three to the gambler.

It was the biggest gap to turn up yet. The two had been betting dollar pieces and the pot, growing steadily, was approaching a hundred. The gambler bet the pot. Bridger threw him a three. The card fell and Bridger drank down another shot of whisky. He looked straight at the gambler, who slammed his fist on the table and threw in a batch of money.

Bridger winked and dealt himself a ten and a seven. He laughed out loud, bet the pot and threw a nine. It was as if he had perfect foresight. He could almost feel the card was right before he tossed it. He felt powerful, unbeatable. It made him laugh harder. He raked in the huge pot while the gambler swore.

"You cheating Yankee scum, you mama's boy drunk!"

Bridger froze. Then he rose slowly and deliberately and turned toward the bar, taking two unsteady steps. He was already dizzy from the drinking. Now anger twisted through his brain. The last four words the gambler uttered were almost exactly the last words Bridger's father had spoken to him. He took another measured step toward the bar, moving his right hand slowly toward one of the guns in his belt. The saloon was still. Bridger heard a rustle behind him, a whisper of flesh brushing a vest, so soft it could hardly be heard.

Yet Bridger knew. His drunkenness, as it sometimes did, had given him a fleeting clarity of thought. He knew what was happening behind him. He could see it in his mind. He heard a hammer's click and knew the gambler was going to shoot.

Bridger whirled, pulling a pistol, cocking, and firing with a single contraction of his hand. A staggering thunder filled the saloon as two guns exploded, and Bridger heard the gambler's shot snap past his face.

The gambler slammed back in his chair, tipping it over and crashing to the floor. He fell full-length on his back, his boots rising and coming down hard on the planks. He lay still, his open mouth and staring eyes giving him a dazed, dumb look. Bridger spied a damp hole in the gambler's black coat, and a tint of red beginning to color his exposed shirt. The man lay still and silent as a stone. Shocked, Bridger still held the pistol. It was at full cock, but pointed at the floor. He began to shout.

"I'm not a killer. He's the killer. I'm just looking for Big Mike. We're gonna be rich because of all the treasure, and then by jiminy, I'll buy you all the drinks you can drink.

'Cause you're all my friends."

He waved the pistol at the gambler. "He wasn't my friend. He's just an old killer." Bridger waved the pistol again and accidentally pulled the trigger. A shot slammed into the floor.

"Killing the rats," he bellowed. "Kill all the rats!" The other customers held very still, glancing this way and that. They were jittery. One or two slipped out a door. Bridger was breathing hard and looking around, his eyes starting to roll. He, too, backed out a door and ran down a dirt street, blindly, trying to get anywhere away.

The lone man at a corner table watched and never moved a muscle.

# 18 🌿

BRIDGER CAME TO IN THE DARK.
Something was trying to kick its way out of his head. His
stomach heaved and he had to urinate. He couldn't figure out
where he was. He started to crawl, vomited, and fell face
down in the bile. Then he wet himself. He didn't care.

He wanted to be unconscious, but felt too bad to sleep.
It must have been some party, he told himself. It must have
been some good time. He tried to keep thinking that. But it
was no use. Bridger knew he couldn't think all was right with
the world, however hard he tried. And a terror washed over
him; something horrible had happened. He had been a part
of it. What had he done?

He couldn't remember. Maybe he didn't want to. He
felt sick, adrift, as if some part of his soul had been torn away.
Then he heard a rustling and felt something wet splash over
his head. He cried out in shock. "Yer a right mess there,
young fella, an' it takes one to know one. But you could be
worse, an' a lot a people think you oughta be the sheriff by
now or at least a town marshal. We'll just get you straight-

ened right back up and see what we can do."

It was an old man. Bridger struggled to remember; he'd met him last night. He thought. Yes. Corkeye, he called himself. Corkeye Slim. He'd poured water on Bridger and now he was offering him water to drink. "Take as much of it as you can, and then take some more, and then we'll get you washed down. Some smelly, you are, and I oughta know."

Bridger slowly came to. He wondered if he dared move. He was on the ground, under the hull of an overturned boat. He perceived it was early morning, barely past dawn. He had no idea how he'd gotten there, no idea where he'd been for the past many hours. What was it that had happened? Something terribly bad. But he couldn't bring himself to ask. Then Corkeye made the questions unnecessary.

"You shot Pardner Low, and a lotta people think he'd needed shooting for a long time. He near shot you in the back, like he done a few folks around here. He's just a mean cuss. He'll live, I hear, but it ain't likely he'll have much of a shootin' and gamblin' career around here for a while. And he won't be missed, I'll tell you, and if you lay low awhile, the sheriff won't be around asking many questions. Just another saloon shooting. He's too busy politickin' that highfalutin railroad crowd anyhow."

Bridger felt too sick to do anything but listen. He'd lost control of himself again, lost all memory of what he'd done. He'd shot a man, and it didn't feel right, even if the man were a scoundrel. He ached, head and belly and spirit, and again his greatest fear weighed on him: he couldn't handle himself the way a man should. His father had planted that doubt a long time ago. Maybe he'd been right.

Bridger couldn't even remember the fight that some

evidently said had made him a hero. A menace, that's what I really am, thought Bridger, and someone should shoot me. I should shoot myself. He thought of the pistols and reached for them on reflex. Gone!

"Right here," said Corkeye. "Thought I'd hold 'em just in case you woke up nervous. It's plain you know how to handle 'em, but you were some scary last night. Want 'em now?" He held them out to Bridger, who took them with shaking hands.

"That one there," said Corkeye, pointing to the pistol Bridger had taken from the rider during the stage race. "I don't know what to make of it. Looks like it's pieced together with parts of a lot of different guns. Wonder it didn't blow up in your hand. As it was, it half misfired. You shot straight, but the slug didn't have a punch. Now if you'd shot'm with that"—he pointed to Miss Lily's Colt—"they'd be organizin' a buryin' this morning."

"Ah gahd," said Bridger. "I feel like the devil."

"Sure ya do," said Corkeye. "But I got a plan, 'cause you did me a favor by layin' that skunk low." He chuckled at his play on Pardner Low's name. "Let's get you cleaned up, at least, and then I'm sailin' you across the bay. Best thing you can do is stay put for a while and breathe up the sea breeze and eat some oysters." Corkeye winked his good eye. "And I'm thinkin a generous young fella like you might remember old Corkeye for doin' it."

Bridger shook his head, although the movement hurt. "I have to see someone. Two people, really, if I can find them."

"Go to town and you will ask for trouble," said Corkeye. "Folks don't care you shot Low. Most of 'em probably glad, like I said. But they don't want to see you walkin' around, big as you please. They might start thinkin', here's one more no-good takin' the place of the one he shot. Now listen here. You stay outta sight. Folks will respect you more if they don't see much of you. You go shovin' around, they might worry you're gonna shoot them next. You were a wild sight last night, shootin' up the place."

Bridger cringed at Corkeye's last few words. He had no memory at all of what had happened. He watched a seagull pecking at a scrap. That bird, he thought, has more worth than I do. But he had to press on, or at least make the try. He thought of Mr. Satin and Miss Lily. Either one might tell him something more about the Point of Pines. He really wanted to see Miss Lily more right now, but not until he got to feeling better. If he started feeling better.

"Can you take a message to someone for me? Tell him where I've gone and that I've got to see him? It's important." With a sudden move, Bridger felt inside his coat. Thank goodness, at least he hadn't gotten himself robbed this time. "I'll pay you if you'll take a message."

Corkeye looked interested. "Wouldn't ever turn down a few coins," he said. "Who's your man? Or lady, mayhap?" He winked again.

"Man calls himself Mr. Satin," said Bridger. "Tall, wears an alligator coat, like the hide's around the shoulders. Nice mustache, pretty well dressed, talks like he's educated."

Corkeye's face fell. "Don't think so. Don't think you want that one."

"Yes, he's exactly the one I want. What do you mean?"

"Why, that fella, that one calls himself Satin, he and Low are partners." He smiled again at the pun on Low's name. "Partners in crime, you might say."

❖ ❖ ❖

"I just don't believe it," Bridger said. "He treated me fairly. More than fairly."

He relented and let Corkeye talk him into sailing somewhere away from Tampa. Now they were on a great bay, and Bridger could barely discern land in any direction as Corkeye's little sailboat, which he called a sharpie, kicked along on a crisp northeast breeze.

"He was settin' you up, likely as not," Corkeye answered. "Like he did me. He paid me real nice to do the odd job, and me bein' a man most always in need of money, I did what he asked. Then one day he asked me to burn somebody out. A homesteader over here across the bay. I told him no, and he got real mean. Said he knew all about me, could have me put in prison if he wanted. Not that I've been an angel, but anything I ever done was a long time ago, and I never killed nobody or stole. Not much, anyway. But around here a man can wind up in jail, or dead, if they cross someone with money or connections. I just tried to stay out of his way.

"Then one day that homesteader's place got set on fire. That Low, he was the one finally got hooked up with Satin, and he was the one who done it. I know, 'cause he was careless enough to let me see him loadin' a boat with kerosene. Sure, he got a couple of fishermen to take him over. Next day word come that homesteader got clean burned out. No one ever saw those fishermen again. But I saw Low and Satin together in town a lot. I was usually drunk, and they knew it, but I wasn't that drunk. Low said if I ever said anything, he'd blame the burnin' on me—if he didn't kill me first."

Bridger mulled it all. "Just doesn't seem the same man. He lives in Jacksonville, for one thing. And why'd he want to burn anyone out, anyway?"

Corkeye snorted. "Money, of course. He's tryin' to put together land for a railroad comin' to the Point. This homesteader wouldn't sell at Satin's price, so Satin figured he'd just force him to leave. Worked, too, and now he's thinkin' he can scare others off, or buy 'em out cheap. As far as Jacksonville, he might live there. But he works all over this state, trying to put together land deals. And now railroad deals. There's a lot of em like him out there tryin' to get rich these days. Except he's meaner than most."

Corkeye's railroad references startled Bridger. He knew for sure Mr. Satin was interested in the trains opening up the Florida wilderness. But he couldn't believe the man was desperate enough to destroy settlers' property. Bridger thought he might just ask Mr. Satin straight out when he saw him next. After all, he'd probably head back to Tampa after a few days of hiding out. He wanted to see Miss Lily, too—although it was hard to think about that today. He felt as if he weren't worthy of her.

"Where are we headed?" he asked.

"Pinellas village, over on a bayou off the bay. Point Pinellas, some people say. Be there shortly, way this wind's going."

Bridger looked up sharply. "Point Pinellas? Point, point, anyone ever call it the Point of Pines?" A surge of excitement rolled through him. It cleared his head a little. Corkeye grinned. "Well, that's kind of the old-fashioned name, but sure enough, Point of Pines it is. Spanish words are Punta Pinal." Corkeye said it differently, with the accent on the last syllable. But it was close enough for Bridger to know.

He trembled. His head spun. And it wasn't entirely the hangover's fault. He gripped the boat's gunwales and tried to calm himself. After journeying more than a thousand miles by land and sea, after all that had happened, he was about to reach his destination, almost by accident.

It was a jarring realization, as if he needed one this morning. What would he do now?

# 19 ☀

"THIS IS THE PLACE I've been dreaming of," said Bridger, peering at a rapidly approaching shoreline that from a distance looked like a low-lying wall of green. "It's the end of my journey, Corkeye."

"Well, you could do worse, young fella," answered the old man, misunderstanding Bridger's excitement. "When things are right, this spot can be a paradise." Bridger smiled. Maybe he'd tell Corkeye specifics later.

The sharpie cut south across a stretch of shallows. Bridger could see a school of fish so thick it looked as though he could step out of the boat and walk on them. "What are they?"

"Trouts, them are. You can see 'em all, though. Mullets, reds, perches. Catch hundreds of pounds of 'em in a day, if you wanted. Thousands, maybe. Up there on shore, you can grow whatever you want. Oranges, melons. Yams, all kinds of vegetables. Man could live here forever on what he caught and grew." Bridger thought Corkeye was trying to describe a paradise on earth, but he sensed some sincerity in what the old man said.

He spied blackened pilings and what looked like burnt pieces of wood on shore. He pointed them out to Corkeye, who clouded up. "That's the homestead Low burned out. Or what's left of it."

"What happened to the people?"

"Sold out. To your friend Satin, just like he wanted 'em to."

"And you say others are being threatened?"

"He wants others to sell to him, that's for sure. And they know what happened to the first bunch. Guess you could call that a threat."

"Why doesn't the law step in?"

"I guess 'cause there's no law against talkin' property deals, and nobody can prove anything about the burn-out. That's to start. The other thing, no one pays much attention to what happens over here on Pinellas. It's the same law as it is for Tampa, but it's hard to get here from there. You have to sail over like we're doin, or come around the top of the point. And there aren't any roads into it, just a few cow trails. It's always been a wild place with just a few folks livin' here, and them a pretty hard, standoffish bunch. 'Course now, there are some new folks comin' in. Some a those English foks, even. One of these days, we'll get a railroad in here and turn down-right civilized."

Bridger asked: "Corkeye, why don't you just go to the law yourself and tell them what you know?"

Corkeye frowned. "I'm lucky someone like Satin hasn't done me in already," he said. "Maybe the only reason they haven't is that they think I'm an old drunk—which I am—and no one would take me serious, which they probably wouldn't. But a course if I were to go talkin', and maybe I should at that, they'd come after me for sure. Guess I'd like to hang on to what years I got left."

Bridger wanted to ask about lost treasure, and whether Corkeye had ever heard of a Big Mike McGinnis. But maybe now was not the time. The old man was tacking the sharpie past two small keys and into a kind of lagoon. Neither man noticed the white wing of a sail far behind on the bay.

Ahead of them, tall trees and low, pointy bushes marched almost to the water's edge. Bridger saw some rickety docks, a few wooden buildings huddled close to the shore, and a small boatworks nearby. Two or three unpainted frame houses stood further back.

"Welcome to Pinellas village," said Corkeye, easing his boat next to a dock and roping it to a post. There wasn't a soul in sight. Their footsteps knocked on dock planking and echoed off the water. Ripples from the bay spanked a narrow beach where Bridger could see spidery, gray creatures popping in and out of coin-sized holes in the sand. Aromas of fish and saltwater washed over him, and the sight of nets stretched to dry across overturned boats reminded him of a fishing village he'd once visited on Long Island.

But this one lay silent, almost ghostlike in the morning. There was no hint of the bustle Bridger had witnessed in Jacksonville and Tampa, or even of the ambition in smaller Ocala and Brooksville. At least those villages had railway or stage stops. "Ain't this quiet, usually," Corkeye said, heading for a weathered building with a sign proclaiming it to be a store.

Two nailed-up posters at least suggested some lively interests might be concealed within the settlement. One announced a Saturday-night dance at the San Jose Hotel.

The other, like several Bridger had seen in Tampa, promoted the coming of the itinerant pugilist Bongo Jones, the Key West Slasher. Corkeye pushed open the door, which caused a set of bells to jangle overhead. Two men were inside. "Gents," Corkeye greeted them. "Pretty quiet around here today."

They glanced at Corkeye, then looked at Bridger in none too friendly a fashion. The man behind the counter spoke. "Word is, there's gonna be more trouble," he said. "Old Man Stroud got a letter. Last offer, it said. Everybody figure's there's gonna be more burnin'. They're stayin' at home. On guard, you might say."

He continued to stare at Bridger but spoke to Corkeye. "Who's your friend?"

"Now, Romano, don't start gettin' riled," Corkeye said quickly. "This here's young Bridger. Matter of fact, he put the one did the last burnin' out of commission for a while. You oughta thank him. Bridger, this here's Joe Romano, runs the store here. Also mayor of Pinellas village, kinda like. Man there's Archie Hankins, come all the way from England."

There were cool nods all around. No one said a word for a few seconds. Then Romano broke the silence. "Fact is, no one knows who did the burnin'. Fact is, old man, some people think you had a lot to do with it. You're the one with all those connections in Tampa."

Corkeye bristled. "That's how come I got a idea who did do it, Romano. And for that matter, you have a few Tampa connections yourself, as I recollect. Ain't that where your daddy started out fishin'? If he was livin', he wouldn't take kindly to his baby boy talkin' down one of his old pals." The speech quieted Romano. The men waited to see who would make the next comment.

Bridger glanced around the store. He saw barrels of nails, shelves filled with dry goods, trousers, boots. Some rifles and a shotgun or two hung on the wall, and Bridger could smell gun oil, along with tobacco and a comfortable grocery-store aroma of spices and coffee. Despite the suspicion rolling off Romano and Hankins, there was something here that pleased him. He couldn't blame the men, under the circumstances, for not welcoming him with open arms. But he wondered if he could win them over. He would have to, he thought, if he were to get any further with his quest.

"Men, I'm looking to stay for a while," he said. "Maybe after you get to know me, you'll see that I'm not here to do anyone harm. What I'd like is a place to stay, and maybe some work to do. I've traveled a long way and a long while to get here. I've some mysteries of my own to solve and by and by, maybe I can tell you about them, if you'll let me. Meantime, I'll do my best to help you." He looked in turn at Hankins and Romano, trying his best to look pleasant without putting on a huge smile the men might think insincere.

It seemed to break the ice a little. "Right, fair enough, then," said Hankins, the Englishman.

Romano began studying some paperwork on the counter. "Probly got a room for you at the San Jose," he said, poking his thumb in what Bridger took to be a hotel's general direction.

"Say," Corkeye butted in. "Who signed that letter to Stroud, anyway?"

"Didn't see it myself," Romano answered without looking up. "Heard it was from someone named Sam Satin, though. Called himself a land agent. For the Gulf and Citrus railway."

❖ ❖ ❖

Bridger took a room at the San Jose. Still a bit sore from the race, shaky from his binge, and depressed about his misadventures in Tampa, he spent the next two days resting mind and body, and thinking about what he would do next. He talked to almost no one. Corkeye had sailed back to Tampa, and few in the village seemed inclined to get acquainted.

Bridger stayed close to the hotel, or strolled around the village, nodding to people he saw and hoping to be seen by as many as possible. If someone's property were burned, he wanted his own whereabouts easily established. He took care not to appear furtive in any way. He bought a few items from the general store, but Romano, while coolly polite, showed no interest in conversation. And Bridger did not bring up any of his own questions.

There were no burnings. And gradually, the village assumed what Bridger took to be its more typical routine. He watched a boat-building project and observed the comings and goings at the little post office, which with Romano's store seemed to be the village's main source of information and speculation. Bridger learned there was strong feeling in favor of a railroad coming to the Point and that in fact two or three syndicates were rumored to be interested in pushing through to a rail terminus on Tampa Bay or the Gulf of Mexico. Besides bringing growth and a probable rise in property values, farmers would have a quicker way to transport their produce to markets.

But there were some—"old backwoods ignoramuses," Bridger heard them called—who preferred their wilderness and wanted nothing to do with a new way of life they feared a railroad would bring. And still others, while hoping the rails eventually would bring prosperity, were not yet willing to part with any of their property for right-of-way—except at the high price they demanded.

Business on the frontier, bringing good and bad, Bridger observed. He thought of the things he had taken for granted in New York—good railroads, easy transportation, cities and towns with plenty of advantages and lots to see and buy— and how the few people here were beginning to yearn for those pleasures, scheming to get them. Well, they'd probably be better off with them, Bridger speculated. Probably. But in a very short time, he had begun to appreciate the peaceful, unhurried ways of the little settlement, surrounded by its tall pines and placid bayou waters.

After a few nights, he'd risked a beer or two in the San Jose's small saloon, but hadn't really enjoyed them. He found himself wanting to be outside and decided to walk along the docks. He gazed across the lagoon, Big Bayou, the locals called it, and it was a pretty sight with the moon glistening on the water. He thought of Miss Lily and wondered what she was doing.

"Bridger. Bridger!"

He jumped, startled, and looked toward the shadows along the shore.

"Over here. Bridger!"

He stepped off a dock and moved toward a tree line, carefully. There was a movement in the shadows, and out stepped Corkeye. "Man wants to see you. Come on over here." Corkeye's voiced sounded odd, and he was moving very slowly and deliberately. Bridger wondered if he was drunk. Then he saw another man appear.

"Young Mr. Bridger," a voice said. "You are a hard one to keep track of." It was Mr. Satin. Bridger peered closer and saw he held some kind of gun in his hand. It looked like a derringer. Seeing the weapon displayed, on top of all he'd lately heard about Mr. Satin, got Bridger annoyed. "Why the gun?" he asked abruptly.

"Because your friend here—two birds of a feather, I wager—didn't want to help an honest businessman looking for his employee. He needed some persuasion, to be frank."

"Put it away and we'll talk," answered Bridger, still curt.

Mr. Satin stuck the weapon in a coat pocket and waved off Corkeye. "You can disappear for a while," he said. "This young fellow and I are going to set some things straight."

Bridger watched Corkeye move off. He didn't like Mr. Satin's attitude, so different than when he'd last seen him, after the stage race. "All right," Bridger said. "Let's set some things straight."

"First, young man, it's customary for employees—well-paid employees, I might add—to stay close at hand to their employers in case there might be actual work for them. You've deserted me at least twice now. Then, I understand you get intoxicated, gamble recklessly, and shoot down innocent people. I come to find a person I trusted is now wanted in not one but two cities! I can take you to the law and may well do so, as it would enhance my own stature in a community still somewhat new to me."

Bridger felt his heart start thumping and his breathing tighten. He liked to fight physically, but he hated this kind of confrontation. "There's more to it," he said. "I didn't just shoot a man. There was a, a . . . altercation." Bridger hated this. His throat was tight and his voice was trembling.

"Nevertheless, you shot a man. In your drunkenness. You have to answer for it. You can come with me now, or I can return with the law. And don't think you can get away. Your recent history suggests you wouldn't do well as a swamp refugee."

Bridger's brain reeled. His options weren't attractive. Then Mr. Satin added another. "There is, of course, an alternative. I have another job for you, coincidentally very close to where we are at this moment. Do it well, and, as far as I'm concerned, you can remain at large. I'd not breathe a word of your whereabouts."

Bridger truly did not want to deal with the law. Perhaps what Corkeye had said about no law really caring about the Low shooting was true. But then Corkeye was a ne'er-do-well and he himself was a stranger. Things might not go so well. It was tempting to jump at.

"What would you want me to do?" Bridger asked cautiously.

"I want you to light a fire," Mr. Satin said smoothly. "That's all. Just a little fire."

The statement hit Bridger like a punch. Corkeye said Mr. Satin was behind the first fire. He had signed the letter to . . . what was the name? Old Man something? Now it all was starting to come clear. Bridger tried to calm down. He wanted to see if he could prove what he was thinking. He decided to play innocent at first. "What kind of a fire? And where would it be?"

Mr. Satin smiled. "Just to clear some fields for a friend, you might say. For progress. Right here on the point."

Bridger plunged in. He remembered the name of the

man who'd received Sam Satin's letter.

"You mean Old Man Stroud's place? I hear he's selling out."

Mr. Satin's smile stayed, but the humor left his eyes. "You evidently hear a lot for someone new to this area."

"He has a letter people are talking about. Signed by you. Word is, he's afraid something will happen if he doesn't sell. Like what happened to the last folks who had some good land here."

The last of Mr. Satin's smile vanished. "You hear too much, but I would hate to think you also talk too much," he started. Bridger's voice rose, his heart racing. Now his words came easily, and he let them roll. "Yes, and I'm not going to stop hearing or talking, and I'm not going to burn anything for you. You go to the law if you want. You're blackmailing me. I have a feeling they might be just as interested in you."

He saw Mr. Satin fumbling in his coat pocket, perhaps feeling for the derringer.

"Bring that gun out and I'll stick it down your throat," threatened Bridger, his blood up now.

Mr. Satin put on an oily smile again and stopped groping in his pocket. "Oh, I wouldn't shoot you. There is, after all, the matter of that money I've given you. I think you owe me something."

"You gave me money, I did what I could to earn it. I'm not taking anything more from you, and I'm not doing your work any longer. It's that simple," Bridger said. "I don't like the way I think you're operating. I don't like the way you do business. An honest businessman doesn't come threatening with guns, trying to scare people into committing crimes. And I'll take my chances with the law. If they want to see me, they can come ahead. I'm staying right here." Bridger's heart was still racing, but now it was from exhilaration, not fear of what Mr. Satin might do.

He reached into his pocket, brought out a wad of money and threw it down. "Take this back, too, if you want. I don't want anything to do with it."

Mr. Satin turned and looked as if he would spit. Instead, he called out. "Old man. Get out of the shadows. I know you're listening. We're going back across the bay. Now." He bent to take the money and looked at Bridger one more time, smirking and nodding as he spoke. "Why, it's always a grand sight to see a boy give his own life direction. But you, you will take your chances. That you will, indeed."

Leg Dicken knew he could not stall much longer. Mizell's reports from Tampa were puzzling—but one of them frightened Dicken badly. Bridger was on Point Pinellas. What he planned to do there was not clear.

While drunk, Bridger had shot a man in Tampa, Mizell reported. Then he had traveled—or escaped—across Tampa Bay to the Point. Dicken rotated the cylinder of a revolver, letting the cartridges slide out. Then he slipped them in again, slowly, listening to the cylinder's click.

He was afraid to leave his schemes in Jacksonville. But he was even more afraid to ignore what might be happening to the south. He decided he would retrace Bridger's route as closely as possible and see what there was to be learned about this audacious pup. Then he would seek him out on Point Pinellas. After that, he would decide how to make his approach.

If only he doesn't know the treasure's whereabouts and go straight to it. Dicken brooded about it. But care and planning before what seemed to be a sudden move had gotten him along—most of the time.

He would take care with young Mr. Bridger, too. Drunk or sober, he seemed a man who didn't mind a fight. Dicken opened the revolver's cylinder and snapped it shut one more time.

# 20

IT WAS DANCE NIGHT at the San Jose Hotel. Two days after his confrontation with Mr. Satin, Bridger had heard nothing, either about fires or of lawmen seeking him. He felt good about having made a stand, relieved that no one had come to cause him difficulty. And now that Saturday night had arrived, he was curious to see what the social occasion might offer.

Glancing around the hotel's "ballroom"—really just the small building's main room with the furniture moved out—Bridger could see the gathering wouldn't rival in sophistication what Jacksonville had to offer, not to mention the posh affairs he'd attended in New York.

But it seemed the entire population of Point Pinellas had turned out. Men, women, and children crowded the dancing area, porches, alcoves, and stairway. It was, he reflected, probably the best entertainment available in this remote backwater.

He smiled at the fierce energy burned on the dance floor. A fiddle, banjo, and harmonica cranked out spirited jigs and quick two-steps, with several people rattling spoons for rhythm. Once in a while the little band would play a drifty waltz. But the faster "Cindy" seemed to be a particular favorite. Bridger heard it requested three times, and the hotel shook with the stomping of boots on the thin plank floor.

He let his eyes pass over a line of young women apparently without husbands or beaus. Or at least they seemed to have no permanent companions, although he noticed that several danced when asked. He liked what he saw a time or two—but then, no one lately seemed to compare well with Miss Lily. He wished she were here now.

Then he spied the young Englishman he'd met the day he'd arrived. "Well, how d'ya do," he said. "Tom Bridger's the name. Met you at the store the other day."

"Yes, Archie Hankins is mine," said the Englishman, extending his hand. He was a small, wiry man with a wispy mustache and pale skin that looked sunburned. "Sorry we weren't terribly friendly the other day. Didn't know quite what to make of you." His eyes danced over the rowdy crowd and he seemed on the verge of laughing. "Quite the do here, wouldn't you say?"

"Very lively." Bridger gestured to a young man capering alone, waving his arms and kicking his feet in kind of a hammering tap dance. "He seems to be enjoying himself."

Hankins chuckled. "That's Boy Thompson. He does get rather exuberant. Most of them do after they've had a chance to sample the evening's beverage of choice. Though Boy seems to be that way with or without refreshment."

Bridger had noticed many of the young men nipping out of flasks, some openly but most sneaking outside. He sorely wanted to follow and see if he might find a drink or two himself. But for the moment, at least, he thought he would abstain, hoping instead to make some acquaintances and learn what he could. Uncle Mike still was the first object of his quest, then the treasure—and he'd been wasting time. For now, he'd try to socialize, making do without the liquor.

Someone shouldered past Hankins, jostling him roughly, then turning to look as if expecting a challenge. Bridger noticed the man was dressed in rougher clothes than most of the others. And though most of the revelers presented a rough-and-ready demeanor, this one was a step beyond that, a wild-looking fellow. Bridger watched to see how Hankins would respond.

"Awkward of me, old chap. I'll have to watch where I'm going, won't I?" The man started to say something, then closed his mouth and walked away, a scowl on his face.

"And that's Elbert DeBell, of the infamous DeBell clan," said Hankins. "Always charming, Elbert is."

Bridger thought the name sounded familiar. DeBell. He watched Elbert make his way around the room, finally edging into a knot of hard-eyed men forming a group unto themselves, away from the rest. In their midst stood a huge man, a great, black beard hanging down his chest. Bridger recognized him. It was the man he had arm-wrestled in Tampa!

"The tall one with the long beard. What's his name?"

"That's Nathan DeBell, head of the clan. He is as hard as they come. Not mean, precisely, just very set in his beliefs. His people were here first—years ago, I suppose—and Nathan refuses to allow anyone to crowd him. Newcomers are strictly unwelcome. They're here to see who might have an unfamiliar face, and to see whom they might intimidate."

Bridger saw DeBell staring at him across the dance

floor. He said something to a lean companion, who began working through the crowd of dancers. "Here comes Esaw," said Hankins. "One of Nathan's sons, brother to Elbert and a few others. Though he's the most unpleasant of the lot."

Esaw navigated the room, passed close to Bridger and shouldered him. He was shorter than Bridger, but stockier. Bridger decided to follow Hankins' example. "I beg your pardon, I should be more careful."

Esaw jerked around. "You should be more scarce, is what ya should be. And watch yer mouth. I'll take you apart."

"Do," Bridger smiled. He felt relaxed, but watched Esaw closely, prepared for a surprise punch. But his politely uttered one-word response seemed to baffle the man. He looked toward his kin for a moment, then recovered. "Let's go outside. You and me need to get a few things straight."

Bridger smiled again. "If you want to go, please do. I'll be along in a while."

Esaw bristled. "I mean now, sonny. You don't understand." He put his hand on Bridger's chest and pushed. Bridger squared around to face Esaw. The music kept up, but a few of the dancers stopped to look.

"No, you're the one who doesn't understand," said Bridger, still holding back. "I don't want to get things straight right now. I don't even know you. Maybe we can get acquainted later." Esaw tensed and Bridger braced for the punch he thought would come for sure. Then a shout came from outside. The music stopped suddenly and the cry came again, a note of rising panic in the voice.

"Hey, help! Come out here! Help! It's a dead man!"

Men, women, and children streamed outside. Bridger saw a man standing near the docks, looking down at something. He jostled through the crowd to the front. Lying face down on the narrow, low-tide beach, a body sprawled. "Who is it?" someone yelled. "Is he dead?"

Emboldened now that he had support, the man who had called out rolled the corpse over. Bridger tried to focus on the face. Then he choked back a gasp. It was Corkeye Slim.

The inquest took several hours, although at first it promised to be brief. "He was a simple fisherman known to drink," intoned the justice of the peace, whose usual occupation was raising citrus trees. "No doubt he drowned." It would have ended there had Dr. Amos Partington, the Point's only physician, not noted the injuries on the back of Corkeye's head. Thus began the argument. Did Corkeye hit his head, fall in the water, and drown, or was he clubbed and thrown in the water? The answer might mean murder.

At first suspicion fell upon Bridger. He had admitted to the hastily assembled coroner's jury that he had spoken with Corkeye not two or three nights ago and was the last person known to have seen him alive. But Dr. Partington noted that the condition of the body when it was found suggested Corkeye had been dead just a few hours. And enough people had seen and talked to Bridger the day of the dance to make him seem a less likely suspect—though not one entirely in the clear. Somewhat reluctantly, because he had no particular evidence and because he was hesitant to cross his former employer, Bridger mentioned that Mr. Satin had been with Corkeye, too.

"The railroad man," someone pointed out. It brought a

rumble of suspicion. "Maybe we should ask him a thing or two," said another man. But no one offered another word. Bridger, though his silence shamed him, did not say Mr. Satin had wanted him to commit arson and that perhaps Corkeye had heard.

In the end, the coroner's jury ruled accidental death by drowning, probably after injuries by a fall, perhaps on the victim's boat. "There is not enough evidence to say this is a murder," said the justice. Bridger thought it was a matter of the people not wanting to admit a killer might be among them. As the justice had said, Corkeye was a simple fisherman, not a pillar of the community.

"So they don't want to trouble themselves," he complained to Archie Hankins. "Never mind they don't explain how he got out of his boat if he fell. Never mind they don't know where that boat is now. Never mind a lot of things." Bridger was angry, shaken, and hurt. Corkeye had been one of the few people who had been kind to him, old drunk or not. He had a feeling he had let his friend down.

"I think that some people in this community know, deep down, that something a lot bigger than they must be at work here," offered Hankins. "There was a fire. There was a death that may have been murder. If they can help it, they don't want to offend the powers, whoever they may be. And so they don't complain to authorities in Tampa when property is burned. They prefer to call a suspicious death a drowning and nothing more."

"Yes, but it is more." Bridger grumbled. "People can't just ignore things. They want some kind of civilization here. Don't they?"

"Well, not everyone," laughed Hankins. "You saw

DeBell and his crowd. They'd just as soon things stayed the same. And there's others like them. On the other hand, you have people like Romano, who runs the store, and Mr. Sheppard, the hotel owner, and even Jim Proctor, the justice today. They'd love for civilization, as you call it, to rear its head here. They think it would mean money for them. So they're afraid to annoy anyone who might help them make that happen. When it comes down to it, they're not that concerned about the fire. It wasn't their property, after all. And maybe it'll make the way easier for a railroad. And then DeBell and his group would just as soon that no one from the outside would pay attention to what happens on Point Pinellas.

"So in one way, the two groups are allies. But in another they're at odds, and sooner or later, the groups will clash. It might be only politics. Or it could be something uglier—if that's possible."

Bridger smiled. He was beginning to like Hankins, and he said what he could to encourage conversation. "Could DeBell's bunch be behind it? Corkeye's death, I mean."

"Not likely," said Hankins. "He was much like they are, an old-timer. And he was basically harmless. No, I think someone had other reasons to kill Corkeye. But people don't want to pursue it for the same reason they don't want to pursue the burning. They don't want to stir things up."

Bridger understood the reluctance. He'd felt a version of it when he'd decided to bring Mr. Satin's name before the coroner's jury. He admitted as much to Hankins and told him a little about his relationship with Mr. Satin.

Hankins, in turn, offered a little of his background. The Englishman had come to Pinellas with his clergyman father, mother, brother, and sister. They had been lured by a real estate promoter's flashy advertising campaign in England that had described Florida as a healthy, subtropical paradise ripe for settlement and bursting with potential for riches in citrus crops.

"Of course, we found out the truth soon enough," Hankins said. "It's hellish, hard work to make a go here. You'll find out how hot it gets this summer. The soil is full of roots and rocks. And at night the insects will carry you off if the mosquitoes don't bleed you to death. Would you believe it, we have to put the legs of our bedsteads in cans of water to keep the ants from crawling over us at night."

Hankins shook his head. "We believed a big lie, it seems. And now sometimes, I can hear mother crying herself to sleep." Bridger listened politely. He was interested in Hankins' views. But he was dying to ask him if he'd ever heard stories of a lost treasure, or if he'd run into a big man named Mike McGinnis.

But once started, Hankins chatted on. "Tell you what. You say you're interested in working, and we could use an extra hand. There's a cabin at the edge of father's property no one's lived in for some time. Why don't you take up residence? You could live for free, we'd feed you—most of the time—and maybe offer a little stipend on top of that, in return for your help."

Bridger considered. It might be a way for him to get established on the Point, and maybe its residents would come to see him as more than a mere hotel transient.

"Why do you think Corkeye was murdered?" Hankins asked suddenly.

"I agree with your theory," Bridger said. "Probably

because he knew something somebody didn't want him to." Bridger didn't want to come right out and say he suspected Mr. Satin. Corkeye had thought he'd been behind the burning. Maybe Corkeye had threatened to tell the authorities after all.

But Hankins had attended the inquest. He knew Bridger had talked with Mr. Satin when Corkeye had been nearby. "If Corkeye knew something, then you know it, too, I wager. And if so, you could be the next target." Bridger recognized the possibility, but had not really admitted it to himself. Hankins' remark startled him. If it were true, it might mean two sets of lawmen and a local killer were after him—not to mention the mysterious ambushers who'd been at him during the steamboat trip and the train journey and then during the stagecoach race.

All of that helped him make up his mind to accept Hankins' offer. It was time he started winning some allies here. Miss Lily had been one—but who knew when, if ever, he'd see her again?

# 21 🌴

BRIDGER MOVED INTO THE "CABIN," though it was more of a shack, and began working the groves and the land, soon learning it was true what Hankins had said about the difficulty of digging out a living in Florida. It was moving into early spring, but a day clearing land left Bridger feeling as though he'd run a long race or engaged in a hard fistfight.

Yet every day was not the same. Now and then he and Hankins would take time away and go exploring, poking into every corner of Point Pinellas. "It's a peninsula, too, like the main part of the state," said Hankins. "But this one isn't big. Seems to get birds and fish from all directions. It rains gallons in the summer and this jungle turns into a veritable aviary. Has other animals, too. Wildcats, wild pigs, wild this, and wild that. I've heard stories of bears, but I've never seen one."

The Englishman, it turned out, was an amateur naturalist and loved the wilderness. He introduced Bridger to birds: majestic herons and egrets, the sleek cormorants, and the ungainly pelicans that looked awkward when standing around the docks but could plunge on fish like a bolt from the sky.

On his own, Bridger began to run the forest paths. He exercised in the early morning. Sometimes he sparred with Henry Wilton, a strapping Englishman who'd been a booth fighter in his native land, battling all comers at fairs and carnivals.

With all that and the work, and the regular meals the Hankinses provided, he was beginning to feel trimmer and healthier than he had in weeks. Now and then, he felt like finding a drink. Each time, he fought back the temptation. But one night late, Bridger awakened to a scratching and scrabbling outside his shack. At first he thought it was an animal. Then he heard a strange voice, speaking conversationally—though there was no one answering.

"Ah, yez think ye'll have it beaten, behind yez, then it'll come on yez when yeh was t'inkin' it was finished. That old feelin'll come a creepin' to yez, talkin' to yez when ye're alone. 'Come on,' it'll say, 'just you an me, we'll go off together, ye'll get away from yer cares, it'll make yez feel grand.' "

Bridger did not recognize the voice, and, though he apparently wasn't being threatened, the eerie disturbance gave him shivers. Was this one of his pursuers? If so, it was an odd approach. What was he talking about? Bridger lay in the dark and felt for Miss Lily's Colt, which he always kept nearby. The speaker went on for a while, worrying the theme of temptation, it seemed, and then he ended with a chortle and a giggle. Bridger could hear him thrashing away through the night.

"Why, you just made the acquaintance of Kenny Kilkenny," Hankins said next morning. "He is an inveterate tippler and simple on top of that, kind of a hermit of the woods. From our part of the world, but Irish, you see.

Harmless, though. Probably didn't even know there was someone inside. Surprised he didn't come in and lie down beside you."

Hankins's enlightenment made the episode seem even stranger to Bridger. The day before he had been thinking he'd not tasted drink since Tampa—and that he felt good about it. Odd that an "inveterate tippler" should then come calling, practically voicing a warning. Bridger ignored his friend's slight disparagement of the Irish. But it was several days before Bridger could put the episode out of his mind. The irony was, he recalled it the next time or two he felt like having a few drinks. The opportunity was ever-present, should he feel like taking it.

Down one of the more well-used trails, several miles from Pinellas Village, was another settlement. It was a little bigger and boasted, besides its waterfront enterprises, a few more business establishments, some of them saloons. Bridger thought he'd continue to stay out of them, at least for a while longer. Truth was, living and working as he had been, he didn't feel the temptation as much. He was comfortable in his situation, though he knew he should be pursuing his own business.

One day he confessed to the Englishman that he had probably made a habit of drinking too much from time to time, and that despite the heat and hard work, he believed he was living as well right now as he had for years. "And Archie," he said, "I'm going to tell you something else. This is just between you and me. I came to Florida for one reason. Two, really. But the most important one was to find my Uncle Mike McGinnis. He is—or was—a soldier, a kind of adventurer. He came to Florida and somehow found his way to this Point. He said there was a lost Spanish fortune here. It was in a letter, the last we heard from him. More than four years ago.

"I got here myself by accident and luck. Went through a lot, too, and now I'm here, I'm not sure what to do next. But it's time to do something, and I want to start by asking you. Did you ever see or hear of a Mike McGinnis? He's a big, husky, fun-loving Irishman. Not like Kenny. If you'd ever met him, you'd know who I mean. And then the other thing— did you ever hear legends about a lost treasure like the one my uncle mentioned?"

Hankins stayed quiet for perhaps half a minute. Bridger wondered if he were going to ignore the questions. When Hankins finally answered it was in all seriousness. "Tom, I've never met or heard of anyone like the man you describe. Of course, my family and most of us English have been here only a year or so. I daresay there is much we don't know."

Hankins paused to let that sink in. "As for your mysterious treasure, yes, we've heard some stories. I understand there are stories all up and down Florida's Gulf Coast, what with it supposed to have been a pirate haven and all that. I discount most of those tales, frankly. But there is one version I've heard from some old-timers, who speak of it—and they don't, often—as though it were simple matter of fact."

"There is supposed to be a great wealth here on the Point, a wealth that came from some old, old source long before any of us were here. And that wealth is supposedly under the guardianship of one very old-time family here. That family's name is DeBell."

A dozen questions jumped into Bridger's mind. But Hankins held up a hand. "Tom," he said, "I don't know anything about it, whether it's true, whether it's a tall tale, as you Americans say. As I say, my family hasn't been here long. While we have, we've been busy just trying to get by, trying to make a living. We haven't had the time or, frankly, the interest in chasing old myths. I debated even telling you, because I think worrying about it would be a waste of time."

Bridger let it drop. But he continued to mull the possibilities. So far, no one had told him absolutely the treasure was nothing more than legend. And here was a suggestion it could in fact be true!

But while Bridger was trying to figure how he could ever get close enough to the DeBell clan to learn anything more, two things happened. Neither appeared likely to help him in his quest, and each seemed at odds with the other. The first was that a letter from Miss Lily came to him at the Pinellas Village post office. She was coming to visit. The second was that big Henry Wilton asked for his help in some serious training. Bongo Jones, the Key West Slasher as advertised, was coming to the Point, in addition to Tampa. Romano, the storekeeper, had heard about the pugilist through his Tampa relatives, and was now promoting a fight on the Pinellas side of the bay.

"There's prize money," said Wilton. "Help me win it and I'll cut you in." Bridger sniffed Miss Lily's envelope and read her letter several times. It was written in a precise, nearly formal hand:

"Dear Thomas,

"As you read this, I hope to be bound for Tampa and thence to the Point of Pines, as you call it.

"I am sorry we were not able to meet in Tampa previously. I did stay there for several days, but eventually learned that you crossed the bay for business purposes. I decided to return to Ocala, but now find I would like a longer stay in Tampa. My plan is to return there in a few days. There are many old acquaintances I wish to visit, and perhaps we will find it convenient to meet as well.

"In addition, I believe you retain some of my late husband's property. If this finds you willing, please leave word with the postmaster as to your availability.

I am, sincerely,
Your friend,
Regal Lily Frazer "

Hardly suggestive of anything beyond a desire to say hello and probably to retrieve the pistol and the watch, the letter nonetheless excited Bridger. And he was relieved that Miss Lily seemed not to be aware of his indiscretions and violence in Tampa. Or perhaps she was being polite when she referred to his flight across the bay as being "for business purposes."

He wondered why she had gone back to Ocala and hoped she hadn't thought him rude for not meeting her. But she was coming back, and that was good. He did an about face and marched back inside the post office. "I want to leave a message for a Mrs. Regal Lily Frazer," he said. "That I'll meet her where and when she pleases. When she arrives, please tell her I'm staying with the Hankinses."

"When she arrives," grumped old Shelton, the postmaster. "Not like there's not enough strangers coming in here already." It was true. The past few days had seen heavier than usual traffic in and out of the village, and Bridger had heard business had picked up in Disston City, the other settlement. Several new settlers were building homes, though all were avoiding the area of the burning.

Some new faces were obvious around the San Jose, too. "Matter of fact," said Shelton, "Someone was asking if I knew a tall young fella with a mustache, probably come not long ago." He looked at Bridger for reaction. "Man? Woman?" Bridger had Miss Lily on his mind.

"Man. Told him that description fit a lot of folks."

Henry Wilton, who had attached himself to Bridger since asking for his help, spoke up. "This lady now, she won't interfere with our training, will she?" Bridger shook his head. "It's all right, Henry. Don't worry. We'll start today." He was thinking about Miss Lily, hardly recognizing that someone else might be interested in his whereabouts.

So intense was the English community's interest in the upcoming prize fight that the Hankinses gave Bridger time off to do nothing but work with Wilton, now the Britons' favorite son. And fight fever had spread throughout the Point. Without having seen either Wilton or the Key West Slasher in battle, some of the more reckless settlers were already making large bets on the Englishman.

Romano, the store owner, had taken seriously his promoter's role. He printed more placards, these announcing a fight for the championship of the Caribbean Sea and the Eastern Gulf of Mexico, hoping word would spread as far north as Cedar Key, and south through Bradentown, Punta Rassa, and Fort Myers. He hoped to attract growers, cowmen, backwoodsmen, anyone who liked a good fight and might be willing to spend some money.

"Who knows?" Romano kept repeating. "Maybe we

could get John L. Sullivan himself down here someday." The heavyweight champ was touring everywhere else, he said. Why not Point Pinellas?

Bridger knew that boxing, though scorned by many of the "elite" his father socialized with, indeed was enjoying a heyday. In New York's larger cities, wealthy young men were learning from professional fighters. Bridger still smirked about the introduction of small gloves. In his opinion they merely added a false sense of gentility and only seemed to make matches less brutal. But they seemed to mollify some of boxing's more vocal opponents, though bouts under the bare knuckle rules still were popular.

The excitement made Bridger think of the hullabaloo that always seemed to surround his own hero back in Troy, Paddy Ryan—"The Trojan Giant." He wished he were going in the ring himself. But though he enjoyed this Florida version of fight fever, Miss Lily was never far from his thoughts. He wondered if she were as eager to visit him as he was to see her.

Meanwhile, a boat excursion to Tampa was organized to see the Slasher there—three nights before he was due on the Point. And the San Jose scheduled another dance for the night of the fight, seeing a chance to prime the festivities and make a few dollars. Romano ordered a huge liquor supply boated over from Tampa. Moreover, word around the point was that some of the backwoods recluses had their stills burning overtime to produce their own brand of spirits to sell. It was clear the people of the Point—the new English and American settlers and the dour oldtimers all—were eager for a diversion.

Bridger, meanwhile, began to feel his sparring partner

was likely to be overmatched—unless Bongo Jones, the Key West Slasher, was even slower afoot, more sluggish of reflex, and easier to hit than Wilton himself. Bridger cuffed the Englishman around with ease (and great care), adroitly dodging Wilton's flailing counter-pawings.

"That's all right, Henry," Bridger said. "You're just rusty. You've got plenty of time to get in shape."

In fact, he had about two weeks. And Bridger thought his friend's fantasies might be over-reaching his prowess. Maybe Wilton had sparred, as he claimed, with such English greats as Charles Mitchell and Jem Smith—but it was plain to see he had been out of action a long time. Bridger tried not to take it too seriously. After all, he could only help so much. And between sessions, Bridger hung around the post office.

"Any word?" he inquired of Shelton, who invariably shook his head. But one time he looked up. "Man outside, over yonder by the fishermen's shed, he's the one asked about someone like you awhile back."

Bridger strolled past the shack and took a discreet look. The man looked up once but showed no particular interest. Bridger studied him. The man was big and looked rough enough to be one of the Rotten Row denizens in Jacksonville, Bridger thought. But this one looked healthier and was better dressed.

As much as he'd been pursued already, Bridger was tempted to go up and ask the fellow point blank what his business was. But he was getting along comfortably here. Why risk trouble? Besides, what if Shelton were wrong? Bridger decided to let the matter drop. Certainly he was around the village enough if someone wanted to find him. If someone did, then he'd deal with it. For now, he'd put it out of his mind, concentrate on what he'd say to Miss Lily, and keep on training with Wilton.

But during a sparring session, he stepped inside too quickly with a left hook and accidentally buried his fist in Wilton's solar plexus. Wilton groaned and collapsed heavily. Bridger rolled his eyes. "Henry, I'm sorry," he said. "That was the next thing to a dirty punch. It was an accident." But it finished Wilton for the day. Bridger wondered guiltily if he hadn't sensed the opening and taken advantage of the slower man. And during his long runs in the forest, he began to worry. Every day people asked about Wilton's progress.

"He's coming along, coming along," Bridger always answered. But he knew Wilton wasn't coming along, and wouldn't. He wondered what he could do to discourage the wagers being placed on the big man. There were strangers watching for who knew what, a crowd of betting men from Tampa would likely come to the fight, and people here were likely to lose what little money they had managed to save.

One of his runs took him a good eight miles along the trail to Disston City. Two schooners were in port, both from Cedar Key. One unloaded lumber, the other a few passengers. A generally busy atmosphere seemed to have taken over the hamlet. The latest rumor had it the railroad would come there, not to Pinellas Village, nor to any other spot on the Gulf side of Tampa Bay.

Turning to make his return run, Bridger was surprised to see several members of the DeBell clan, including Nathan himself, standing outside a saloon staring at him. Bridger slowed on an impulse. He thought: Take a chance now. Surprise him. Who knows what the old character might say? He jogged right up to DeBell and stopped, ignoring the glares he received.

"Hello, sir, d'ya remember me? You beat me at arm wrestling in Tampa awhile back. Twice, actually. I'm living over here now on the Point. Saw you and thought I'd say hello. And ask you something, if I could."

DeBell gazed at him in a strange way. Not exactly in a hostile way, but as if he were some sort of specimen that had jumped off a table and begun to speak. "Yer the drunk," DeBell said. "What d'ya want with me?"

Bridger felt the blood go to his head, but he kept his voice steady. "Folks tell me you've been here a long time. I'm looking for a relative of mine. Last I heard from him, he was here on the Point. I thought you might have run into him."

DeBell glowered and moved back a step, putting some distance between himself and Bridger. He put a hand on the pistol butt sticking out of his belt. "I don't care for strangers," he said, staring into Bridger's eyes. "Don't care to remember 'em, neither. They don't last long around here."

He paused to let his words sink in. "Don't expect you will, neither." DeBell's kinsman smirked and the one Bridger thought the one he remembered as Esaw laughed out loud. DeBell turned to go.

"Hold it!" Bridger's voice cracked out. Nathan DeBell stopped dead. The rest looked stunned, as if they'd never heard their patriarch addressed in such a way. "I talked to you in a civil way," Bridger grated out. "You don't have to talk to me if you don't want, but you could show some manners. I was always told that's what you Southerns are known for."

Nathan DeBell continued to stare. Bridger saw from the corner of his eye that one of the clan was loosening a long knife tied to his belt. DeBell spoke very softly and deliberately. "What do you want to know?" His hard eyes never left Bridger.

"I've got an uncle, a big tall fellow, like you and me. Name of Mike McGinnis. He was here for a while, maybe four years ago. Something about the Point interested him." Bridger did not want to say what that was just yet. "We had a letter from him, then we never heard from him again. I'm trying to pick up his trail. I thought you might know something about him, or might have seen him."

DeBell waited until he was sure Bridger was through. "Never heard of him," he said, contempt filling his voice. "He wouldn't a lasted long here, he was a Yankee like you. There ain't a one of you man enough." Bridger puffed up and moved forward a step. DeBell turned to him square.

"Do it," he challenged. "Make a move. We'll kill ya where ya stand and leave ya ta rot in the dirt. And no one'll lift a finger against us." Bridger wanted to fight but knew he didn't dare. Every one of the half-dozen men surrounding him now either had out wicked-looking blades or wrapped their fists around pistol butts. He couldn't get a word out. He was afraid to try.

DeBell saw soon enough there'd be no fight this day. He turned to go, spitting in the dirt. His kinsmen followed. Each glanced at Bridger and spat on the ground.

"They don't appear in force like that very often, unless it's some kind of occasion," Archie Hankins observed later. "Maybe they just wanted to see who was on and off the ships. They will have their hands full watching everyone's comings and goings once the railroad comes, wherever it ends up."

Hankins looked troubled. "Bridger, I heard today that this Satin fellow might be near. Lurking about in the woods somewhere."

"Where did you hear it?"

"Kenny Kilkenny. The fellow who came rustling around your cottage that night. He lurks about in the woods himself and, well, he sees and hears things. He's also not entirely as thick as he might seem, or as people may think."

"How would he know Satin?"

"Says he saw him the night Corkeye brought him to you."

"Where is he supposed to be?"

"A few miles away. Stays in a cowman's old shack, Kenny says."

It was bad news if, as Bridger feared, he was on Mr. Satin's list of people to do away with.

Then Hankins put the thought in words. "Tom, I don't think you should run alone, or go anywhere by yourself until we find out what this fellow's up to."

"You're right, I think. Maybe I should see what I can get out of Kenny and then pay this camp of Mr. Satin's a visit. Instead of just waiting for something to happen." But too much already was happening for Bridger to organize a scouting expedition. It would be hard enough finding Kenny and finding him sober enough to talk sense. There was still no word from Miss Lily. Bridger waited and stewed about it. And he tried to put some kind of finishing touch on Henry Wilton's training.

Wilton's punching had sharpened and he was moving less awkwardly. But he was slow and Bridger thought still far too easy to hit. At least he was big and strong, and seemed to take pride in his ability to take a punch to the head. Maybe he would get lucky and land a good, hard blow of his own. Bridger had very big doubts.

But he dared not express them strongly to Wilton's Point Pinellas backers. Most of them were too caught up in the event emotionally and financially to listen. They looked at Bridger as if he were a traitor when he sometimes shook his head and scowled when asked about Wilton's chances.

Bridger went so far as to ask Hankins' father, The Reverend Archibald Hankins, if he could find a way to contribute some sense to the affair. The elder Hankins smiled indulgently while shaking his head. "Even though I, as a clergyman, must deplore violence, you can see that many people here love pugilism, including not a few of my countrymen. They don't see it as an act of willful barbarism, but as a display of courage and skill. And they like the idea of having a champion." The benign old man paused, made bony fists and flicked them in the air. Bridger knew he had lost the argument before it had truly begun.

"They need the diversion, you see. It takes their minds off the hard labor and the heat and the hardships out here. It's an antidote to monotony. If it excites them, if it pleases them, if it makes them happier only for a while, then perhaps it brings them closer to God."

Bridger had never mulled the theology of a fistfight. He decided not to wade in now. The Reverend Hankins was probably planning to take in the Slasher's Tampa appearance in addition to his bout on the Point. He thought of the staid clergyman cheering at a fight and smiled.

"I myself can't go with you to Tampa," Bridger later

confessed to Wilton. "I know I should, to take a look at this fellow. But . . . I think Tampa may not be a healthy place for me right now." He had spoken a bit about his adventures across the bay, and Wilton had heard more through gossip. "Don't worry yerself, me lad. I'll spy out this 'ere Bongo Jones and mark 'is every weakness."

Several boats carrying twenty or twenty-five Point men were sailing to Tampa later in the afternoon, and to celebrate the occasion, Wilton had opened one of his precious few bottles of English ale. "Want a taste?" he asked Bridger, though not with enthusiasm. The ale had come with him from England, Bridger knew, and Wilton was chary of sharing. Though he was at least half-interested in a taste—or several—Bridger declined.

"I'll save it for a victory celebration, Henry." He wondered how sincere he sounded.

The boats left together under a fine breeze and great bombast from the passengers. "We'll come dragging this Slasher's carcass back," bawled Nick Watford, another one of the Englishmen who had clearly been at his own ale.

"We'll have to drag him after he sees the likes of us," answered Boy Thompson, whom Bridger recognized as the energetic dancer at the San Jose. Even Jim Proctor, the citrus man who also served as Justice of the Peace, was along. Bridger thought he looked like he could sail to Tampa without benefit of a boat.

Bridger drew Archie Hankins aside. "Try to look this Bongo Jones over pretty well, can you? See if you can spot his weaknesses. Maybe we can still give Henry something to work on these last few days."

Wilton by now was singing the fifth verse of a bawdy

version of "Barbara Allen." Hankins just shook his head. "I'll do what I can, Tom. I may have my hands full just keeping this lot out of stir."

Bridger finally saw off the fleet and renewed his vigil at the Post Office. "Nothing," growled Shelton.

Still mulling what he would say to Miss Lily, how he might learn more about the DeBells and what, if anything, he could do to help Henry Wilton, Bridger retired to his cabin, where he fidgeted into the night. Every noise tightened his belly. Sometime after midnight, a squall raked the Point with sharp, pelting rain. Several shots of lightning cracked like rifle fire, and cannonades of thunder rattled the cabin. Bridger finally dozed off as the storm abated. He dreamed that he was drunk and lost in the forest.

In the morning the boats had not returned. They drifted in one by one during the afternoon, not looking the worse for storm wear. But those aboard were grim. They tied up their boats and came ashore, barely uttering a word in contrast to their noisy departure. Bridger attributed the near-silence to the after-effects of drink. Which was partly true, but there was more to it.

"A monster," Bridger heard Boy Thompson mutter. Henry Wilton came in pale and shaken. "Seasick, Henry?" Bridger asked. The big man just shook his head and walked away, leaving Bridger puzzled and a bit annoyed. Finally Archie Hankins came in alone in a sharpie. Bridger grabbed a line and threw it toward the boat. "What's the business, Archie? Everyone looks like he lost his money or his last friend."

Hankins looked as glum as everyone else. "That Bongo Jones," he answered. "The man's a brute."

"Well, the man's a traveling fighter and this is the frontier. What did you expect?"

"I expected someone with at least a trace of humanity. This fellow has none that I could see. He simply butchered the poor fool who had a go at him. He may be dead for all I know. Jones pinned him on the ropes and hit him and hit him and hit him. The man's face was pulp. And this Jones . . . he looks like a creature out of your worst nightmare. Deformed. In a horrible accident perhaps. I don't know."

Henry Wilton was down and out with no punches thrown. "The man's a beast. I've never seen 'is like and I will not get near 'im," he said flatly.

Panic overran the Point promoters. Romano, the storekeeper, had heavily invested. People expected a good bout and could be expected in return to buy plenty of drinks and more. No fight meant a disgusted crowd would hang on to its money. People would be unhappy, especially the gamblers, and they were many. Trouble was a given, and there was a concern that, depending on how surly the prevailing attitude, disgruntled, drunken fight fans could cause a major ruckus.

"They could break up my store," worried Romano.

"You fight him, then," retorted Wilton. "Maybe you'll make enough to pay your doctor."

Bridger listened to all the talk. His opinion was that none of it amounted to much. He couldn't imagine a sporting crowd, no matter the depths of its disappointment, resorting to destruction. And he didn't believe Bongo Jones could be the demon pugilist he was made out to be.

Puffed-up notions in unsophisticated minds, he thought. Well, he'd fix it all.

"I'll fight Bongo Jones myself," Bridger told Romano. "You'll have your fight, you'll have your crowd, everyone will be happy." He smiled slightly. "Maybe I'll even make some money."

Archie Hankins was the only one who tried to talk him out of it. He didn't come close to succeeding.

# 22 ☀

THE FIGHT WAS SET for a Saturday night, and by the Friday afternoon, gamblers, thrill-seekers, and the bored or curious began drifting to the Point. Some had come by boat; others had meandered down by land, on horseback, in buggies, in wagons, and afoot.

Word had gotten around that two professionals would fight, a strong youngster against a fearsome warrior with hundreds of fights behind him. And rumor had it the bout would yield a genuine champion of the Florida frontier, who might next fight Sullivan, the national champion.

It was said that the Key West Slasher had battled throughout Cuba, South America, and the mysterious islands of the Caribbean; and that the youngster from the North had beaten the English champion Mitchell in a secret bout witnessed only by a few—and then covered up by the press to avoid embarrassing the pugilistic establishment.

It was rumored that Young Tom Bridger—for so he was being called by the fight crowd—had killed a Jacksonville man with his fists. What Bridger heard of this merely made him shake his head and laugh. And wonder how much he had helped spread similar talk when he followed the fights back home in New York.

Now that he was participating, he worried only about the shape he was in. He felt good physically; he liked the way his muscles popped out, and the running had built his endurance nearly to what it was during his racing days. But he worried about how he would react in a genuine fight. It had been months since his last real one. Cuffing the buffoon on Jacksonville's Rotten Row hardly qualified.

Alone in his cabin, throwing combinations at half-speed, he worried about his instincts and timing. Sparring with Henry Wilton at least had been exercise, but more often he held back, never testing his own limits or polishing his talent. He tried to remember all the lessons from Big Mike and the pros at Paddy Ryan's place. He practiced the quick, short, and sneaky hook to the solar plexus that would stop most any man. He thought about the few formal fights he had had, and how he'd learned to be patient, waiting for the other man's mistake while constantly stabbing his hard, straight left.

He went to bed and when he closed his eyes, he thought of himself fighting, jabbing swiftly, moving smoothly, feeling strong. On such visions he slept.

He awoke to a sour, hot sensation stinging his nostrils. Something was making his eyes water. A rustling, scuffling sound came from the door, and a throaty shout. "Ge' out! Tom Bridger, are yez in there? Wake up, ge' out! Ye're burnin'!"

Bridger sat up in bed, confused. Had he slept through the day? Was it time for the fight? Then he smelled the smoke and heard a crackling and recognized the voice of

Kenny Kilkenny. And he spied a flame shoot up outside one window. Bridger jumped up and bolted through the door, running outside barefoot. A healthy blaze was eating at one end of his cabin. He felt a hand claw at his arm and flinched.

It was Kenny, babbling. "Ge' away, ye mus ge' away from here. Ye're burnin' and they'll kill yez!"

"No, we've got to put it out!" Bridger yelled. He sprinted to the back of the house and saw the growing fire raging at dry wood and old palm logs. The palmetto thatching on the roof had caught, too. Bridger looked around, stunned. There was no water to fight a fire; the closest was a creek a quarter-mile away. Desperate, he scooped up dirt and threw it on the fire.

The effort only winded him and served to increase his panic as he watched the blaze expand on itself like a monstrous orange flower. It cracked like a pistol and a growling rush of air sizzled from its core. A blast of heat tightened Bridger's skin and he stumbled backward, tripped on a root, and fell.

He struggled up and dashed to the door, but plumes of smoke were spewing out. He knew he dared not risk going in; he probably wouldn't come out. And where was Kenny!

"Kenny! Kilkenny!" he bawled, throwing his arm in front of his face and lurching toward the door. Another blast of heat threw him back. Then he heard shouting from the edge of the woods and the sound of running steps. It was Archie, followed closely by Henry Wilton.

"I can't find Kenny!" Bridger shouted. "He woke me up and now I can't find him! I'm afraid he's . . . " He looked helplessly at the blazing cabin.

"No, it's all right," Archie shouted back, straining to be

heard over the roar of the fire. "He came and woke us up, too. He's behind us. But we can't save this shack. The only thing we can do is try to keep it from spreading into the woods."

For the rest of the night, Bridger, Hankins, Wilton, and Kenny kept vigil, stamping out embers that drifted from the shack, clearing nearby brush that might catch, clawing up dirt with their hands and throwing it on smaller fires blossoming around the main blaze. When the night finally turned gray with dawn, blackened chips and splinters lay in the shack's ashes. A scorched iron bed frame missing a support leaned drunkenly in the ruins. A stinking pall of smoke mixed with the morning fog.

The four men, exhausted, sprawled a few yards away. They stared with red and hollow eyes. Kenny took out a bottle and passed it around. Bridger held it for a long time.

"Kenny," Hankins asked. "D'you know who started it?"

Kilkenny shook his head. "Saw an orange glow, and it got bigger," he said.

"Tom? Any ideas?"

Bridger finally passed the bottle to Archie without taking a drink. He told them about the confrontation with DeBell. "Then, too, maybe it was Satin."

"Or someone who wanted to make dead certain you didn't win the fight," spoke up Wilton.

The men looked at each other. "My God," said Bridger. "It's daylight. The fight's tonight."

Bridger tried to rest at the Hankins' home all day. But he was too wound up and worried to make a good job of it. Finally, he rose in the mid-afternoon. He ate some salted beef, drank coffee, and munched some orange slices, the juice dripping down his chin. Then he tried reading a copy of *Ivanhoe* he found in the house. But he was too nervous to concentrate. He went outside to do some light calisthenics.

Archie showed up almost immediately, scolding Bridger for not resting. But he was waving an envelope. "You have it, man. It came and old Shelton let me bring it to you." He thrust it and Bridger grabbed it. Immediately he recognized Miss Lily's elegant script and tore it open.

"Dear Thomas, I shall be arriving on Saturday instanter"—he smiled at the somewhat old-fashioned usage—"and hope that we can meet at your earliest convenience to discuss subjects of mutual interest.

"I understand that there is a sporting event taking place and that the lower point may be quite crowded with sightseers. I pray you can arrange to meet me at the San Jose Hotel, an establishment I am told is convenient.

"The information came to me from a fellow passenger on the Ocala stage, who said he is from Jacksonville and seemed very interested in your researches. He told me he hoped to visit the Point himself."

Bridger laughed and cursed in the same breath. Of all the days for Miss Lily to arrive! "Archie, I'm a little overwhelmed," said Bridger, filling in Hankins on the letter. "I need to stop and think. That fire has addled me, I admit, but I've got to pull myself together."

Hankins agreed strongly. "It's very clear you can't have your mind playing over all this at once. All things considered—and your own well-being is one of them—you had better not be too far distracted from this prize-ring business. Tell you what: I'll keep vigil at the San Jose for your friend. When she arrives, if she does, I'll get her stashed away and come back straightaway. You, in the meantime, you just go about your preparations. You must—you absolutely must—keep your mind on this Bongo Jones. Believe me, he is a dangerous man."

Bridger thought it unlikely Miss Lily would allow herself to be "stashed away," but did not argue. "Well, you're right," he said. "One crisis at a time." As much as he wanted to see Miss Lily, Bridger realized he was eager for the contest tonight. Thinking about it took his mind off the fire and who might be behind it.

Besides, he wanted to do well, to prove himself to the men of the Point, to carry their banner. And certainly, if he didn't concentrate, he could be injured by Bongo Jones, if all that was being said about him proved even close to the truth. But it was more than wanting to win the approval of his neighbors, he realized. He wanted to prove something to himself: that he was strong, that he had heart and character and courage. And that he had those qualities while sober.

A good showing would help him put away some of his recent unsavory activities, he realized. It would make him feel worthy again, and whole. It occurred to him that was probably why he had so quickly volunteered to fight in place of Wilton. This battle, he thought, was one he needed for the good of his soul.

The fight was to be held in a clearing off the main trail, about halfway between Pinellas Village and Disston City. In the center, a crude ring had been constructed, two strands of rope wrapped around four posts. There was no flooring to cover the patch of dusty ground inside the enclosure. Although it was still more than an hour before the battle would start, a crowd had gathered, jovial, boisterous men in various stages of exuberance.

Leg Dicken's man, Wade Mizell, was there. He mingled but did not take part in the socializing. He noted that most of the men were armed in one way or another, and that many were drinking or seemed to have been earlier. Mizell himself had bet heavily on Bongo Jones, and he planned on being sober enough to collect every bet. Every bet, he thought grimly. For sure, he had bet every penny he had in his name on Jones, betting small with every Point sucker he could find, and there were plenty. He had seen Jones batter his Tampa opponent, a huge, tough cowman known for his cruelty in fights. This Slasher had finished the cowman in less than five minutes, leaving him torn and helpless.

Mizell had watched Bridger gun down Pardner Low, and the kid had stomach, no question—at least when he was drunk. But he'd also seen that bearded old peckerwood take him down in arm wrestling. He couldn't be that tough. Anyway, this Slasher looked to be inhuman. He would win, and Mizell would double his fortune and take it back to Jacksonville. It would bring him pretty close to where he could strike out on his own, away from old one-leg.

Mizell scanned the crowd for Leg Dicken. He had come to the Point, for whatever reason. It annoyed Mizell, as if Dicken were looking over his shoulder. He'd never done that before. But then maybe it had to do with his big interest in this kid Yank, whatever that was about.

He watched two youngsters jump into the ring, scuffling and drawing laughter from the crowd. A man with bushy muttonchop whiskers shooed them and tried to chase them out of the clearing. The boys dodged into the woods, but Mizell saw them pop out a few minutes later and head for another vantage point. It made Mizell smile.

Satin cursed the two children. They had nearly trampled through his hiding place. He wanted to be nearby, but did not want to make an appearance while it was still light. He doubted few, if anyone, on the Point could easily recognize him. He hadn't shown himself much. But there was no sense in risking an encounter with young Mr. Bridger just now, or running across someone the young jackanapes might have looking out for a man of his distinguished description.

He would confront Bridger soon enough. After he was shattered and had been beaten senseless, perhaps unto the point of death. Then he would once more come close to this man-boy and once more help him right himself. Perhaps he would even be called upon to nurse him back to health. He hoped so. Then he would draw this boy to him once and for all, make him a part of his life forever.

He had hoped to accomplish it all with the fire. He had hoped to rescue Tom at the last minute, thus proving his continuing devotion—despite the way the boy had disappointed him. The drunken yahoo had spoiled it by his warning. Still, he believed their partnership would come about. It would be of classic proportion: he with the brains and cunning, Tom Bridger with the strength and innocence of youth. The combination would be irresistible. Together, they would grow rich and powerful. Satin edged a little deeper into the jungle. He would show himself soon enough.

Nathan DeBell watched the early carousing with disgust. He rarely took drink in public, believing it degraded him. Yet he spent time in saloons and at social gatherings so that he might be knowledgable about his community. He himself preferred to stay in the background. But he read what newspapers were available and attended such public meetings as might be held. He also mingled whenever men of sporting or political nature came together. In this way, he gathered knowledge, which he believed could be turned to influence. And tonight he planned to influence the course of events on the Point.

Too many of these speculators, landgrabbers, and railroaders were coming into the territory. They would bring more settlers and there were too many already. What they needed was a little discouragement. He and his boys would provide it. DeBell touched his pistol and caressed the cylinder. He'd made sure all of his boys had come well-armed. Three of his sons and three nephews all carried pistols and two had shotguns. And if there were any need for close quarters, they all carried hunting knives.

Things would heat up when that fight started. There'd be more drinking, a lot of shouting, and just naturally a few of the more spirited boys would shoot off their guns. If a ruckus didn't start, Nathan planned to start one himself. And if a mob caused a riot, well, those things happened. And if someone got shot, those things happened, too. Sometimes people died down here where the territory got rough. People had to understand that. They had to understand it was risky to stay too long or show too much interest. They had to understand it might be better to stay away. Forever.

❖ ❖ ❖

Bridger glanced at the pocket watch Miss Lily had given him. It was 10:30 p.m., thirty minutes before the fight. Outside, the wind was picking up. "Hope it doesn't storm again," Bridger said, mostly just to say something. Henry Wilton was there in the Hankins' home with him, taciturn and worried. He paced, stopped, and constantly rubbed his hands on his hips. He would gaze at Bridger, then turn away and blink rapidly.

"Henry, settle down. I'm trying to relax." In truth, Bridger knew he couldn't. For one thing, he was worried about his hands. Some fighters soaked their hands for months in a brine mixture or walnut juice to harden them. He hadn't had time. His hands felt soft and he wondered if they would break on Bongo Jones's skull. Perhaps a body attack was his best chance. It would be both a surprise and a possible method to preserve his fists.

And Bridger was worried about Miss Lily. Where was she? Was she coming at all? "Where the deuce is Archie?" he muttered.

Wilton shrugged. "You should warm up some more," he said.

Bridger stood and repeated his routine of easy punching motions, putting together the combinations he hoped would be effective. He knew the moves by heart. Some of them Big Mike had taught him years ago, and he could do them like lightning when necessary. The thought excited him. He let it chase away other concerns. He was ready to be tested.

"The buggy's ready," Wilton said. "We might as well go." It was a short ride to the clearing. They saw a dozen men straggling toward it. When Bridger and Wilton reached the site, they found a huge crowd already waiting. Bridger had expected sixty or seventy people to show up, counting the revelers who would fuel up at the San Jose before finding their way to the fight the best way they could.

But this mob must have numbered several hundred, Bridger thought. It looked like a fairgrounds without the booths. Surely there weren't this many people on the Point, Bridger thought. People must have come from Tampa, Bradentown, and up and down the Gulf coast, just as Romano had wanted. They were everywhere, standing, talking, drinking in small groups, or milling about. There were even men up trees, hoping for the best possible vantage point.

A number of the spectators started up a cheer when they saw Bridger, and over the din Bridger heard someone shouting, "'Hey now, Mr. Water. Go it, Mr. Water." Glancing toward the commotion, Bridger spied the young fellow who had helped him during the race with the stage. Cheese! Just thinking of the name made him laugh, and Bridger flicked the boy a jaunty wave. He thought he recognized some others from Brooksville; one or two might have been among the men Mr. Satin had tried to persuade that stages were outmoded conveyances.

Bridger let Wilton clear a path toward the ring, and that was one thing the big man was good at. "Step aside now, there's a good chap," he bellowed, once or twice using a beefy arm to sweep aside those more firmly rooted.

"Sonny, you better win," shouted a man with a cigar. He puffed out smoke with every word. "I bet my little farm on you."

Such imprudence bothered Bridger, not because he thought he might lose but because people had bet on him without ever seeing him or the Slasher fight. They bet on him because they knew him. If he didn't win, no one would want to know him. Such was the plight of losers. But now the people were cheering, and Bridger liked it.

He walked lightly behind Wilton, fists loosely bunched, arms bent at the elbows and bouncing in rhythm with his stride. He felt strong. He was sinewy, not bulky, his muscles long like thick ropes. His taut belly showed not a pinch of fat, and when he breathed deeply, his chest muscles looked like a pair of armor plates.

They got to the ring and Bridger climbed through the ropes, shuffling lightly. Just the act of seeing one of the fighters clamber into the ring excited the crowd; cheers, hollers, and whistles resounded. Bridger looked out at the mob. Dozens of faces stared back, some with eyes hard as bricks and others dewy-eyed with pride. The scene began to transport Bridger. He looked at the tall torches, fixed in the ground. Thick, guttering, blue-orange flames threw skittering shadows around the people and into the trees, and rags of stringy moss swayed in a fresh breeze. A thrill of anticipation crept along his neck. *I was born for this*, he thought.

Another commotion began toward the rear of the crowd, and those in the front turned, craning to see. It was Bongo Jones, heading for the ring. Bridger could see that he was tall, perhaps taller than Bridger himself. But he could not see his face, which was partly covered by a hood on the short, black cloak he wore.

Then Archie Hankins appeared at ringside. "Your friend is here!" He had to shout, for more yelling began as

Bongo Jones made his approach. A gust of wind shook the ring ropes and there was a rumble of thunder. Bridger looked at Archie, then out over the roiling crowd. "Where?"

"I say, Tom, the lady has a mind of her own. She absolutely would not wait at the hotel. The idea of you in a prize fight seemed to intrigue her no end."

"But where is she?"

Archie gestured vaguely. "Here in this mob somewhere. She said they'd never abide a woman at one of these—I agree with her there—so she's gotten herself up as a man. Buckskins and all. And I tell you I wouldn't dare to cross her. I believe she has armed herself, too."

Bridger grinned, remembering Miss Lily's cool use of the pistol when the outlaw had tried to pull him off the train. He liked her being here to see him now; he puffed up a little and practiced a combination of punches. The movement seemed to puzzle Archie. "Tom, she wanted you to know something. She said the man she met on the train is named Mr. Elijah Dicken—and that he has a wooden leg." Archie flicked his head to one side. "Actually, there's a chap like that right there."

Bridger glanced and saw a tall man. He wore a slouch hat and a frock coat with the alligator hide, and he had a wooden leg. There was no mistaking that it was the man he had first seen in Jacksonville—and doubtless the one he had heard so much about later. And Leg Dicken was staring a hole through Tom Bridger.

Bridger stared staight back, still doing his easy shadow-box shuffle. It was certainly the man he had seen on the Jacksonville docks. The mighty Leg Dicken he had heard so much about. Even with his handicap, he looked powerful, capable, a match for someone like Nathan DeBell. But what was he doing here? Had word of the fight stretched all the way to Jacksonville? And it puzzled Bridger that the man was looking at him so intently, as if he knew him. They had never been introduced—so far as Bridger could remember. But there was no time to ponder. Bridger heard gasps from the crowd, and disgusted oaths. People were talking fast and loud, their rhythms excited and argumentative, as if they suddenly had been told war had been declared.

Bongo Jones had entered the ring. Bridger looked over—and recoiled in shock. Jones had thrown off the cowl covering his head, revealing grotesque disfigurement. He was entirely bald, with not even an eyebrow. What appeared to be thick streaks of scar tissue criss-crossed the top of his head. Both ears were gone, with nubs of flesh covering the holes. One eye blazed hostility, but the other merely stared, unmoving, lifeless. A piece of jagged flesh constituted what was left of his lower lip, most of which seemed to have been removed or torn away, exposing a bottom row of teeth and some gum. Yet the freak seemed fit and alert. He moved like any prize fighter Bridger had ever seen, smoothly and confidently. He was tall, indeed taller than Bridger, but lean almost to the point of thinness.

Bridger watched, fascinated. Jones was horrific, either deformed or horribly injured. But he moved liked a snake ready to strike. Two others were in the ring with him: Romano, the storekeeper who had acted as fight promoter, and another man Bridger didn't recognize who carried a bucket and towels.

Romano gestured for quiet. The crowd calmed down and, from the center of the ring, Romano cupped his hands and bellowed, enjoying his own bombast. "Gentlemen and sportsmen all, an epic of fistiana for your entertainment and inspiration, also for a purse of one hundred dollars and the championship of the Caribbean and the eastern Gulf of Mexico, heavyweights. A fight to the finish, London Prize Ring rules. No gouging, biting, or butting."

The London rules meant bare-knuckle fighting until one of the combatants could not continue. Under the brutal code, if a fighter was knocked or wrestled down, he had thirty seconds to "come to scratch" —get to the center of the fighting enclosure ready to do battle—or be declared the loser.

"I introduce to you," the promoter went on, "your brave gladiators. First, your guest, a most distinguished professor of pugilism and a veteran of more than three hundred bloody battles, never defeated, the scourge of the Caribbean and the Indies, the cruel, the merciless BONGO JONES, the Key West SLASHER!" There were some cheers, but more hoots and jeers. Jones refused to acknowledge the introduction, but glared across the ring at Tom.

"And now your hometown favorite, a likely lad and well set-up, his courage unquestioned, his talent unmatched, a worthy challenger in any arena, the pride of Point Pinellas, I give you Young . . .Tom . . . Bridger!"

The spectators exploded in shouts, hoorahs, and applause. Bridger held his head high, lifting both hands. A man who would act as referee hopped inside the ring and brought the two fighters to the center. For the first time, Bridger got a close-up look at the Key West Slasher. And for the first time, he felt his confidence slip.

The Slasher's hideous countenance was intimidating in

itself. But a terrible, purposeful hostility rolled off the man. He jerked one shoulder toward Bridger, then the other, as if he were coiled, as if he could not wait to spring and devastate. He flexed his muscles and moved his head menacingly, his one baleful eye glittering in the torchlight, contemptuous and filled with hatred, and he moved in closer to Bridger, emphasizing his height, angling his head so he appeared to look down his nose in derision.

Bridger felt a tremor in his belly, and knew that he was afraid, and yet that in itself did not bother him. He had been through enough athletic contests to know that fear could be used. But another thought lurked underneath. He knew Bongo Jones's intimidating use of movement, the rolling of the shoulders and the crowding, the ugly staring. He had seen it all before, down to the order of the moves and the peculiar tilt of the head.

Uncle Mike used to go into a fight the same way. Could Bongo Jones have known him, learned from him?

# 23

Bridger never saw the blow that knocked him down. Something that felt like a mallet hit his face, and dim shades of gray and black filled his vision. He hit the ground flat, the impact hammering out his wind. The crowd's moan built to a far-away roar. He rolled instinctively, rose, and nearly stumbled. Upright, he pedaled backward.

"Get to the middle! The middle!" screamed Henry Wilton. Bridger gaped at him, baffled, dizzy, and dumb. He managed to speak. "Did I get up? Am I up?"

"Get to the middle, man! Now!" Wilton was hysterical, urging Bridger to come to scratch, or the fight would be over with one punch. Bridger bumbled forward, still dazed. He smiled and held out his hand to shake the referee's. The referee waved him off. "Knockdown, Mr. Jones, Round 1," he called. Bongo Jones stood at ring center, then leaped forward.

Bridger, still grinning like an ape, ducked slightly and slipped to the side. It was a move on instinct, done without calculation, but it threw off the Slasher's timing just enough to make him miss. Now Jones backed off a bit, assessing.

Bridger began to emerge from a kind of dream state, realizing again he was in the ring. The brutal opening had jarred him into a kind of calm. It shoved aside the fear. Bridger felt a kind of comfortable warmth spread through his body. He felt no pain and he saw clearly, as if the impact had focused his perceptions. He had taken a tremendous blow and gotten back up. It gave him confidence.

When Jones moved toward him and threw punches, it seemed as though he could see them starting before they came at him. He smiled. He retreated a small step, then another, and watched Jones miss. He stepped in and rapped two quick jabs to the Slasher's face, then ducked and retreated. He knew his moves looked good. He heard shouts of encouragement.

As he circled, stopped, and jabbed crisply, Bridger watched the Slasher bob and weave, and he couldn't help the thought: The man moves just like Uncle Mike. Could Mike have trained him? Bridger retreated, dodged, staying away from Jones while studying him.

Jones closed again, feinting twice with his left. He paused for a moment, then shot over a straight right. It glanced off Bridger's head, but the impact made him stumble. And Jones was on him like a panther, digging short, hooking blows to Bridger's sides. Then he grabbed Bridger in a bear hug, lifted him off the ground and threw him down hard. Bridger's sides ached, but he thought his ribs had survived. He would have to be careful, whether fighting at long range or in close. Jones probably knew every dirty trick in the book.

Again he came to scratch and again he moved warily, probing for a weakness in Jones's defense, still mystified by the stance and movements so like Big Mike's. He couldn't shake the eerie feeling about his uncle. And it broke his concentration. The Slasher moved close, crowding Bridger and ripping hooks to the body, going for the soft spots. It was how Bridger himself had planned to fight. He lowered his arms to block the belly punches—and once more found himself flat on his back, looking up at the sky. He was amused to see lightning streaking it. Oddly, it occurred to him the thunder harmonized with the rumble and buzz of the crowd, like low-pitched music. It made him smile. But still he felt no pain, despite the the blows he had just taken.

Bleeding from the nose, Bridger got up, and Jones knocked him down again. Two more times he rose, and twice more he went down hard. Bridger's partisans fell silent, while a few who bet on the Slasher were shouting to the skies, calling for the kill. Bridger looked wobbly and uncertain. But he moved on instinct, evading, sliding this way and that, and when Jones moved in too quickly and carelessly, Bridger stuck a stone fist straight to the solar plexus. Jones moaned and went down on a knee, and Bridger's friends set up a howl.

Hearing it and seeing Jones down sent a bolt of new life through Bridger. While he waited for the Slasher to rise, a flurry of rain swept in on a crisp breeze and the squall's cool energy further lifted Bridger's spirits. He liked rain, and the storm excited him. But the Slasher was too tough and hard. In a few seconds, he'd shaken off the smash to his midsection and attacked with a frightening ferocity, raining punches, shouldering, butting, and elbowing.

The referee ignored the dirty tactics, despite Wilton's braying protests. Jones head-butted Bridger, opening a cut on his face and putting him down again. The fighters tore at one another like dogs for ten, fifteen, twenty more rounds, their faces ripped and bloody, red rivulets running off their bodies with the rainwater. The storm had turned the dust to mud, and several times the men slipped in the goo and fell. Some rounds ended with one man beaten down and others when one simply dropped to a knee for a few seconds rest. And Jones began to do that as often as Bridger did.

But it was clear neither man would surrender. It was going to be a true fight to the finish. For a while, the rowdiness among the spectators subsided, as if the squall that seemed to send energy to the fighters had sapped their own. During one pause after a Jones had wrestled him down, Bridger looked over the crowd, hoping to catch sight of Miss Lily. Instead, he saw numerous jugs and other liquid-filled vessels moving from hand to hand. It was apparent many were reinvigorating their spirits with a fresh batch of homemade whisky from somewhere.

Bridger came to scratch and the Slasher charged, raining blows from all angles, clubbing Bridger's head and hammering his ribs. This time it hurt, but Bridger absorbed the pain. And though the blows were hard, they now lacked the devastating power of Jones's earlier punches. And a kind of numbness had crept through Bridger so that he felt each jolt but not the searing sting. He stood his ground and hit back. With a pair of left-right combinations that pained his bruised knucles, Bridger bloodied Jones' nose and tore the flesh around an eye. Something rolled out of the socket and Bridger thought for a horrible instant he'd knocked out Jones's eyeball. The socket was empty and Bridger realized— still shocked—it must have held an artifical eye that dropped out.

Blood spread down the side of the Slasher's face. He

leaped at Bridger, using his left arm to circle Bridger's neck while pummeling his face with a right. "I'll kill you out here." Jones spat the words, spewing saliva and blood through a ruined mouth, and Bridger, surprised, took a step back. From nowhere a punch exploded on the side of his head, ripping his ear and driving him into the dirt. His head buzzed but he floated without pain, as though he were out of his body looking down at the fray.

He rose, slowly, deliberately, never taking his eyes off Jones. The mob bellowed, excited by fresh blood and the fight's renewed viciousness. They sounded like wild animals. Red lightning tore the sky and thunder dropped like cannon shots. Bridger gestured for Jones to come ahead.

And on the men fought. Bridger shot a straight right, crunching it into Jones's mouth. It caved in the row of exposed teeth. Bridger heard and felt them tear away, even as he felt them rip the flesh of his knuckles. The Slasher fell, and Bridger stumbled backward. Both men were exhausted. Yet Jones was up on his knees, ready to rise. It made Bridger think of what Big Mike had told him years ago: "'Make 'em carry ya out, if it comes to that. It's a sin to give up."

There certainly was no quit in the Slasher. But he swayed as he stood. The referee called it the fifty-third round. Bridger knew the long bout worked in his favor. Jones was accustomed to dispatching his cow-camp opponents in a few minutes. This brutal fight was well into its second hour. Jones shot a punch, but it was slow and slipped off the gore on one side of Bridger's face. Bridger fired back, his fist connecting on the Slasher's forehead. A streak of pain tore through the back of his hand and into his wrist, eclipsed in a moment by the sting of a hard blow to his ear.

Bridger knew he needed to work on softer targets. His hands throbbed. It was time to go to the body, even though it meant close-quarters fighting. Standing his ground, he let Jones move in.

He coiled his strength and feinted twice to the head. Then he stepped close, driving bent-arm punches to Jones' belly and sides. Five, six, seven blows and he felt the Slasher's ribs give way on his left side and knew he'd broken several. He tried to screw in a solar plexus punch, and was off-target a fraction. But it still paralyzed the Slasher, who looked ready to fall.

He lunged instead, smashing his forehead squarely on Bridger's face. Bridger's nose popped like a nut. Then Jones aimed a hard right hook and missed, using the follow-through to slam his elbow into Bridger's jaw, nearly falling as he committed the foul. Jones wobbled, bent over, and, hands dangling, vomited on the ground. Bridger, dizzy, couldn't focus his eyes. The front of his face felt smashed flat. Blood cascaded across his mouth and chin, painting his chest. He spat out a tooth, and the small movement shot what felt like nails through his cracked jaw.

But neither man would go down. They groped, pawed for each other, reeling, shoving now more than punching. The bloodletting had driven the crowd to frenzy. Several fights broke out. Gunshots echoed as several men in their excitement fired rifles and pistols in the air. Another lightning bolt sizzled close by, its thunder exploding a second later. Huge raindrops pelted down hard.

Mr. Satin had come out of his hiding place. Now, lurching with the milling crowd and struggling to keep his feet, he spied Leg Dicken and fear stabbed at his belly. Dicken! He must be here with a plan of his own. Some kind of scheme. And ready to horn in, as always, Satin thought, fury washing over him. Ready to do him in, maybe, like he'd always wanted to do, ever since that day they'd ridden off together for the Olustee fight.

Dicken, smiling grimly, was stumping deliberately toward a man gazing glumly at the action in the ring. He whirled the fellow around. The rough handling surprised Wade Mizell. He looked at his boss in shock. Then Dicken let go a punch to the jaw that put Mizell on his seat.

"I've been wanting to do that," Dicken grated. "You're an incompetent fool. Don't ever let me see you again." He clumped away, still wearing a glowering half-smile, as if pleased with himself. He paid no attention to anything around him.

Satin reached into his coat and palmed his derringer. In all the confusion, there might never be a better chance! He could rid himself once and for all of at least one problem. And in another part of the crowd, Nathan DeBell was furious. At himself. Angry because he had not killed two men when he'd had the chance. Now they were back—and he'd make a clean sweep this time—first the freak, then the peg-leg. He'd lost sight of the peg-leg for a while, but there he was now.

The shooting had already started, just as he'd planned. Pretty soon his boys would gun down one or two men at random, and in the panic he'd finish what he'd started years ago. He drifted through the jostling throng, edging closer to the one-legged man, but staying near the ring. First he'd take out the fighter, the last stinking thief who'd tried to rob him. And it was him, all right, no matter that ugly face. DeBell knew from the way he moved. And the fact that he'd torn the man's ears off himself. Somebody had ruined the rest of his looks, too, but they hadn't changed that cat-like way he had of moving.

On the mob's edge, more shots went off. There were shouts and cries. People craned to see what was happening. DeBell stepped to the ring ropes, drew a pistol, and shot Bongo Jones in the chest. No one seemed to notice one more gunshot or the man who fired it. DeBell lowered the gun and stepped quickly back into the crowd, moving toward the one-legged man. He moved quickly, cocking his gun as he held it low, close to his thigh. Satin, too, shouldered through the crowd. A gap opened and he practically ran toward Dicken, intending to fire point-blank. Startled, Dicken backed up as Satin charged closer.

DeBell saw the rapid movement and, afraid his quarry would dodge away, fired from the hip, quicker than he'd intended. His shot missed Dicken and Satin, rushing forward, took it through the right eye. The bullet blew off the back of his head as it went out. Leg Dicken saw Satin fall, and his eyes locked for several seconds on the man's ruined face. Then he turned to see who had fired the shot. But Nathan DeBell had melted away.

One after another, several more shots rang through the clearing. People hit the ground, covering their heads, while others dived behind trees and into bushes. At least three more fistfights broke out as cursing men stumbled over one another trying to get away. One skinny fellow stood stock still amid the chaos, draining a flask of whisky as fast as he could.

In the ring, Bongo Jones reeled, staggered, pawed at his

wound and spat blood but still would not fall. Bridger, at first unaware his opponent had been shot, looked wildly about, trying to sort out the pandemonium. He craned to see Miss Lily. Then he saw the blood pulsing in rhythm from Jones' chest. He stepped and grabbed the man, lowering him to the ground. As he did, the Slasher's eye blazed straight at him.

For the first time, Bridger saw the chilling blue he remembered as the shade of Mike McGinnis's eyes! "Get away! Touch me an' I'll kill ya yet, ya little puke!" The fighter wrenched away from Bridger, cursing. "I know ya! Pokey, that's who. Followed me, didja? Want the money for yerself. Well, ya can't have it. Yer a weakling, and I'll kill ya first!" The rant dissolved in a coughing fit.

Bridger's heart hammered. Pokey, he'd said, that silly name Mike used to call him! Bridger fought off a wave of dizziness. The monster of a man he'd been fighting was his lost uncle! "Mike, oh dear God," he finally got out. "What in the name of . . . what happened? Let me help you. We'll get a doctor . . . just be still . . . " Then Archie Hankins and Miss Lily were in the ring, at his side. Cheese was right behind them, looking solemn. "Henry went for the wagon, Tom," Archie said. "We shouldn't tarry here." He looked curiously at the man Bridger held in his arms.

"He's my Uncle Mike." Bridger gulped for air, nearly sobbing. He saw Miss Lily and felt a surge of relief. Surely everything would be all right now. She wore trousers and a shirt and as she knelt, she pulled out the shirttail and tried to tear off a piece of the rain-soaked cloth. Cheese handed her his knife and she cut out a square. She folded it into a pad, placing it over Mike McGinnis's wound and tying it on with string. Around them, the riot had begun to subside. Afraid now, men had disappeared into the woods or back onto the trail. There was no more gunfire, although there were several wounded. Satin lay dead.

Bridger saw the one-legged man just outside the ring ropes, staring at him. He nearly hailed him to come help. Then he saw the gun dangling muzzle down in the man's hand, and checked his impulse to call out. He turned back to Mike McGinnis, who was writhing and drooling scarlet threads of saliva, cursing with every cough. No one else paid attention to the fighters they had been cheering. The clearing, turning into a bog now, was nearly empty. A dozen or so men sprawled or sat, some nursing wounds. One knot of men argued about their wagers. "Let's just hush about it," one whispered. "The law's bound to be around anyway."

Rain still came down steadily. It had extinguished most of the torches that weren't knocked over, although one still burned gamely. Cheese set it upright. Henry Wilton pulled up in the wagon. "We'll have to hurry," he said. "That trail's going to be part of the swamp in a few minutes."

Bridger, Archie, Cheese, and Miss Lily had a job to get Mike McGinnis into the wagon. Even the bullet wound hadn't stopped his thrashing, and he backhanded Cheese on an ear. "He sure is strong, Mr. Water," Cheese commented, "ain't he?" At last Wilton flicked the reins and the wagon lurched ahead, pointed toward Doc Partington's. The passengers sat or sprawled across Mike McGinnis's limbs to keep him still. But the fighter raved on. Bridger glanced back one time. Leg Dicken still stared, gun in hand, marking the wagon's departure.

# 24

MIKE MCGINNIS WEAKENED, but would not give up. During one of his quieter moments, Doc Partington looked at the wound and shook his head. "Bullet's buried deep. I can't save him. He'd die on the table if I tried."

Bridger yelled at him. "You have to try, we can't just let him go, not after all this!"

"It's no use, son. I'm more concerned about you. You're exhausted and you look like you've been beaten with clubs. What a vicious business you got yourself into." Bridger let the doctor clean the worst of his injuries. He insisted on staying with his uncle, kneeling beside him. "Mike, Mike, why'd they . . . who shot you, d'ya know?" But McGinnis rebuffed every attempt Bridger made to communicate. "I'll tell you nothin'. Get away. All you want is that fortune. You'n that miser father of yours, the rich puke, couldn't ever get enough, could he? You did this to me. All of you."

Bridger shook his head. Mike seemed to be delirious, living on will, forcing out words that made no sense. "You're a fool," McGinnis shrieked. "You can't stop me! Nobody can!" He lashed out and slammed the heel of a hand into Bridger's face. Bridger reeled back, nearly blind with new pain on top of his other injuries.

"That devil with the long beard, I saw his treasure, all hidden away. That's the one who shot me. Same one who tortured me before, cut off my ears, ripped out an eye. Guess you hired him to finish the job, did ya? And when he couldn't do it, you made sure he handed me over to that sea scum, those pirates, that's what they were." McGinnis began to shout. "Human waste! I lived in it, do you know that? They branded me! They tried to burn me to death, God rot them straight to hell! And they did it for you. You wanted it all!"

The outburst shocked Bridger and the others, as much for its ferocity as for the words.

"I can't see how he's lasting, where the man gets his strength," marveled Doc Partington. Cheese looked ready to flee. Bridger looked at Miss Lily, praying she would not believe his uncle's raving. "He's not himself, he can't be," he pleaded. "Can't you see? No one, not me, not anyone in our family even knew where he was—or what he was doing!" Miss Lily responded softly. "Of course you didn't. The poor man's mind must have been broken."

"No!" McGinnis bellowed. Somehow he struggled swaying to his feet, the crude bandage on his chest soaked and running red. "I'm a whole man! I'm rich! The treasure is real! I saw it, it's why he tore my eye out!" His voice dropped almost to a whisper and he looked ready to topple. Bridger stood to catch him. McGinnis skewered his nephew with one glittering eye. "They tried to blind me. And I'll blind you, by God!" He lunged, clutching at Bridger's eyes with two clawed hands. Then he flinched and seemed to stiffen. His shoulders slumped and his hands dragged down Bridger's chest. Bridger caught his uncle, lowering him back to the floor. Mike McGinnis never knew how gently. He had died on his feet.

Miss Lily, Doc Partington, Archie, and Cheese watched silently. Bridger wept at last. "He knew who I was," he said. "But he didn't know what I was about, why I was here. I came here to find him. Not kill him."

Doc cleared his throat. "Oh, now wait a minute, son. You didn't kill him. The bullet did, not the beating. He wouldn't have survived even if he hadn't been battered. You can rest on that count."

"Doc, I meant I didn't come here to hurt him. Didn't come here to steal from him. Wanted my uncle back, that's all. He was my best friend. When we . . . when we understood each other."

Now Archie spoke up. "Tom, I think we all know you well. I do, at least. And I believe you. Your uncle . . . he must have been tortured out of his mind." The first gray light was pushing away the dark, and it was no longer storming. Bridger heard the treble song of a mockingbird. He caressed his uncle's head, running his fingers gently over the scars. "Mike, Mike, there's so much more I want to know." At last he lay down, and at last he slept. He did not wake when some people came and took away McGinnis's body. He barely roused when Miss Lily brought him pillow and blankets to make him more comfortable on the floor.

Toward noon he awoke, aware someone was in the room with him. He peered and saw a tall man looking down at him. The man had a peg leg. Then he saw the drooping mustache, the slouch hat, and the duster with the alligator hide.

"Leg Dicken," he said, almost to himself. But his visitor heard it. "I've stomped men for sayin' less than that to me, you whelp," Dicken said. "I should stomp you right now." Bridger started up but Dicken kicked him back down.

"You stay put," he ordered. "I want you right on your backside where I can watch you squirm. You slimy pup. See if you can get away now. You're done runnin'." Dicken pulled aside the front of his coat, exposing a holstered pistol.

Sprawled on the floor exhausted, aching though he was, Bridger felt his anger rise.

"How'd you get in here? Come to that, what d'you want with me? Is this something to do with Jacksonville? Because of it does, you're the one who needs to do some explaining, not me."

Bridger made as if to get up again, but sharp pains in his side—and the fact Dicken pulled his gun partway out—made him sit back down. "I'll tell you what I feel like tellin'," said Dicken. "As far as how I got in here, your friends evidently thought their little pup needed some quiet. There's no one around. Which is a good thing, because it'll give us time to talk. And if you don't tell me what I want to hear, I'll burn this place down, and if any of your friends come back, I'll kill them. Without a thought. I'd like to do it anyway."

Bridger could feel the menace. His heart started to hammer. "What am I supposed to tell you?"

"You start by telling me exactly what a Yankee boy like you wants in this kind of pesthole. And if you lie, I'll cut your tongue out." Dicken knelt on a knee. His eyes burned on Bridger's face.

"Looking for a relative," Bridger got out, struggling to keep his voice steady. "This is where he was, last we heard from him."

"What else? What else were you doin'?"

Bridger hesitated before answering: "That's it. That's why I'm here." Dicken's hard fist lashed out, and smashed Bridger's nose, already broken and raw. Pain tore through his head. He cried out and lurched backward. He saw more jagged flashes of red and white. Then he felt something hard, oily, and vaguely smoky slam through his lips and teeth. He felt the other man's weight press him down. Dicken had jumped on Bridger knees first and rammed the gun into his mouth.

"You ran drunk all over Jacksonville, screamin' about a treasure. Right here, right here in this jungle. By God, you tell me about it. Now! Or you're dead! A dead man, by God!"

Bridger could barely put a thought together. He jerked his head and got Dicken's gun out of his mouth. "All right! It doesn't matter now. I'll tell you what I know, and it isn't much. I just don't care anymore. My Uncle Mike, he's the relative I was looking for. He told me in a letter about a huge fortune hidden here. Or maybe lost. It was the last we heard from him. I came here looking for him, and yes, hoping to find the treasure. But Mike's dead now. As far as that treasure goes—maybe he knew where it was. Once. But he didn't tell me, and I just don't care anymore. Let the money-grubbers take it. You fight over it. I'm trying to get away from people like you."

Dicken kept his gun pointed at Bridger, who noticed it wasn't cocked; nor was Dicken's finger near the trigger. "If I knew where it was, I'd tell you. Let you and old Nathan DeBell go at it. He's the one I think is guarding it. Maybe you old goats could settle each other once and for all. But I don't know, so I can't tell you. Can't tell you anything else. You want to kill me, now's your chance."

Dicken relaxed a little and, looking thoughtful, got himself upright. "Say," he asked suddenly. "What was that ugly fighter to you, anyway?" The question annoyed Bridger, even in his weariness. He started to flare back, but decided Dicken knew no better. "He was my uncle. Mike McGinnis," Bridger said wearily.

Dicken raised an eyebrow. "The uncle you came here to find? That the one who said he knew all about that treasure?"

"It was him."

Dicken smirked. "It's strange. I lost a relative of mine out there tonight, too. Elihu Dicken, Lou Dicken, that was his name. You knew him as Sam Satin, I came to hear a while ago. He was my brother."

Bridger blinked. "Mr. Satin? He was my employer—for a while."

"As I said, I happened to hear that awhile ago. A very strange thing, too. And a shame you fell in with him."

"Probably," said Bridger, looking straight at Dicken. "But I might have done worse."

Dicken smirked again. "You can at least trust me to be what I am. Lou, now, anyone who ever knew him, he let 'em down in the end. He was an odd one, besides a liar—goin' by that fool name. Like he didn't want anyone to think we were related. My big brother. A coward. I rode off with him to fight the Yanks at Olustee. He left me for dead on the battlefield. And I lost my leg because of it. Infected. Two days I was layin' out there."

Then Dicken gestured at a ragged bag in the corner of the room. "That's his luggage, such as it was. Your uncle's, I mean. His second brought it, said you'd be here, too. Was interested to know if you might want a fight manager. I told him you had other plans. But that's how I knew to find you. I just followed him over."

Bridger sat on the floor and watched Dicken clump over to the bag. He placed his gun on the floor next to it, and pulled at the bag's top. "Guess I'll just have a look," Dicken said. "Maybe there's a rich clue in here." A new anger blazed up in Bridger. "Hold it!" He stood and glared. "You're not going through his things. They're private. Family things!"

Dicken feigned surprise. "Why, hell, son, you haven't even seen 'im for years. He wasn't the same man. You saw him. Why, he wasn't even human." Dicken bent to the bag and missed Bridger's first, sudden move. Putting aside pain, he shot across the floor. Startled, Dicken tried to stand but Bridger grabbed his lapels and shoved him against the wall. Then he punched Dicken in the face.

But his steam was gone and Dicken was strong. The older man took the blow, laced his own fists together, and hammered Bridger in the belly. Bridger felt his wind go out and dropped to his knees. Dicken's pistol lay there and Bridger picked it up. Still in a rage, he struggled up, flailing with one hand. With the the other, he slammed the pistol into the side of Dicken's face.

The blow shocked the older man and he stumbled against the wall. Wide-eyed, he put a hand to his face. Bridger thought he saw flash of fear in it. But Dicken slipped his other hand inside his coat. Bridger thumbed back the pistol's hammer and stuck the barrel in Dicken's face.

"Get out of here," he said. "Just get out."

Dicken didn't speak. He squeezed his eyes shut, rubbed

his cheek, pulled his hand away, and opened his eyes slowly, staring at his hand as if to look for blood. Bridger watched the facial gestures, followed the movement of Dicken's hand. Then he felt the hard cylinder of a gun barrel pressed into his aching ribs. With his other hand, Dicken had pulled a derringer.

"Back off me," Dicken gritted. "You're dead if you don't."

"Then we both are." Bridger didn't blink. "You shoot, so do I." For a few seconds, the two glared into each other's eyes. Bridger was tempted to pull the trigger. But he knew Dicken would shoot him in reflex, just as he had threatened Dicken. He wanted to speak but could think of nothing to say. Then Dicken offered another of his nasty smiles.

"All right, young'n. I'm going to step back and point my gun at the floor. When you see me do that, why don't you do the same?" Bridger gave a bare nod. Dicken moved and pointed the derringer down. Watching carefully, Bridger took a step back and lowered the gun he held.

"I believe," Dicken said, "they call that disengagement."

Again, Bridger nodded. "What now?"

"Let me try one more time," Dicken said. "Just let me talk. Maybe you can understand that I'm still interested in that fortune we both know about. Used to be hidden in a cavern. I've thought of it every day since the first time I ever saw it. I had some old papers I got from a sutler, Mighty Miles was his name. Not that you'd know him. I met him right after Olustee. But there was a map amongst his things and some kind of instructions. One day I came here lookin', just on a hunch, you might say. And I stumbled right into it. I got away with a little bit, before some of these backwoodsmen came after me.

"But there was plenty left, if it's there anymore. Any of those people guarding it got even a lick of sense, they'd a moved it out. But I've got a feeling it's still around somewhere. People like that don't think much of banks. And I'm not gonna get a good night's sleep until I find out one way or another." He paused, watching the younger man before him. And Bridger thought about what Mike McGinnis had said. He'd been talking crazy, yes—but Leg Dicken didn't seem so crazy, and he said he'd seen the fortune, too.

"Thing is, I've still got the map," Dicken said. "I'm strong—but maybe not as strong as I was. I want help. Someone who can shoot and fight and doesn't mind doing it. This time, when I go after that treasure, I want someone guarding my back. If we have to fight our way to a fortune, I want someone beside me. And you, you've already fought your way through half of Florida."

Dicken laughed a bit. "I know, because I paid the people who had to fight you. Not that they were any good at it." Then he gave Bridger a straight-on gaze. "People usually work for me. I don't take many partners, but something tells me I can count on you. Anyway, I know that treasure's what you come for, too. You have your dream, like I got mine. There's enough of it to make us both wealthy. Forever. We get rich, we go our separate ways."

Bridger stayed quiet awhile. Dicken was trying another approach, though obviously pursuing his own interests. Still, he liked it that someone as hard as Dicken had acknowledged him as a good man in a fight.

"Whaddya say, boy?"

Bridger thought: *This could be the next adventure*. He cleared his throat to speak, not quite sure what he was going to say until the words started coming out. "Tell you what, Mr. Dicken. I came here to find Uncle Mike. That treasure was something extra, something on the side. I had this idea Mike and I could find it together. It'd be our adventure, he and I. But Mike's dead, and anyway, he wasn't the man who helped me grow up, the man I knew. I think the treasure, or the thought of it, did something to him. It made him careless, reckless. And it led him to a place that broke him. And to people who killed him, finally. I don't want that for myself."

"Like I told you. I don't care about that treasure anymore. I'm finished with it. I meant what I said." Now Dicken stayed quiet, giving Bridger the stare that had intimidated so many men.

"Forget it, Mr. Dicken. You won't change my mind. You'd have a better chance of shooting me down. Try it if you want." Dicken's arm jerked, almost in reflex at the challenge. Perhaps thinking twice, he didn't bring it all the way up—but Bridger leveled his weapon at Dicken's head, thumbing back the hammer again.

"Do you think I'm just going to give up what I've dreamed about for years?" Dicken grated out the words. Bridger shot back: "Do you think you can come here and order me around? I don't live to make you happy. I don't care about your money. And I'll kill you if I have to."

Dicken backed a few steps, glancing down to keep from stumbling with his peg. And Bridger moved an equal distance forward, keeping the gun point-blank at Dicken's head. Finally Dicken turned around and carefully he walked out of the house. Watching him closely, Bridger followed him onto the porch. Dicken clumped down the house's walkway with his swaying, stump-legged gait. There was a horse hitched to a wagon near the road and Dicken headed for it. He turned and Bridger tensed. "Give me the gun back. We're done. Here and now, anyway."

"Nope. Wouldn't make much sense," Bridger said, "not here and now." He let the remark sink in. Dicken glared. "But I'll tell you what. I suspect someone you know has a nice Sharps carbine he got not too long ago, probably the same one I lost in Jacksonville. You get me that gun back and I'll get you back yours."

Still scowling, Dicken turned toward the wagon. When he reached it, he turned back to Bridger and snarled: "You'll be watched. Count on it. We're finished today. But not forever." Bridger sat on the porch steps and shook his head. He didn't bother to answer. He watched Dicken haul himself into the wagon. He heard him cluck at the horse. And he felt something like relief when the wagon wound down the trail and out of sight. He would have taken a deep breath, but his sides pained too much. Instead, he leaned back on the steps, stretching.

The sun was up high and the warmth felt good to Bridger's battered hide. For the first time he noticed the golden sunlight falling through the deep green of the forest around Doc Partington's house. A light breeze moved among leaves and branches, and the night's rain had left a sparkle. Bridger figured he would ache for quite a while. His body was beaten and his heart hurt. Mike was dead. He wondered how close he himself had come. His head throbbed enough that he thought maybe he should be. And Dicken had ruined what was left of his nose. What's more, he sounded like he'd be back to finish the rest of him.

He sighed, puffing his cheeks and blowing out the air. He'd solved some things, but life didn't get easier. Stretching once more, he caused a dozen bruises and cuts to protest. Bridger grimaced and swore, then let the warmth wash over him. He figured he'd be moving around pretty well in a few days. He wanted—he needed—to talk to Miss Lily.

And he'd get through this. An inch at a time. Sometimes that's the way it had to be. Big Mike had always told him so.

# AFTERWORD

Tom Bridger stayed in Florida. He bought headstones for Mike McGinnis and, surprised that he wanted to, for Elihu Dicken. Leg Dicken was never far from his mind, but for at least a while, his enemy stayed away from Point Pinellas. One day old Shelton, the postmaster, delivered a package. It contained a Sharps carbine. The next day, Bridger shipped a pistol to Jacksonville.

Mike McGinnis left a kind of journal, parts of it more eloquent that Bridger would have believed possible. It described an odyssey and an ordeal. He had indeed made his way to Point Pinellas and had found a treasure. Then he had been ambushed.

Shot, beaten, and tortured, "by a cruel-eyed, black-bearded devil of a man." McGinnis told how, weak and desperate, he literally had been sold to a party of fishermen. They had taken him aboard their boats and worked him as if he were a slave. Manacled when he wasn't laboring, fed garbage and scraps, McGinnis was taken to a virtual fortress somewhere in the Caribbean.

"They pretended to be innocent fishermen, but in truth they were the lowest of men, preying on the unarmed, robbing the helpless, and murdering the weak," McGinnis wrote. He wrote of the torment they visited upon him. For amusement, they burned him, twisted and tore his flesh, whipped him.

"Some of it was done to loosen my tongue, to tell what I knew of riches on Point Pinellas. For they, too, had heard the stories. Perhaps I should have told them of the very man who stood sentinel over it; perhaps I could have turned them on him and in some way, they could have helped me. But I did not care to be in league with such brigands. Through some fortitude, I was able to keep silent, for I wished to return alone and, if not claim the treasure for my own, avenge myself on the one who sold me into this hell."

McGinnis made friends with the filth shovellers and scullions of the camp. They gave him extra food and he regained his strength. One day, he climbed into a barrel of human waste, hauled aboard a garbage ship bound for parts unknown. "Anywhere beyond the horizon suited me," McGinnis wrote. "I had nothing to lose but a life, and losing it in a pile of dung was preferable to living as I had been. And if I lived, I could continue my way back to Point Pinellas. Then, as now, I wanted revenge. And if can, to take that fortune as part of it."

The stinking cargo was dumped at sea, and McGinnis floated for a day amid the refuse before drifting ashore on another island. There he survived, finally persuading the crew of another fishing boat to take him aboard. And thus begin his odyssey through the Caribbean, to the Florida Keys, and through south Florida. "I trade on my skill as a prize-fighter (doubtless my terrible visage enhances my reputation as particularly vicious). I fight as often as I can, sometimes twice a night, in fish camps, aboard ships, in salvage yards and back yards, in cow camps, and saloons. I have never lost. Most take a look at me and are finished before they ever try to land a blow.

"Somewhere along the way, I took the name Bongo Jones. There was no reason for it. I just liked the way the name sounded. I think it is a good fit for a pugilist of my degree. It is just a convenient label, at any rate, for I no longer consider myself the man Michael McGinnis. My body and soul have been twisted away from the person I once was. It is a labor for me to write, and I grow less interested in doing so, though perhaps someone one day will read this and come to understand what torment I have endured, and why I live now only to inflict pain."

The journal contained just one more entry. It was scrawled, slashed diagonally across a page, the letters shaky and misshapen, with none of the flowing language of McGinnis's earlier prose. "Evil man is me," the words read. "Now all are against me. They wait to kill. They will die by me, the stinking man of Florida. I smell the treasure so close, am so close, I will revenge."

The words made it clear to Bridger his uncle's mind had begun to unravel; the journal's next-to-last last entry suggested that even McGinnis knew he was deteriorating in some way. Bridger thought it a wonder he had sustained himself at all after the weeks of torture and deprivation. And surely the vicious and violent life of a camp fighter had taken a further toll.

Bridger wrote to his mother, sister, and father. To the

women, he told selected parts of his adventure. He broke the news about Mike, saying only that he had died in Florida. To his father, he wrote that he would stay in Florida and make his fortune "on this Southern frontier, where a man's worth is what he makes of himself, and not what others have given him."

Bridger worked as a laborer until he had money to buy Point Pinellas land. He raised citrus and decided to read law. He spent much time discussing life's matters with Regal Lily Frazer. He stopped calling her Miss Lily and by mutual agreement the couple henceforth referred to one another in public and in private as Lily and Tom.

Bridger returned to Lily the pistol and watch, but did not give them up, precisely. After the wedding, he occasionally shot the pistol, and he was quite undisturbed to know his wife kept a box of mementos, including the watch, that had belonged to her first husband. Lily always thought it amusing that she had ridden the stage from Brooksville with Bridger's enemy, Leg Dicken. Sometimes she teased her husband about it. "He was quite a charming fellow, you know."

Archie Hankins's family, subdued by the Florida climate and unable to make money farming, returned to England. Archie stayed on the Point. He and Bridger became lifelong friends. Cheese stayed, too, and became a cow hunter. He joined Teddy Roosevelt's Rough Riders when they came to Tampa near the turn of the century. He returned as one of the heroes of San Juan Hill—a hospital corpsman who refused to carry a gun.

Henry Wilton died in a yellow fever epidemic in 1887. Simon Puig, the chess player, was killed in the 1901 Jacksonville fire. Wade Mizell tried robbery for a living, was arrested in Tater Hill Bluff south of Tampa, and died in a prison fight in 1902. Kenny Kilkenny came in from the woods one day and got sober and surprised all by revealing a great talent for woodcarving. He fashioned dolls, tiny houses with all the furniture, and toy soldiers. He sold them for a pittance and managed to get by. Kenny fell off the wagon from time to time. Bridger almost never did; but many times he struggled with temptation.

Abner Banks, Regal Lily Frazer's faithful sergeant, continued to take care of her land near Ocala, occasionally visiting Point Pinellas to do his duty by Miz Captain Frazer—which he called her to his dying day. He and Bridger continued to regard one another with suspicion until discovering their mutual interest in chess.

The railroad came to the Point in 1888 but it ended on Tampa Bay several miles north of Pinellas Village. The city of St. Petersburg grew up around it. Bridger never did find out about some things: how he had been carried battered to Miss Lily's door after his experience in the jungle, for instance, or that it was Sam Satin who tried to burn him out the night before the fight. Some things in life, he decided, remained forever mysterious.

He did not raise the matter of the hidden fortune with Lily. But he could not forget it. The notion of it remained, itching and burning, ever calling.

Nathan DeBell continued to hate the development erasing the frontier and bringing more people to his paradise. His clan, though it appeared to be nothing more than a collection of rough farmers, seemed never to want for anything, as though it had an unknown source of wealth. One day, some of its members would become influential, holding positions of power and building a formidable machine to oppose the outsiders who would wreak change on the Point. Nathan, who held to the old ways, would be seen in town, saying little, but watching and listening, ever the guardian.

## THE END

# HISTORICAL NOTES 🌾

BARE-KNUCKLE PRIZEFIGHTS—Considered by some historians to be England's national sport in the eighteenth century, such bouts were conducted in America until the late nineteenth century. A set of rules established in 1743 called for the end of a round when a fighter was knocked or wrestled down. He then had thirty seconds to come to a mark in the middle of the ring called the "scratch." The London Prize Ring rules developed in 1838 refined the code to forbid such tactics as head-butting and eye-gouging, although such strictures were not always obeyed. The last bare-knuckle fight is usually dated as July 8, 1889, when John L. Sullivan kept his heavyweight championship by stopping Jake Kilrain in seventy-five rounds. Thereafter, gloves were used in sanctioned fights.

DEERFOOT—A Seneca Indian whose real name was Lewis Bennett. He ran many races in New York but won his greatest fame in England, where he competed against many of that nation's best runners during a tour in the early 1860s.

Deerfoot's career lasted into the 1870s, when he was more than forty years old.

FIREARMS—Sharps rifles and carbines were popular with both armies during the Civil War and were the weapons used by abolitionist John Brown during the Harpers Ferry Arsenal raid. Texas Rangers also carried the Sharps for awhile. The Winchester caliber .44 was a good rifle said to have helped win the West. As a game rifle, it was favored more in the East than in the West, where many sportsmen believed it too light to knock down larger animals such as bears. The Colt model 1873, developed for the Army, also became a symbol of the old West. The single-action .45-caliber revolver weighed more than two pounds. Single-shot derringers were favored as back-up or concealed weapons because of their small size and large-caliber bullets, lethal at close range.

FOOTRACES—Long-distance running was extremely popular in England and America during the 1870s and 1880s. New York City's Madison Square Garden was host to many of these, including the famous Astley Belt events in which competitors covered hundreds of miles in six-day races for prizes of up to $20,000. Capacity crowds often turned out to watch. Amateurs and traveling professionals also engaged in races of two and three days' length, or over set distances of up to one hundred miles.

RICHARD KYLE FOX—Owner and publisher of the National Police Gazette, a mass-circulation sporting journal. Fox was an enemy of John L. Sullivan and supported many of his opponents, including Paddy Ryan and Jake Kilrain.

FORT BROOKE—It was established as a military post in 1824. Confederates occupied it when the Civil War started, but federal soldiers took over again in 1864. Occupation troops stayed until 1869. The last Army contingent left about 1882, and homesteaders settled on the land. The town of Fort Brooke was established in 1885; it was absorbed by Tampa early in the twentieth century.

JOHN WESLEY HARDIN—The Texas gunslinger spent time in Florida during the 1870s. Using the alias J. H. Swain, Hardin killed several men in Florida, operated a saloon in Gainesville, and was a butcher in Jacksonville, according to Drew Gomber, a historian specializing in gunfighters and who is affiliated with the Lincoln County (New Mexico) Heritage Museum.

PAUL MORPHY—The son of a prominent antebellum New Orleans family, he was the United States chess champion from 1857 to 1871.

MUSIC—"Remember Boy, You're Irish" was written in 1885 and became a music hall hit of the time. "Grandfather's Clock" came out in 1875 and is still heard as the twentieth century closes. There are various versions of "The Minstrel Boy." The words to the one Tom Bridger sang appeared in Irish Melodies, by Thomas Moore, published in 1857. The melody is believed to be a Gaelic air first heard as early as 1600. "When You and I Were Young, Maggie" was a poem written by George Johnson, a Canadian. J. A. Butterfield, an English musician, is sometimes credited as having written the music during his Tampa stay in the 1850s and 1860s. Butterfield opened a music academy and organized a cornet band, one of many popular in Florida during the second half of the nineteenth century. Surely they played "Bonnie Blue Flag" and "Dixie," standard Southern songs since the Civil War.

OLUSTEE—The largest Civil War battle in Florida took place on February 20, 1864, a few miles east of Lake City. Union forces were beaten in a six-hour battle considered the Federals' third-bloodiest defeat of the war (when casualties are measured in proportion to the number of troops engaged). Of 5,115 federal troops, 1,355 were killed or wounded. Many African-American soldiers fought, including men of the 54th Massachusetts, the black infantry regiment celebrated in the movie *Glory*. Some evidence suggests Confederates executed many wounded African-American troops on the battlefield as Union forces withdrew.

PADDY RYAN—Born in Ireland, he was one in a series of nineteenth-century heavyweight champions from Troy, New York. John L. Sullivan stopped Ryan in nine rounds to win the title in 1882.

PIRATES AND TREASURE—Tales of lost or hidden treasure on land or at sea abound on Florida's Gulf coast. Some are documented, some are lore. Pirates, or at least the characters designated as such by the government, are officially noted in the Territorial Papers of the United States as infesting the Gulf of Mexico near Florida during the 1820s and 1830s. Commodore David Porter's Key West naval squadron chased some of them. By the 1880s, pirate stories were rare. But parts of remote south Florida still were feared as a haven for the lawless, and various scoundrels drifted in the seagoing traffic between Florida and the Caribbean. Mike McGinnis referred to his captors as pirates; as long as there is no romantic or "Jolly Roger" connotation, it was probably as good a name as any for thugs with a boat.

POINT PINELLAS—It became the anglicized version of Punta Pinal, meaning Point of Pines, which a Spanish explorer named a tip of land near Tampa Bay's mouth. Sometimes the name was used to refer to the entire southern section of the Pinellas peninsula. The sparsely populated backwater was beginning to be noticed in 1885, when it was a part of Florida's Hillsborough County. More settlers were arriving, including a group from England lured by an intense advertising campaign. There were old-timers scattered throughout, but none was known to have a hidden fortune. The DeBells and their treasure are fictional. So is the concept of settlers being burned off their homesteads for railroad right-of-way. The Pinellas peninsula split from Hillsborough and became Pinellas County on January 1, 1912. Its earlier name echoes today in a southern section of St. Petersburg called Pinellas Point.

RAILROADS—Railroad construction boomed in Florida during the 1880s. More than two thousand miles were built, many into south Florida to help open the frontier. The Florida Southern Railway had a charter from Lake City to Charlotte Harbor, with stops at Ocala and Brooksville. Its engine Sherman Conant was built in 1884. For purposes of the story, Tom Bridger arrived in Brooksville in early 1885, although the line actually was not completed there until a few months later.

STAGECOACHES—Stage travel in Florida began to pick up in the 1830s, and by 1845 most mail was carried by stage. In 1858, Hubbard Hart started a six-horse stagecoach between Palatka and Ocala. Stages were used later between Gainesville, Ocala, Brooksville, and Tampa. Some of those employed four-horse teams such as the one Tom Bridger raced.

STEAMBOATS—Steam-powered vessels regularly traveled the Ocklawaha River from the mid-nineteenth century until as late as 1920. Because of its exotic scenery, the twisting, shallow river was a tourist destination and carried passengers to Silver Springs near Ocala. The Okeehumkee was built in 1873 in Palatka by Hubbard Hart, the same entrepreneur who organized a stage line. Gasoline engines, not railroads, spelled the end of the steamboat era.

BOY THOMPSON—He is the only genuine Point Pinellas character depicted, although others, such as some of the English people and Doc Partington, are based on early settlers. Boy Thompson won no mention in history books. His name comes up occasionally in journals and notes left by Pinellas old-timers. He is described as a laborer, and there is the suggestion that he was a person who had friends, liked a good time, and cut an exuberant figure while dancing. The few references offer no clue as to where life ultimately led him. Perhaps his spirit lives on in this story.

## CRACKER WESTERNS:

*Ghosts of the Green Swamp* by Lee Gramling. Features that rough-and-ready but soft-hearted Florida cowboy, Tate Barkley, introduced in *Riders of the Suwannee*. ISBN 1-56164-120-0 (HB); 1-56164-126-X (PB)

*Guns of the Palmetto Plains* by Rick Tonyan. Tree Hooker dodges Union soldiers and Florida outlaws to drive cattle to feed the starving Confederacy. ISBN 1-56164-061-1 (HB); 1-56164-070-0 (PB)

*Riders of the Suwannee* by Lee Gramling. Tate Barkley returns to 1870s' Florida to save a young widow's homestead from outlaws. ISBN 1-56164-046-8 (HB); 1-56164-043-3 (PB)

*Thunder on the St. Johns* by Lee Gramling. Riverboat gambler Chance Ramsay combats a slew of greedy outlaws seeking to destroy the dreams of honest homesteaders. ISBN 1-56164-064-6 (HB); 1-56164-080-8 (PB)

*Trail from St. Augustine* by Lee Gramling. A trapper, an ex-sailor, and a servant girl cross the Florida wilderness in search of buried treasure and a new life. ISBN 1-56164-047-6 (HB); 1-56164-042-5 (PB)

*Wiregrass Country* by Herb and Muncy Chapman. In 1835, the Dover family battles Indians and cattle rustlers to preserve their way of life on Three Springs Ranch. ISBN 1-56164-164-2 (HB); 1-56164-156-1 (PB)